The

CARETAKERS

ALSO BY ELIZA MAXWELL

The Grave Tender
The Kinfolk
The Unremembered Girl
The Widow's Watcher
The Shadow Writer

The
CARETAKERS

ELIZA MAXWELL

LAKE UNION
PUBLISHING

Published by Lake Union Publishing, Seattle

www.apub.com

Amazon, the Amazon logo, and Lake Union Publishing are trademarks of Amazon.com, Inc., or its affiliates.

ISBN-13: 9781542044578
ISBN-10: 154204457X

Cover design by David Drummond

Printed in the United States of America

For Max

Your kindness is my greatest joy.
To you, and the man you'll grow to be.

PROLOGUE

The screams have long since died away. The bloodstains, like the memories, have faded brown with time, obscured beneath a fine layer of dust. Mildew creeps along the peeling floral wallpaper. The window frames are soft with rot.

A skylight of colored glass softly illuminates the slow and steady decay.

Once, laughter filled the spaces between the tired walls. Running feet and mother's hugs and whispers under covers at night. Hearts beat, as hearts do, then broke, then beat again. Until they didn't.

An elderly woman stands inside the remains of what used to be a home. Her head is tilted to one side, and an observer might wonder if her thoughts are anchored in reality. She wonders the same.

Wings flutter in the silence, disturbing the dust and sending a shower of particles down through the beam of sun soldiering on across the room. Starlings, roosting in the attic. Pests, some would say, but she doesn't begrudge them a dry eave to shelter beneath. The desiccated old place has little else to offer.

Yet something feels different. Changed. This is the thought that occupies her as she stands, listening for sounds that aren't there, feeling blindly for a pulse that ceased many years before.

She shakes her head. Foolish old woman. Nothing has changed. This house is a corpse, too large to move, decomposing where it lies. A victim, as much as any of them, to the madness that lived, grew, and died within its walls a long time ago.

She leaves the house, her steps unhurried. The sun warms her hunched shoulders, then gives way to shadows that shelter the path to the ivy-covered caretaker's cottage tucked far back in the trees.

Home. The way was shorter when she was a girl. She would fly through these woods, branches slapping at her, cheeks flushed as she joined her family waiting up ahead.

A memory calls, some vague shape hidden behind the bothersome fog that's taken permanent residence at the edges of her mind.

Mam's voice, a lilting brogue that whispers of green hills an ocean away. "'Tis the gravedigger's bell you hear, lass."

She waits, feigning disinterest. Impatience will get her nothing. The harder she tries to capture a memory, the deeper into the fog it retreats. But if she's quiet and still, sometimes it will come, stepping lightly like a doe emerging from the woods.

Sometimes.

Today, though, it bounds away, skittish and shy.

A different memory comes instead. A ghost of a memory, back to greet her as an old friend might.

"Keep my secrets," it whispers in her ear. "For my secrets are yours."

She's not frightened. At her age, there's little left to fear save death, and even death brings the haunting scent of something new and unknown. An enticement of what might come next.

But as is the nature of ghosts and memories alike, this one has no concern for the future, and even less concern for death. It is fully encapsulated by the past.

The old woman frowns and thinks of the gravedigger's bell.
A small, dark seed of worry burrows down deep, settling in.
Something is rising.
If only she could remember what it is.

1

TESSA

Tessa stands near the back and surveys the crowd. The crush of reporters in their dark overcoats brings to mind a flock of blackbirds. Unsavory creatures that travel in packs, aware they possess no great beauty alone. Only the power of the mob. They vie with one another, jostling to prove their dominance, and turn their glassy eyes to the object of their curiosity.

Oliver Barlow.

Wondering if he'll make a good meal, no doubt.

Tessa shakes off the thought. She's no better. Not really.

"Mr. Barlow, what are your plans now that you're a free man?" one of them shouts over the rest.

"I . . . I don't know," Oliver stammers in response, overwhelmed by the strangers and microphones pushing in on him, questions coming quick and sharp from all directions.

He glances at his wife, a full head shorter than his lanky six-foot frame. She stares at her shoes, intimidated by the mass of humanity blocking their way.

Oliver's father, a truck driver who manned a wall of stoicism during the fourteen years of his son's incarceration, stands beside the couple and mops at tears that show no sign of stopping.

Oliver scans the crowd. Searching for an answer, perhaps. Or an escape. Or simply a familiar face in a sea of strangers.

When his eyes find Tessa, they light with relief, and she sends him what she hopes is a reassuring smile.

"I just want to live my life," he says, his voice stronger. "Hug my kids. Have a home-cooked meal. Watch a ball game with my old man."

The elder Mr. Barlow chokes back a sob and hides his face behind his hands. Oliver glances at him, bemused. After a slight hesitation, he gives his father an awkward one-armed side hug, which only causes the heaving of the old man's shoulders to increase.

Oliver's words are honest, if simple, and leave the reporters hungry for more.

"Do you plan to return to the Bonham community permanently, Mr. Barlow?"

"Chief Winters and the district attorney still deny any wrongdoing in the handling of your case. Would you care to comment on that?"

"Are you angry at the system, Oliver?"

Tessa holds her breath as each barbed question lands, questions that if directed her way would send her into an anxious spiral of self-doubt. Each one steals a little more happiness from Ollie's face. He opens his mouth to reply, and for a moment it seems he might hand the reporters the sound bite they're baiting him for.

Then his gaze meets Tessa's once more. With a nearly imperceptible shake of her head, she silently implores him, *Don't let them win.*

Ollie bites back the response ready to spring from his lips. He takes a deep breath instead, then glances over his shoulder at the Merrivale Correctional Facility. His home, for better and for worse, for far too many years.

The hulking gray structure stands resolute. Uncaring and unapologetic.

"What's done is done," he says when he finally turns back to the waiting crowd. "Today I'm on this side of those walls. That makes it a better day than yesterday."

Tessa lets out a relieved breath, but any hint of celebration has fizzled. When Oliver Barlow walked into prison he was a young man, twenty-two years old and brimming with righteous anger and protestations of innocence. Now he's old and he's tired. A man clocking out after the longest, darkest shift a person could imagine.

"So if you don't mind, I'd like to go home now."

After a few last-ditch attempts, the news crews begin packing to go, unrewarded for their efforts. Ollie steers his family toward their waiting car, a faded gold sedan that hasn't been new for a long time.

He holds the door for his wife, who quickly ducks inside, her head still bent low. Mr. Barlow Senior drops into the front passenger seat and burrows in, trying to control his emotions.

Oliver looks up as Tessa makes her way toward him. A smile breaks through the clouds on his face, erasing some of the signs of premature aging. Even the gray, gloomy day can't dampen it, and Tessa feels her own face respond in kind.

Before she realizes it, he's pulled her in for a hug that lifts her off her feet and swings her around. They're both laughing when he sets her down.

"You did it," he says, his grin wide and amazed. "I didn't believe it, but you really did it."

She smiles, but her voice is serious when she speaks again. "It's your story, Ollie. I was just the messenger."

He raises a brow. "Maybe, but no one was listening before you came along. I wish Mom was here to see this."

Donna Barlow, a plump, soft-spoken woman who devoted her life to her youngest son, never wavered in her commitment to proving his innocence. After more than a decade of dedication to what many saw as a lost cause, she died when an aneurysm burst inside her skull weeks before the appellate judge's ruling excluded the tainted evidence that had led to Oliver's conviction.

"She liked you a lot," Ollie says. "She trusted you, even with your fancy car and your city ways."

He's teasing her. Tessa has adapted to urban life and looks the part. Her dark hair is cut into a sleek bob with long bangs. Her clothes are stylish and of good quality. But beneath the surface, she'll always be a small-town girl.

"I liked her too, Ollie," Tessa says. "It was an honor to know her."

"Thank you for coming, Tessa. Thank you for everything." Ollie hugs her again.

"Seeing you walk out of that place is all the thanks I need. So why are you wasting time? Get out of here. Be happy, Oliver. Go live your life."

"Yes, ma'am," he says with a grin and a salute.

She waits and watches until the gold sedan turns out of the parking lot. The horn honks once as it drives away, then disappears into the distance.

"Tessa Shepherd?"

She turns, surprised when a straggling reporter calls her name.

The documentary Tessa produced and directed about the case was a huge success and made Oliver Barlow a household name practically overnight, but Tessa is never on camera. She's rarely, if ever, recognized outside of professional circles.

"How does it feel to know you helped free an innocent man?"

"No comment," Tessa says with a half smile and a quick shake of her head. She knows he has a job to do, but today isn't about her.

She tucks her hands into her coat and walks slowly back to her car.

How does it feel?

Tessa turns the key in the ignition.

Ollie's conviction was a travesty. A breakdown of justice at the most basic level, and Tessa played a part in righting that wrong. Tonight, Oliver Barlow will celebrate with his family, a free man at last.

How does it feel?

It feels amazing.

Her gaze falls on the phone she left charging. There are hundreds of numbers programmed into it, hundreds of people she could call. People who would meet her for celebratory drinks or dinner. Acquaintances, friends, coworkers. Her mother's number is there—Tessa's biggest supporter.

She can picture her with a cup of coffee on the front porch of her Pennsylvania farmhouse, hear the pleasure in her voice at an unexpected call from one of her daughters. She can hear, also, the tension that would eventually creep in between all the things they'd leave unsaid, because they've been said so many times before and gotten them nowhere.

There's one number that isn't there. It doesn't need to be. Tessa knows it by heart. She never dials it, but there's a part of her that hopes each time her phone rings that she'll see that number displayed, reaching out to connect after all this time.

But that's never happened, and Tessa can't remember the last time she felt so alone.

2

Eighteen months later

The wrap party is in full swing when Tessa clinks a fork against a glass of champagne. She waits patiently while the small but lively crowd quiets down.

Carefully chosen, her team is an eclectic group. Despite their current and varied levels of intoxication, each is outstanding at what they do. They've earned the chance to relax.

Their latest project, a three-part documentary delving into the child sex trade, was harrowing. No one walked away unaffected. Tessa discovered one of the interns crying in the bathroom last month and sent the girl home early. She didn't expect her to come back, to be honest, yet there she was the next day.

Tessa schools her face into a neutral expression.

"I don't need to tell any of you this one wasn't easy, so I won't," she says. "What I will say is, rest up and enjoy your weekend, because next week we've got work to do."

That gets the full attention of the room. There are a few groans, but they all come from the plus-ones. A twinge of guilt tugs at her conscience, but she chose this crew for their talent and dedication. That doesn't always equate to an easy family life.

The empty apartment waiting for her is a testament to that.

Tessa's phone vibrates on the table in front of her. She glances at the number.

It's Oliver. Again.

Tessa bites her lip, conflicted. She lets the call go to voice mail. Now isn't the best time, but she'll reach out tomorrow. She will.

She turns her attention back to her crew. "I've just gotten word that the pitch for our next project has been selected."

"Since when do we pitch?" asks Anne, Tessa's production assistant. Anne's been with Tessa longer than anyone and looks peeved to be hearing this for the first time. Tessa didn't want to get anyone's hopes up only to disappoint them if the project fell through.

"When the former first lady wants a biopic, and her people ask for a pitch, then you pitch," she says with a shrug.

Tessa smiles as the words sink in. There's a beat of silence as mouths drop, but it doesn't last. The room erupts into cheers. It's a once-in-a-lifetime opportunity, and for the rest of the evening they celebrate accordingly.

Even Anne manages to forgive Tessa's secrecy.

By the time she lets herself into her apartment a few hours later, Tessa's ears are still ringing and her cheeks are tired from grinning.

She tosses her keys into a decorative bowl on the kitchen counter and kicks off her shoes before dropping onto the sofa with a sigh of relief.

Her phone buzzes again in her bag. The possibility of ignoring it crosses her mind, but she can't do that. Checking her phone is a compulsion, one that all the therapy in the world can't cure her of.

With an exhausted stretch, Tessa digs it out of her bag and cracks one eye open to peek at the number.

She sits up straighter and answers the call.

"Mom?" Tessa glances at the clock. It's after midnight.

"Hi, sweetheart," her mother says. "I didn't wake you, did I?"

"No, I just got in. A little late for you, though. Is everything all right?"

"Of course. I couldn't sleep and you're always up late working, so I thought I'd say hello."

There's a pause while Tessa takes that in.

"O-kay," she says, drawing out the word. Jane Shepherd is an early-to-bed, early-to-rise sort of person. "Hello to you too. Now, what's going on?"

From the other end of the line, Tessa hears the refrigerator door open, then a clink of ice cubes hitting the bottom of a glass. This is followed by the faint but distinctive sound of a screw top lid and liquid splashing.

"Mom, are you drinking?" Tessa asks. Her mother drinks alcohol about as often as she makes phone calls after nine o'clock.

"Tessa. Brace yourself. This may come as a shock, but according to my records, I am, in fact, an adult. I know it's difficult to wrap your head around, but if I choose to pour a drink to help me sleep, I'm well within the bounds of acceptability."

Tessa sits up fully, the remnants of her champagne buzz fading. Jane Shepherd only gets snippy when something is on her mind.

The late hour, the liquor, and now snark. A trifecta that has all of Tessa's alarm bells ringing.

"Whoa. Not judging, just surprised, that's all," she says carefully.

"I'm sorry," Jane replies a moment later. "I didn't mean to snap. I've been a little under the weather lately."

Concern knits Tessa's brows together. "Have you seen the doctor?" she asks, suspecting the answer.

"It's nothing to worry about, sweetheart, and that's not why I called anyway."

"All right," Tessa says slowly. Her mind is racing with possibilities, none of them good.

"It's about my birthday," Jane says finally.

That's the last thing Tessa expects, but a far cry from the potential disasters she's been imagining.

"Mom, if you're not up to it, we can postpone until you feel better. Reservations can be changed. I may have to call in a few favors to trade out the theater tickets, but that's not the end of the world."

"I'm not postponing, Tessa. I'm not coming."

It takes a moment to process the full implication of her mother's words.

"But . . . why?" Tessa asks, taken aback by the wave of hurt that washes over her. "We always . . ."

"Not anymore," Jane says, her voice bristling with determination.

Tessa is speechless. She casts her gaze around her apartment. It's neat, tidy, and very, very solitary. Most of the time that's okay, but the week her mother spends with Tessa in the city brings a warmth into the space that sustains her.

It's little enough to ask, especially since Margot has her the rest of the year.

The thought is so selfish that Tessa determinedly pushes it away. She's a grown woman, not a jealous child.

"This year, instead of me coming to you, I want you to come home to Linlea," Jane says.

A cold sliver of fear pierces Tessa at these words.

"This has gone on long enough," Jane says. Her voice has a practiced rhythm. She's rehearsed this. "It was a mistake to allow you girls to continue this ridiculous estrangement, and I should have put a stop to it years ago."

Tessa stands, wraps her arms around herself, and paces her apartment, an attempt to stave off the sensation of being cornered. She counts her breaths—one, two, three—a trick that sometimes holds the anxiety at bay, but it has little effect.

"I can't do that, Mom. You know I can't," she says quietly. "Please don't ask me to."

Jane is silent for a moment. Tessa stops breathing altogether, hoping her mother will reconsider.

"I'm not asking, Tessa. I'm telling you. I expect you here. One week, at home, with your family. Your *entire* family."

Unconsciously, Tessa reaches to her throat. She grips the brass key on a gold chain her mother gave her the day she left. Tessa knew then she wouldn't be back for a very long time, if ever.

Jane had slipped the chain with the small key from around her own neck and placed it on Tessa's. It was the first time she could recall seeing her mother without it.

"I've had this for as long as I can remember," Jane said with a soft smile. "I've never known what it unlocks, but I suppose the mystery is part of the appeal. Take it with you, Tessa. Let it remind you that you always have a home to come to, no matter how far life takes you."

Even as her mother said the words, Tessa wondered if that was true.

"Mom, I can't come home. Not if Margot's going to be there." Her sister's name catches in her throat.

"You can. You will. And so will your sister. This is coming to an end."

"You act like any of this is up to me. It's not." Tessa's hands are trembling, and she wonders if another drink might not be such a bad idea. "She doesn't want me there."

"How would you know? The two of you haven't spoken since you were eighteen."

"I know *because* we haven't spoken. She doesn't want me there!" Tessa takes a deep breath, forcing her voice into a reasonable tone. "And I don't blame her. Would *you* want to see the person who almost killed you?"

But even the truth, as inelegant and painful as it is, doesn't deter her mother.

"That's an excuse you've hidden behind for far too long, sweetheart. You're going to have to do better than that."

3

The next morning Tessa's head is pounding. She'd like to blame the champagne, but suspects it stems more from her mother's unsettling ultimatum.

After a restless night, she drifted to sleep in the early hours of the morning only to jolt awake gasping for breath. She was falling, her sister's name stolen from her lips by the wind rushing past. It's a dream she's had many times.

But that isn't how it happened. It wasn't Tessa who fell.

She squints at the coffeepot, presses a few random buttons, hoping for the best, then fumbles in a drawer in search of a bottle of aspirin.

There's a mountain of work waiting in her office. Contracts to look over for the upcoming project, production notes to file for the previous one. Phone calls to make and appointments to keep. Tessa's not up to facing any of it.

Her mother has turned on her. Turned on her and her sister both. Ironically, the person Tessa would most like to talk to about that, the one person who would understand, is Margot.

She sighs. Twisting off the cap of the bottle, she palms two white pills and washes them down with water from the tap. It's not the first time she's ached to hear her sister's voice. It won't be the last.

Her phone buzzes, vibrating its way across the kitchen counter. Tessa groans and briefly considers tossing it into the East River. But the satisfaction of watching it hit the water, even in her fantasies, is swept away by the same sensation of falling that overwhelmed her dreams.

She turns and checks the number. It's not Margot. Of course it's not. The logical part of her stopped expecting that years ago, but she's yet to convince her heart.

Tessa presses the button to accept the call.

"Morning, Anne," she says, with a forced brightness that she doesn't feel.

Tessa's false cheeriness is wasted. The greeting is barely out of her mouth before her assistant says in a strained voice, "Have you been online yet?"

"No, I just got up. Why?"

Anne pauses. "You might want to sit down."

———

The video is shaky is Tessa's first inane thought, and the last coherent string of words she's able to pull together as two minutes and seven seconds of deepening horror play out across her computer screen.

When Oliver Barlow's face comes into focus, she gasps. How long has it been since she's seen him? A year? More? His face is gaunt and pale. Prominent cheekbones stand out above a scruffy, unkempt beard. Locks of greasy hair frame red-rimmed eyes.

It isn't the face of a free man, living his best life. It's the face of a prisoner of war.

"My name . . ." His raspy voice breaks, and he stops to lick his lips. His gaze darts at something unseen behind the camera, then he starts again. "My name is Oliver Barlow. You think you know me, but you don't."

Oliver turns and stares directly at the screen, his eyes boring into Tessa's.

"To Chief Winters and the Bonham Police Department, I was a problem to deal with, so they dealt with me, even if they had to break a few laws to do it. They locked me up and patted each other's backs. But they got caught. You'd think cops would make better criminals, wouldn't you?"

Oliver chuckles, but there's no humor in it, only a deep and seething anger Tessa's never seen before.

"Then for a while, I was a story. An underdog to champion, to show off your virtue, and, most importantly, to sell, sell, sell. But hey, who am I to complain? The crooked cops got called out, and a judge let me out of jail. Everybody loves a happy ending, right? *RIGHT?*"

Tessa flinches when he yells the last word, his palpable rage a force that feels directed at her personally.

"But there's one problem. Nobody cares what happens next. Nobody gives a *damn* when their favorite underdog is set free, but the world has closed up around the place that was meant for him. Nobody cares when there's no life left for him to go back to."

Tessa tastes the coppery tang of blood as she bites down on the inside of her cheek.

"Where are the reporters now, huh? The movie people? The lawyers working pro-fucking-bono to spit-shine their own reputation? They got theirs. They got their happy ending. And me? I'm supposed to be grateful for the scraps of a life and shut the hell up.

"But I'm not your pet. You wanted me to sit and shake and roll over like a good dog, but I won't do it anymore."

A slow grin spreads over Oliver's face, and Tessa's skin prickles.

"You took everything from me, Winters. Everything. Now it's my turn." He leans close to the camera, and his voice drops to a low, satisfied whisper. "Do you know where your daughter is, Winters? Pretty little Valerie? I know where she is."

Tessa struggles to breathe.

"You won't find her alive. But if you do what I say, exactly what I say, because make no mistake, I'm the one in charge now, I might tell you where to find her body."

Oliver looks straight into the camera. Tessa doesn't recognize the man staring back at her. She dives for the wastebasket beneath her desk, but even the sounds of retching can't block out the final words of Oliver Barlow's message.

"Then you can bury her like you buried me."

4

Tessa, clammy and dazed, looks up and realizes nearly an hour has passed. Time she's spent wide-eyed and sour-stomached. Her pajamas are soaked with sweat, and the hangover of earlier is a child's tantrum compared to the boulders shifting and grinding between her temples.

Oliver poured a trail of gasoline and lit a match, and the world is burning in his wake. Tessa is burning with it. She scoured the news sites, searching for every detail. Each story is frustratingly the same.

The video was sent directly to the media, to multiple outlets, ensuring that even if some of the networks found the ethics to contact the police rather than broadcast it, at least one of them was bound to leak it. And they did.

The footage was sent from Valerie Winters's phone, which was later found in her empty apartment along with clear signs of a struggle.

Chief Winters's daughter is only twenty-five years old, a student studying to become a vet.

The photograph that runs in most of the stories, likely pulled from a social media account, shows a fresh-faced girl with a large smile. Her shoulder-length hair, cut into choppy waves, is the same deep brown shade as her eyes.

Valerie Winters was last seen leaving a friend's party late the previous night.

Questions lash at Tessa. Her thoughts circle back to the call from Ollie she ignored the night before.

Did he reach out to Tessa as he was waiting outside the girl's apartment? Or was he already inside? Did he kill Valerie, then, with blood on his hands, dial Tessa's number? Would anything be different if she answered his call? If she answered *any* of the calls he made to her in the last few months?

She has no answers.

Facts are scarce, the investigation ongoing, and most articles resort to a rehash of old information. The Morley case is brought up again and again. Inevitably, someone suggests that, given the latest developments, it appears the state had the right man in prison for the murder of Gwen Morley all along. At least until a popular documentary convinced the public of his innocence, prompting a new investigation and the eventual release of a monster.

She slams her laptop closed.

This can't be happening. But even as the words float across her mind, Tessa recognizes them for the denial they are. The low-level dread that normally sits warm and ready at the base of her stomach is awake now and roaring to be fed.

Oliver Barlow is a killer.

She staked so much on that statement being false. Her career, her reputation.

The life of a girl she never met.

Tessa reaches for the wastebasket again. The brass key her mother gave her swings forward on its chain, clinking against the trash can.

There's nothing left in her stomach.

Oh God, what has she done?

5

KITTY

A world away, deep in the northern Pennsylvania forest, a small wooden chest lies in darkness, hidden beneath the floorboards of an ivy-covered cottage. It has brass fittings and a lock with no key.

Two old women sit in the early afternoon light on the front porch. Deirdre, the eldest, holds a pile of green beans on an apron across her lap. She snaps the ends off each before dropping it into a bowl by her side. She works slowly, her movements weighed down by age and the onset of arthritis she refuses to acknowledge.

The other, Kitty, is clearly younger, but not so much as one might think. Generous genetics and a sunnier disposition have left her skin less ravaged by time.

Kitty holds a bone-handled paring knife in one hand and an apple in the other, such a glossy red it borders on profane. Not a speck of yellow mars the relentless crimson.

With a practiced gesture, the younger old woman slices just below the skin and turns the fruit in a slow, smooth motion that peels away the red in a continuous ribbon, revealing the ripe flesh beneath.

"Do you have any regrets, Dee?"

She hadn't realized the question was forming until it fluttered past her lips into the silence between them.

A slight break in the rhythm of the beans snapping is the only indication her sister hears the question.

"I regret I didn't add cinnamon to the grocery order," Deirdre eventually says. "The bit we have will have to do." She eyes the number of apples Kitty has left to peel. Her own hands don't stop their work. "I'd like to get that pie in the oven so it can cool before suppertime."

Kitty makes no effort to increase her pace.

Deirdre squints into the distance where the trees stand between the two of them and the world outside.

It's always been this way. Deirdre never looks back, even now, with far more of their lives behind them than in front.

"You're an irritating woman," Kitty says, common words with no heat behind them.

"Aye," Deirdre replies, but her eyes are still trained on the woods, an extra furrow in her wrinkled brow. "Supposed to be a storm coming."

Kitty follows her gaze, but there's no sign of what, or who, her sister is hoping to see.

"He'll be back when he needs to be," Kitty says. "Aiden knows these woods as well as you or I."

Deirdre frowns. "Aye, and I know him. He'll be putting off coming home, dreading the rain keeping him indoors. He'll drag up at the last possible minute, soaked to the bone and tempting pneumonia."

Kitty shrugs. "At least you've gotten a head start on being mad about it."

Her sister glares at her. Kitty smiles sweetly. Deirdre snaps the last of the beans with more force than necessary and stands, brushing off her apron. She's a tall woman, where Kitty is short and plump. Deirdre is all angles and corners, age having carved away any softness she'd once had. She leans down to pick up the bowl.

"Try to finish those apples sometime before the resurrection, will you," she says as she walks past Kitty toward the door.

"Quit fussing," Kitty says. "If Jesus comes back by suppertime, he'll have a nice apple pie waiting. With not quite enough cinnamon."

"Well, I hope he has enough sense to come in out of the rain, or we'll be nursing *two* men with pneumonia." Deirdre slams the door behind her. Her footsteps echo across the worn floorboards as she heads to the kitchen.

"You can't catch pneumonia from getting wet, Dee!" Kitty calls. "Doctors discovered these crazy things called viruses, and they don't travel by rain."

Kitty smiles when the window between the kitchen and the porch closes with a bang. She turns back to the apple in her hand, but movement catches her eye, and she lifts her gaze to follow it.

They've been there a while now, the figures playing hide-and-seek along the path that leads to the big house. They laugh with an abandon that only comes with youth, and the sound brings Kitty's heart a rare kind of joy.

Deirdre didn't see them, of course. She never does, and Kitty's learned not to ask. She doesn't like to upset her sister.

It's a shame, though. Such wild, lovely children.

She watches them until worry begins to nibble at the edges of her enjoyment like a hungry mouse. They have no idea how beautiful they are. An overwhelming need to protect them comes over her. To warn them.

From what, she doesn't know.

The smallest one spies her, then stops to wave.

Kitty raises her hand to wave back, but they've gone.

She drags in a sharp breath and glances down at her other hand. A line of red, the exact shade as the glossy apple, wells up across her palm where the blade of the knife has sliced her.

Cursing her carelessness, she squeezes her hand tightly into a fist and rises to get a bandage before Deirdre notices.

Her sister worries too much.

6

TESSA

Tessa can't catch her breath. She's left with nothing but her own tangled emotions, and there's little peace to be had, alone with her churning thoughts.

It's a familiar feeling, the sensation of breaking apart in slow motion. It scares her, knowing where it can lead if she can't get a handle on herself.

She's got her feet firmly on the road to a setback.

Setback. Her therapist's term for it. Privately, Tessa thinks the phrase sucks. It's nothing so benign. It's a descent. A descent into a dark, lonely place. A place she's terrified of being trapped again.

Because this time, she won't be alone. The image of Valerie Winters will be there to keep her company.

Her intercom buzzes for the fourth time in the last half hour. The first three were reporters. This one, thank goodness, isn't.

"Tess? Tessa, it's me. Can you buzz me in?"

The voice is distant, mechanical, but there's no doubt who it is. She's been expecting him.

She told him not to come, but she didn't mean it. She wouldn't have called if she hadn't wanted, *needed*, him to come.

She presses a button to open the door downstairs.

When the knock on the door comes, Tessa hesitates. This is the reason she called. A friend. Support. A lifeline.

"Let me in, Tessa," says the voice on the other side of the door. "I know you're there."

She sighs. She's not fooling anyone. Not even herself.

When she opens the door to her apartment, Ben Russell peers at her, concern etched on every line of his face. "You look like shit," he says after a moment.

"Good to see you too." She leaves him standing in the hallway and walks back toward the kitchen. She needs to walk away. If she stares at him too long, she'll lose her composure. "I guess you've seen the news?"

"Yeah." He drops an overnight bag inside her door, then closes it behind him. "The police haven't found her, then?"

"No." Tessa pulls open the door of the fridge and grabs two beers. "I don't think so. I tried to call the Bonham Police Department, but . . ."

"Persona non grata?" Ben guesses, correctly.

She hadn't even made it past the receptionist, whose manner had turned distinctly cold after Tessa had given her name. The chilly reception wasn't a surprise. After fourteen months of exhaustive research and interviews, she produced a series that laid bare every mistake and abuse of authority she could dig up in the Bonham Police Department's handling of the Gwen Morley murder case, and there was no shortage of material to find.

The results were devastating to the small, tight-knit community located just south of Albany. After the documentary was released, there was an outcry for justice from the rest of the country, but in Bonham, many, if not most, of the residents stood firm in their belief that Oliver Barlow was a rapist and a murderer.

Tessa devoted an entire episode to describing what seemed, to an outsider at least, like an inordinate amount of prejudice against the Barlow family that ran like a river through the little town.

"No one is going to let me anywhere near that investigation," she says. "Not that I blame them. I just . . . I don't know. I feel like I should be doing something."

Ben follows her into the kitchen and takes a seat on a barstool. Tessa distractedly notes how kind the years have been to him, and the unfairness of that. By rights, he should have a middle-age paunch and at least a little sagging around the jowls, but no. His strawberry blonde hair, just this side of ginger, is as thick as it ever was, and if there are a few grays lurking in there, they're well camouflaged. Ben moves with the lithe grace of a man comfortable in his skin.

"Have you eaten?" she asks. "I can find something to throw together if you're hungry." She avoids his eyes and clasps her hands together to hide their tremor.

"No, I'm fine."

Tessa crosses to the pantry anyway and rummages through the shelves. "I don't have anything but stale crackers anyway. I'll order something."

She gasps when she turns to find he's moved from his seat. He's standing directly behind her.

"Forget food, Tessa," he says. "I'm not here for you to feed me."

Her eyes are level with the buttons on his shirt, and she slowly raises them. When they meet his, she freezes.

"I came to make sure you're okay." One hand comes up and gently brushes a strand of hair behind her ear.

The worry in his eyes undoes her. Each of the defense mechanisms she uses to hold herself together begins to snap, one by one, and before she's aware it's going to happen, tears fill her eyes.

"I can't get her picture out of my head," she whispers. "She was so young, and so pretty. Her whole life ahead of her, and now she's dead. And it's my fault."

Her face crumples, and she drops the box of crackers between their feet, pulling her hands up to cover her tears. She hasn't seen Ben in years, and he's been in her apartment for less than two minutes before she's turned into a needy mess of insecurities.

She chokes back a sob as his arms close around her. "It's okay, Tess. I'm here."

He doesn't tell her not to cry. He just holds her while the pain and guilt course through her.

Tessa's feet go out from under her, and he supports her as the two of them slide to the floor. She leans her head against his chest and cries the tears that have been building from the moment she saw Ollie smile into the camera that morning.

Tessa doesn't know how long she cries. Long enough to soak the front of Ben's shirt while he strokes her hair. When she finally manages to glance up, his head is leaned back and his eyes are closed. He looks tired, and a new wave of guilt hits her. He was at a conference for work when she called. He should be heading home to his own bed, not babysitting her.

Ben doesn't bother to say any of the well-meaning clichés most people would. It's one of the reasons she loves him. And she *does* love him, no matter what's happened over the years. Ben understands she doesn't need or expect him to fix anything. She only needs him to be there. A friend to remind her she's not alone.

"I'm sorry," she says as she wipes her face on her shirtsleeve. "I hate putting you in this position."

He shrugs. "And I hate seeing you take everything onto your own shoulders like this. You didn't plant evidence. You didn't throw Barlow in jail. You didn't steal years from his life."

"That doesn't make it okay!" she says, sitting up and staring at him. Tessa picks herself up from the floor. Even with her back to him, she's aware of Ben's gaze on her.

"No, it doesn't," he says. "But Tessa . . . this isn't on you. If Winters had done his job, none of this would have happened. I don't know if Barlow's guilty or not—"

"You saw the video."

"Yeah, I saw it. I saw a desperate, angry man whose life has been ruined. If he was guilty the first time around, then Winters should have proven it instead of letting his men railroad him."

Tessa shakes her head, searching for the right words. "Ben, you don't understand. I was convinced Ollie didn't kill Gwen Morley," she says. "Not just that the authorities didn't play fair. Not just that he was a victim of a corrupt system. I believed that he was *innocent*."

Ben shrugs. "Maybe he was."

She stares at him in horror. Each possibility is worse than the other. The idea that she helped put a murderer, a guilty man, back on the streets to strike again . . . or the idea that an innocent man became so warped by events outside of his control that he crossed an unforgiveable line. That he took a life, *murdered* another human being, out of some twisted need for revenge.

"What's happened since doesn't negate what came before," Ben says.

"Doesn't it?" she says softly. "I wish I could believe that."

Ben sighs and pulls up one leg, resting his arm across his knee. "But you don't, do you?" There's no judgment in his face, only a sad acceptance.

"I can't." Not because she doesn't want to, but because she does. If Tessa can separate the two crimes, she can absolve herself of responsibility for the second. She can still believe, in her heart, that she did the right thing. The desire to do so is nearly overwhelming. And incredibly self-serving.

"By his own admission, Oliver Barlow is a man capable of terrible things. Regardless of how he landed there, prison is where I found him, and prison is where he'd still be if I hadn't gotten involved."

Ben sighs. "All I'm saying is this isn't entirely on you. Don't do that to yourself. It'll take you down roads you don't want to go down again."

Thoughts of the last time flash through her head. The hospital, the meds. The descent that took her there.

"Have you talked to your mom?" Ben asks.

Tessa shakes her head. She should tell him about her mother's ultimatum, but it won't change anything. Ben can't fix her family either.

He doesn't bother asking if she's talked to her sister.

"Look, Tessa, there's nothing good about this situation, but you can't do anything about that. It's out of your hands. The only way you're going to get through this in one piece is to find a way to accept that."

She looks up and meets his eyes. "But how?"

"One step at a time," he says. "Just like everything else."

His smile is warm, and she can still see a glimmer of the boy she fell in love with when she was six. The boy who, if life had dealt them a different hand, she might have married.

7

The next morning, Tom Petty sings about one more time to kill the pain, and Tessa burrows farther under her covers. The music accompanies an unmistakable smell of freshly brewed coffee and frying bacon.

It's an irresistible combination and pulls her from the bed against all odds.

The shower is running in the bathroom as she passes. Tessa rubs sleep from her eyes and stumbles toward the promise of caffeine.

She pours a cup and sees a cast iron pan her mother bought for her sitting on the stove with a tea towel draped over the top.

Tessa's never used that pan. Not once.

Suspiciously, she lifts the edge of the tea towel.

"Biscuits? You made *biscuits*? Ben, how long have you been awake?" she yells.

There's no answer from the bathroom and no one to hear her grumble about farm boys rising with the roosters. She takes a biscuit from the pan. It's flaky and still warm.

As fortified as she's ever going to be, Tessa turns down the music and settles in at her small kitchen table. Her phone has been switched to silent for nearly twenty-four hours. Reporters started blowing it up not long after the story broke.

But she can't hide from the world forever.

Girding herself, Tessa checks her notifications. Her stomach drops at the number. With a sigh, she begins listening to her voice mails, deleting the ones from the press when they've barely begun speaking.

There are three messages from her mother, all sent the day before.

Tessa pauses on the last one.

"Honey, I know you're having a rough day. And I know you need time to process this, but please don't ever forget, you're not alone. You're loved. Always."

Tessa squeezes her eyes shut. She's not going to cry. She's not.

"Goodnight, Tessa," her mom continues. "We'll speak when you're ready."

At the tone, Tessa's thumb hovers, then moves to save the message.

The next is from Anne, left only an hour ago.

"Hey, I'm at the office," her assistant says. "Call me when you get this. We have a problem."

The peace her mother's message settled on her evaporates as Tessa dials Anne's number.

She answers on the first ring.

"What's wrong?"

"Bad news," Anne says.

"I gathered that much. What is it?"

Anne pauses, and while Tessa can appreciate her assistant's flair for drama in the editing room, she bites her tongue when faced with it in real life.

"We got a message from the first lady's team. On the office line."

Tessa drops her head into her hand.

She doesn't need Anne to tell her they've been fired. Good news goes to cell phones. Bad news, though, only bad news is delivered via an office line on a weekend when no one is around to take the call.

"Let me guess. After careful consideration, they've decided to go in a different direction?"

"Got it in one."

More words stream from Anne, but Tessa isn't listening. This is what she deserves. What difference does her professional reputation make, given what the Winters family is going through?

But it's a jagged pill to swallow. Her work. Her life. Like a bad magician, Oliver has pulled the tablecloth out, and everything is crashing to the floor.

"Tessa? Are you there?"

"Yes," she says quietly into the phone. "I'll call you back, Anne."

Her assistant is still talking when Tessa ends the call.

Vaguely, she realizes the shower hasn't stopped. The biscuit sitting next to her coffee is still warm. Very little time has passed, but everything feels different. If yesterday had the surreal sensation of a fevered nightmare, today a stark reality is setting in.

A knock on the apartment door rouses her from the immobility that's taken hold of her limbs, and she drags herself to answer it on autopilot.

If she were thinking, she'd realize she's not expecting anyone and the chances of opening the door to a reporter while still in her pajamas with sleep-tangled hair are better than average.

But when she unlocks the door and swings it open, Tessa's mouth drops. She can't find her voice.

It's not a reporter. It's Margot.

Margot is here.

Tessa drinks in the sight of her sister. In an instant, she comprehends how much of herself she left behind when they parted. There's been a hollow place at the center of her she's carried ever since.

But there's no time to dwell on either the magnitude of that loss or the sensation the sight of her sister brings, the tingling rush of lifeblood into a limb whose circulation has been blocked.

Because something is wrong.

One look at her sister, her face drawn and haggard, hair a cloud of unruly curls around her shoulders, her eyes puffy from tears, and Tessa understands immediately that something is very, very wrong.

Margot reaches out to grasp her without a word, pulling Tessa into a tight embrace that won't allow her to hide the way her body is shaking. Tessa can do nothing but hold on for dear life.

Whatever horrible thing has brought Margot to her door, Tessa's not sure if she has the strength to face it.

"Margot . . ." she whispers. It's a question. One she doesn't want to hear the answer to.

Her twin sister clutches her tightly, and Tessa flashes to the night their lives changed forever when they were ten years old. A single-car accident on an icy road. A policeman at the door. They'd clung to one another while their mother collapsed in the doorway in her pale blue nightgown.

Margot says the words she dreads. Her heart is already breaking.

"It's Mom, Tess."

Like in her dream, Tessa is falling. The wind is rushing past, and all she can do is brace herself for the impact.

"She's gone. She died in her sleep last night. They think it was a heart attack."

Tessa's mouth opens and pulls in a sharp, involuntary gasp, absorbing the blow as it lands.

Footsteps sound in her ears and, with a sinking sensation, Tessa realizes she's not done falling yet.

"Margot?" Ben is standing behind them. The look of concern on his face doesn't negate the fact that he's wearing nothing but a towel around his waist, his hair wet from the shower.

Her sister's grip on her loosens, and Tessa opens her mouth to speak, but it's too late. Margot's face has gone slack and white. Tessa sees the exact moment her confusion gives way to understanding and, in that moment, Tessa loses her sister all over again.

This time maybe for good.

Margot backs away from the scene she's stumbled into, shaking her head like she's been punched. Tessa reaches for her, but Margot bats her hand away.

"No, Margot, it's not . . ."

What's she going to say? It's not what it looks like? Who would believe that tired old line anyway?

"Don't," Margot says, shaking her head again.

"What's happened?" Ben asks, slower to comprehend the monumental shift taking place beneath their feet. He takes a step toward Margot, but she backs up so quickly she bumps against the wall in the hallway outside Tessa's door.

He stops, shocked by her reaction, then the realization of where they are sinks in and his face changes. He glances down at his own bare chest and the towel slung around his waist.

"Margot," he says. "You don't understand—"

"I said *don't*! Don't talk to me." She holds up a hand and Ben falters.

"I should go," Margot mumbles, more to herself than to either Tessa or Ben. "I . . . I'm going now."

She turns and flees down the hallway, bypassing the elevators and heading for the stairwell.

"Margot!" Ben rushes past Tessa, gripping his towel to keep it from falling. "Margot!"

But it's too late. The door slams behind Margot and she's gone, leaving both her sister and her husband in her wake.

Tessa crumples to the floor. Their mother is dead. And Margot will never forgive her.

8

KITTY

"I'll *never* forgive you for this!"

Kitty, seated on a creaky piano bench in the deteriorating old house, turns to watch the drama play out, just as it did once before. The intervening years peel away, and the mold and rot fade into the background, giving way to the warmth of polished wood and the smell of pipe tobacco.

Fallbrook comes alive, at least in Kitty's mind, along with the souls of those who once called it home.

The Cooke family. Their voices carry the hollow echo of time passed.

Ruby Cooke, the eldest daughter, is young still, already showing signs she'll become a beauty one day, but her pretty mouth is tight and her eyes hot with indignation.

"Papa, it's not my fault," cries her younger sister, Cora, while Ruby drags her forward with an iron grip upon her arm.

The sisters, bedraggled and dripping with dirty water and pond muck, stand in the library, presenting themselves before their father's pristine mahogany desk. A puddle forms beneath their feet.

As daughters of the big house, they don't have the immediate sense of having crossed a line, but the Donnelly children, who stand behind them, are servants. At times like this, it hardly matters that they form one band of roving children who wander the grounds together. In the presence of Everett Cooke, the Donnellys know their place.

The youngest of the lot, little Peter Cooke, stands in the back as well. He's only four, but he's recognized the look on his father's face and grips Aiden's hand as he tries to hide himself behind the older boy's legs. Ruby, however, doesn't notice the storm brewing on her father's face. She's concerned only with tossing her sister to the wolves.

"Papa, I demand you punish Cora! She's gone too far this time. First she ruined my new hat—"

"It was an accident! I didn't mean to trample your stupid hat. You were just in the way."

"Then she runs off like a loon, and when I tried to catch her, she pushed me in the pond!"

"That's not what happened—"

A corner of Kitty's mouth twitches upward. Ruby left out the part about trying to drown her sister in the green, murky pond after she tripped over a tree root and fell in herself. The younger girl had laughed, understandably, so Ruby grasped Cora by the ankle and pulled her down into the water too. Aiden had to fish the two of them out.

But the specifics don't interest Everett Cooke any more than they do his eldest daughter.

"Enough!" he roars, staring down the gaggle of children filling his library.

"Everett?" a woman's voice says into the silence that falls over the room. She's pale and delicate, like the china in the cupboard. She sits with her legs crossed at the ankle and a cup of tea poised halfway to her lips. Her eyelashes are so light they seem almost to disappear. "Exactly how many children do you have?"

Mr. Cooke slams his brandy glass down and stands. This time, even the Cooke girls notice he's seething.

"Three," he says darkly. "I have three undisciplined, untidy, untamed offspring who don't have the sense the good Lord gave them. Step forward."

Ruby and Cora hesitate but finally do so, at last comprehending their peril. Cora peeks up at her father's guests, resplendent in their fine clothes and clearly shocked by the tableau in front of them.

"You too, Peter. Stop hiding back there," Everett says.

Peter glances quickly up at Aiden, who nods to the boy. He slowly makes his way forward to stand with his sisters.

The Donnelly siblings step back, grateful for once that their mother is only the housekeeper and they're not expected to be in that line. They do what children of servants learn to do at a young age and fade into the background as best they can, waiting for the opportunity to flee.

"These are my children. Ruby, Cora, and Peter," Everett Cooke says, his voice shaking with barely restrained anger. "And this, children, is your new stepmother, Helena."

The door of Kitty's memory closes softly now on the scene, but not before she recalls the horror on the faces of the Cooke children.

Once again, she's in an empty room filled with dust and memories. Kitty pulls her old bones from the piano bench to make her way slowly home. Deirdre will worry if she's gone too long.

The lure of the past and those who live there doesn't hold the same fascination for Deirdre, who likes to pretend they never existed.

But Kitty can't help staring over her shoulder at what once was. The Cooke children were right to be distressed.

After Helena, everything changed.

9

TESSA

Everything has changed.

Tessa hides in the bathroom of the house she grew up in. In a few hours, she'll watch her mother's casket be lowered into the ground.

But neither Oliver Barlow nor the press salivating over his story stop for Tessa's loss. A second video has been released. She bites her hand to keep quiet while Oliver's face fills the screen of her phone, and his voice echoes off the cold tile.

"My parents put everything they had into getting me out of jail. Their time, their money. Their lives. My mother died. Did you know that, Winters?" A flicker of grief crosses Oliver's face, though it's quickly overtaken by rage.

"What would her life have been like if you hadn't done what you did? What would *your daughter's* life have been like? Will your wife survive the pain? Will she forgive you, do you think?" It's dark wherever Oliver is, and shadows hide much of his face. Tessa thinks he smiles then, but it's brief, there one moment, then stolen by darkness the next.

"Behind my parents' house, on the backside of the property, there's a shed. It's old and falling down. It's been there since I was a kid. Go take a look, Winters. I left something for you to find."

The video ends abruptly.

Tessa catches sight of herself in the mirror. With wide eyes set off by dark circles and pale skin, she looks like a ghost, and feels as substantial as one. As if she might fade entirely away at any minute.

Pull yourself together. Today is about Mom.

No matter how much she wishes it was different, she can't do anything about Oliver. Tessa *needs* to focus.

She splashes water on her face and forces herself to leave the bathroom. A little while later she's putting fresh water in the vases of flowers sent by well-meaning friends and neighbors when the notifications on her social media feeds light up. She braces herself and clicks a link.

A body has been discovered on the Barlows' property. Video shows emergency services in Bonham removing a distinctive covered shape on a stretcher.

The vase of lilies Tessa is holding slips from her grasp and shatters on the floor.

Running feet sound in the hallway, and she quickly kneels to pick up the larger pieces of glass.

"Tessa?" Margot says as she rounds the corner into the kitchen.

"Careful, there's glass," Tessa tells her sister.

Margot opens her mouth to speak, but she changes her mind. Instead, she walks to the cupboard and pulls out the broom and dustpan. She hands them to Tessa, then exits the kitchen without another word.

It's been this way since Tessa arrived. She'd packed an overnight bag, but never expected to be sharing her childhood home. Margot and Ben live on the other side of town, closer to the bakery her sister owns and operates.

Yet Ben's relationship with Margot is as shaky as Tessa's.

She tried to talk to her sister about Ben the night she first arrived home. It didn't go well.

"I know how it looked, Margot, but Ben and I aren't sleeping together," she insisted.

"I'm not going to discuss my husband with you, Tessa," Margot said darkly. "Drop it."

"He loves you," Tessa said, unable to let it go. "I love you. Neither of us would *ever*—"

Margot stood so quickly the kitchen chair she was sitting in toppled to the floor behind her. She elbowed past her sister on her way out of the room.

"Margot!" Tessa cried.

Margot stopped, one hand gripping the doorframe so hard that her knuckles were white. She turned her face halfway back, her profile taut.

"Sex isn't the only way to hurt someone, Tess. You ought to know that."

Tessa hasn't brought up the subject again. The few days since have been filled with funeral arrangements and an uneasy truce. At night, the two of them sleep in their old bedrooms, mirror images with an adjoining bathroom, barely speaking.

The memorial service passes in a bittersweet haze. Her mother was well loved in the community and among her family, and sadness mingles with happy memories. But Tessa can't shake the sense that she's failed her mother.

I've only made things worse, Mom.

The guests return for a reception at Jane's farmhouse. Tessa stays busy refilling glasses and keeping a safe distance from her sister. She knows that once the last guest has gone, and the food and the plates are cleared and put away, she'll get back in her car and leave Margot to sort out the rest of her life.

What choice does she have? She's done enough damage.

Overwhelmed suddenly by the effort it takes to smile and make small talk, Tessa excuses herself. She needs a quiet moment alone. Her feet take her to her mother's bedroom door.

She pushes it open, and Jane's faint scent welcomes her inside. In her creased black dress and heels, Tessa drops slowly onto the edge of the bed and runs a hand over the quilt that drapes it.

Tessa pulls her feet up and lays her head on her mother's pillow, the linen cool against her cheek. Ivory drapes flutter in the breeze from the open door that leads outside where guests are milling about, speaking to one another in somber, hushed voices.

The world has tipped on end, and all the things Tessa once believed true have been lost in some negative space where black is white, up is down, and her mother is gone forever.

When the door opens quietly and her sister walks in the room, Tessa sits up, bracing herself. Margot drops onto the bed beside her, and her eyes roam around the room, searching for somewhere to land other than Tessa.

They sit side by side. Whatever else is between them, in this moment, they share a loss that only the other can comprehend. Margot laces her fingers through Tessa's and they hold on tight.

It can't last. They both know this, but their grip is fierce despite that knowledge. Or because of it.

After a time, the sound of raised voices drifts through the open door, incongruous on a day filled with quiet condolences. Tessa tenses, even as Margot's hand loosens, and she fights the urge to squeeze tighter, to prolong a connection that can't be forced.

Her sister's hand slips from hers as Margot rises to move to the door.

"What now?" Margot says under her breath.

Shaking off the fresh wave of loss, Tessa stands and walks to her sister's side. In their mother's backyard, friends and family are gathered near the giant oak that still has a rope and board swing tied to one of its sturdy, fat branches. A picnic table is loaded with food, but Aunt Nan's broccoli and rice casserole isn't what holds everyone's attention.

Across the yard, where a gate opens to the circle drive, three men are arguing.

"Who is that?" Tessa asks.

Two of the men are recognizable. It's Ben and Uncle Rob, their father's youngest brother. Rob is shaking his finger in the face of a third man while Ben holds an arm across Rob's chest, trying to defuse whatever situation is brewing.

The stranger holds up both hands but doesn't retreat. Instead he pulls a small notebook from his shirt pocket and flips it open, which sets Rob off again.

"I said get the hell out of here, you slimy bastard." Rob's voice carries across the green grass, upsetting the quiet stillness of the scene. "This is private property. You have no business here. Have some goddamned respect, why don't you? And *that* you can quote me on!"

Tessa's heart drops.

The press.

She's out the door, hurrying across the lawn as fast as her heels can take her.

Ben sees her coming. "No," he says, holding a hand up in her direction. "Stay back. I'll get rid of him."

"Ms. Shepherd," the reporter calls over his shoulder. "Ms. Shepherd, would you care to comment on the Oliver Barlow situation?"

Rob draws back a fist, but Ben steps between her uncle and the reporter, gripping the older man by the forearms. It's the opening Tessa needs and she rushes forward, grabbing the reporter by his arm.

She pulls him quickly away from the gathering, toward the privacy of the driveway lined with cars.

"Ms. Shepherd, are you aware that a body was recovered from the Barlows' property earlier today? Given the latest developments, do you stand by the work you did to help Oliver Barlow gain his freedom?"

Now that she has him away from the crowd, Tessa has no idea what to say. If she defends her work, the public will crucify her. If she doesn't, they'll crucify her anyway.

And none of that matters right now.

"I buried my mother today," Tessa says carefully. "This is not the time or the place for an interview. I'd like you to leave. Now."

"The longer you wait, Tessa, the more people are going to talk," the reporter says. She notices the way he's switched to her first name. He can't be a day older than twenty-five. "Public perception is hard to change once it takes hold, and right now you look like you're hiding from a situation you created."

Tessa would like nothing more than to wipe the smugness off his face, but she's in no position to do that. It doesn't help to knows he's right.

"Just one quote. Come on," he says.

She's tempted, if only to get him to leave. *My heart goes out to the friends and family of Valerie Winters during this difficult time. They are in my prayers.*

Two things hold her back. Firstly, the Winters family doesn't give a shit about her thoughts and prayers. No amount of either will bring their daughter home. As far as Lloyd Winters is concerned, Tessa has a seat reserved in hell next to Oliver Barlow. Platitudes would be nothing but a self-serving attempt to salvage her image.

Secondly, though not necessarily of equal importance, she doesn't like him. There may come a time when she speaks to the press, but it won't be to a reporter brazen enough to gate-crash her mother's funeral.

"No comment," Tessa says through gritted teeth. "Now leave, or I'll call the police."

"This isn't going away, you know."

She crosses her arms and clenches her jaw. Seeing she's not going to budge, he shakes his head and tucks his notebook back into his pocket.

"Fine, but—"

"I'm going to get my phone," she says and turns her back on him.

"I've got mine."

Tessa hadn't realized Margot followed them, but she's glad to see her standing a few yards away, holding a cell phone in her hand.

43

"Call the police. Tell them we have a trespasser."

"Fine," the reporter says. "I'm going. No need to be like that."

The sisters stand shoulder to shoulder until he climbs into his vehicle and reverses down the long driveway.

"Margot, I'm sorry—"

"He's right. It isn't going away." Her sister's voice is hard again. Their fleeting moment of solidarity is gone. "And now you've brought it here."

"Margot—"

Her sister turns on her heel. Ben is standing at the gate, watching, but Margot brushes past him. He tries to speak to her, but she walks by him like he doesn't exist.

He waits while Tessa follows at a slower pace.

"I'm sorry, Ben. I'll leave tonight," she says.

He frowns and shoves his hands in his pockets. "How's that going to help?" he asks. The frustration in his voice surprises her.

"That reporter won't be the last to show up, not as long as I'm here. Once I go, there's no reason for them to bother any of you again."

He stares as if he's trying to work out if she has any sense at all.

"What?" Tessa demands.

But Ben shakes his head. "You. You and Margot both. You Shepherd girls are pretty good at running away."

The disgust in his voice stings.

"What's that supposed to mean?" Tessa cries, but she's talking to his back.

10

Aunt Nan washes up while Tessa dries. Her hands and her heart fall into the quiet, domestic rhythm with ease.

There's a dishwasher in the old farmhouse kitchen, but it's understood it's no place for Jane's good china.

"What are you going to do now?" Nan asks.

Tessa glances up and spies her sister in the backyard through the kitchen window. Margot is folding the tablecloth from the picnic table. Her face is drawn, her movements slow and deliberate. The sun is low on the horizon, and a breeze plays with the curls that have fallen from Margot's once neat updo.

We've come unraveled, Tessa thinks.

"I don't know," she says honestly. According to her assistant, Tessa's apartment in New York has press camped at the doors after the release of Oliver's second video.

"You could stay with us for a while," her aunt offers.

Tessa glances at her, surprised. Of course, they all know the situation. Family always does.

"That's nice of you, but I couldn't impose on you and Rob like that."

Still, she's touched by the offer. She's missed this place, these people. Tessa left behind more than her sister all those years ago.

Nan nods. "Well, if you change your mind, you know where to find us. The kids are all grown, and we have the room."

"Thank you," she says. "I'll keep that in mind."

Once the dishes are done, Tessa makes another pass through the house to search out any stray plates or cups and finds Margot speaking quietly with one of Mom's friends. The older man, Tessa can't remember his name, motions for her to join them.

"Margot was telling me you plan to leave town soon," the man says.

She nods but finds herself oddly distracted by his silver-streaked hair and angled features. She would frame him in low light, to accentuate the rugged lines on his face. Maybe firelight. A campfire with snow falling softly in the background.

He's speaking, and she shakes off the vision, struggling to keep up.

"So I'd be happy to see the two of you in my office tomorrow or the next day, if that works for you both."

Tessa frowns. "I'm sorry, I don't understand, Mr. . . ." She trails off, searching for the name he might have already mentioned.

"Smith," he fills in for her. "Jackson Smith."

"Jackson has been Mom's attorney for years," Margot adds, but there's something in the look she gives Tessa that says more.

Tessa's brows rise a little of their own accord, and she struggles to keep her voice neutral.

"I see," is the best she can manage. She meets Margot's eyes. *Really? Mom and the silver fox?*

Her sister's mouth twitches as she tries to hide a smile, but the dimple in her cheek deepens with the effort, and she glances toward the floor.

Tessa's eyes swivel quickly back to Mr. Smith, trying valiantly to hold back the inappropriate laughter that bubbles up.

"Janie was a wonderful woman," he's saying. "I'm deeply sorry for your loss."

"Thank you, Mr. Smith." Tessa manages to keep her voice somber by biting the inside of her lip.

"Well." He clears his throat. "Like I was saying, if you two would like to come by my office, we can get the formalities taken care of right away."

"I'm sorry, what formalities?" Tessa asks.

"Jackson's talking about Mom's will," Margot says.

"Oh." Tessa still doesn't understand. "Okay. But . . . I assume everything is pretty straightforward."

She hasn't considered a will, but it would be out of character for their mother to be anything but evenhanded. A decision will need to be made about the house, and there's the cabin that belonged to their grandparents, but . . .

"Whatever Margot chooses to do will be fine with me," she says. Both faces are studying her, and Tessa squirms beneath their scrutiny. "I plan to leave tonight."

Margot stiffens noticeably and her features go blank. Jackson Smith straightens as well.

"Tonight?" he repeats. "Ms. Shepherd . . . Tessa? May I call you Tessa?"

She nods and avoids her sister's gaze.

"I hope you'll forgive the presumption, but I think it would be best if you could stay for at least another day. I don't have the paperwork at hand, but trust me when I say that Jane's estate is a bit more . . . *complicated* than you might expect."

"What does that mean? Complicated how?" Tessa asks. She glances at her sister, but Margot stands stiffly with her arms crossed. Tessa has been shut out again.

"My office is on the town square," Jackson Smith says, which isn't an answer. He pulls a business card from his wallet and offers it to her. "Come by in the morning, any time you like. I'll explain everything."

Tessa sighs and accepts the card. The low-level headache she's been fighting all day makes a stunning reappearance and suddenly she's exhausted. Exhausted and sad.

One more night. One more night surrounded by memories and past mistakes.

"Fine," Tessa says, giving in. "Tomorrow morning, first thing."

"And after that?" a tiny voice in her head whispers, but there's no answer for that either.

11

Sleep is the easy way out. Sometimes the only way.

But Tessa's body doesn't allow her more than a few hours. She awakens suddenly, frightened for no perceivable reason. Then her heart rate slows as she remembers where she is and why.

Margot is here somewhere too, sheltering her own hurt beneath the same roof. The knowledge pulls at Tessa, magnetic in its insistence.

She rises from the bed, leaving the sheets as tangled as her mind, and pads down the hallway toward the kitchen. She's not searching for her sister. Margot's icy reception has made it clear she doesn't want Tessa's company, but she notices a lamp burning in the living room as she passes.

The two aren't identical twins. Though they resemble one another, the physical features that they share—their mother's eyes, their father's straight, sharp nose—are no more or less than any pair of sisters might.

They do, however, share a connection born of proximity. An unavoidable closeness, having formed side by side in the same womb. At least, they did once.

Before the accident.

Before Tessa's carelessness split them apart.

There's a fresh cup of tea waiting on the counter, steam still wafting upward. Tessa lifts it, letting the heat seep into her hands. The aroma of lemon and chamomile fills her.

It's possible, of course, that Margot made the cup for herself and left it forgotten in the kitchen, and now Tessa is adding tea theft to her growing list of transgressions, but she doesn't believe that's true.

Margot made tea for her, somehow knowing she'd be up soon. Sometimes, broken things retain the shape of their missing half, ragged and unmistakable along their edges. The cup was left for her.

Tea isn't forgiveness, and Tessa doesn't mistake it for such, but it warms her anyway.

She returns to the living room and finds her sister curled beneath a throw, her own cup cooling on the coffee table in front of her. A photo album lies open across her lap.

Tessa hesitates, but Margot doesn't immediately ask her to leave, so she walks slowly into the room.

"Mind if I join you?" she asks.

"It's a free country." Margot doesn't look up from the album and turns another thick page. The riotous curls Margot despaired of as a girl, no matter how many times Tessa said she'd trade her in a heartbeat, fall like a curtain between them, hiding her sister's face.

Tessa sits on the opposite end of the sofa and nurses her tea. Thoughts swirl, but every subject she touches on is out of bounds.

She and Ben will work it out, she tells herself. *They have to. It will be easier once I'm gone.*

Whether that's true or not, it's the best she's got, and Tessa clings to that.

"Do you remember this place?" Margot asks, gesturing to a crooked shot of Jane. It's an opening, and Tessa leans in to take a closer look. There's an old house in the background, looking abandoned and forlorn. She struggles to recall the circumstances of the photo.

"Was that after Granddad's funeral?" Margot asks.

Tessa shrugs and shakes her head. It's been a long time.

"It was," Margot insists. "We stopped here on the drive home, remember? Some historic site Mom wanted to see."

"Maybe," Tessa says. "Look at her face. God, it must have been rough, losing both her parents and Dad, all within a few years. She's not much older there than we are now."

"Life comes at you hard sometimes," Margot says, shifting away from Tessa. And with those words, they slip back into dangerous territory.

Tessa flashes onto the many phone calls from her mother, updates on how Margot was progressing through her recovery. The surgeries, the grueling physical therapy.

The intense desire to be by her sister's side while Margot was fighting to walk again feels like it was only yesterday. Along with the knowledge that she was the last person Margot wanted to see.

Instead, Tessa threw herself into film school. She turned down invitations to parties and avoided making friends, drunk on the guilt of her twin battling her way back onto her feet, while she was blithely walking to class.

She cried when Jane called to tell her Margot had taken her first steps, twenty-one months and eight days after that terrible night.

She cried again, two years later, when Jane haltingly told Tessa that Margot and Ben were engaged to be married.

"He's been by her side the whole time," Jane said, partly as an explanation, part apology. "I didn't want to bring it up before. I know how much you cared about him, but someone has to tell you."

"That's wonderful, Mom," Tessa had said through tears she tried to hide. "I'm happy for them."

But was she?

Before Tessa left town, on that last and final day, she'd gone to see Ben. Their meeting was short.

NYU wasn't a complete shock. Tessa had planned for many months to attend for the upcoming fall semester with the understanding that she and Ben would continue their relationship long distance, at least until he could join her.

Margot's accident had changed everything. There was no more talk of Tessa leaving.

But then, things changed again. Tessa removed the promise ring Ben had given her on her sixteenth birthday, the one she'd worn every day since, and laid it gently in his hand.

She would never forget the hurt on his face.

A clean break. As if such a thing exists.

She didn't have the strength to explain why. If he believed she was a monster for abandoning Margot, for abandoning him, there was nothing she could do about that.

"Please, Ben," she asked quietly. "Please, just be there for my sister while I can't."

Her voice cracked and she left before he could protest any more.

It was the right thing to do, the only thing to do, and Tessa didn't regret it . . . but *engaged*? The news was a shock, to say the least.

The joining in her mind of two separate, damaged bundles of nerve endings that she carried with her everywhere sparked and sizzled as they fused, leaving a new connection. Strong, but tender to the touch.

She forced her mouth to form the words. Margot. And. Ben. *Margot and Ben.*

Once the pain faded, Tessa was overcome with . . . wonderment.

She *was* happy for them. She was.

And now she's selfishly put it all at risk. She glances toward her sister's face, bathed in lamplight as Margot studies the photo album in her lap.

"Margot, I—"

"It wasn't her," Margot says before Tessa has a chance to finish the thought.

Tessa stops and stares at her sister, confused, as Margot closes the album and leans to place it on the coffee table.

"Valerie Winters," she explains when she sees Tessa's face. "It wasn't her in the shed on the Barlow property. It was Oliver Barlow's father."

"What?" Tessa struggles to understand.

"The news broke while you were sleeping. They haven't released the cause of death."

Tessa remembers the small man who couldn't stop crying when his son was released from prison. The way he'd slumped, silent and bereft, during his wife's funeral. "But that means . . ." She trails off, glancing at her sister.

"That means Valerie's body is still out there. Somewhere. And so is Oliver Barlow," Margot finishes for her. "It means this isn't over yet."

12

KITTY

"This isn't over yet! Come back here this instant!"

Kitty moans softly in her sleep, eyes squeezed tight as her limbs move restlessly beneath the sheets.

The voice, one part dream, two parts memory, holds her tightly in its clutches.

Helena Cooke is angry. Again.

Not that she doesn't have cause to be. That cause, as usual, comes careening around the corner into the kitchen. Cora.

The cup Deirdre is raising to her mouth stalls, splashing orange juice on the front of her dress.

Deirdre is closest to Cora in age. Raised in one another's pockets, they formed a friendship that flies in the face of the difference in their stations. But a stranger would be hard-pressed to determine which child is the daughter of the house and which the daughter of the housekeeper, as Cora is generally filthy.

Today, the stink precedes her entrance into the kitchen. Saoirse Donnelly, or Mam, as the children call her, is the housekeeper and closest thing to a mother the Cooke children have known since the death of their own. She wrinkles her nose in Cora's direction.

"Ach, just look at you, you grimy thing." She slaps Cora's hand as she reaches for a biscuit in the center of the table. "What have you done now?" The words are delivered in a cloud of frustration but lined with care.

Cora shrugs, stuffing her mouth full of biscuit she swiped from Peter's breakfast plate instead.

Sharp, quick footsteps follow overhead, then down the staircase. Mam waves her arms and ushers all of them from the room.

"Not you," she says, grabbing Cora by the collar as she tries to sneak past. "May as well face up to whatever this is now rather than later. Sit down. Ach, just look at you, child. You weren't half so dirty when you were off to bed, lass. How is it possible to get filthier in your sleep?"

With the housekeeper's hand on her shoulder, Cora drops mutinously back into her chair. Mrs. Donnelly tucks in a stray strand of hair just before Helena bursts into the room.

"Good morning, Mrs. Cooke," Mam says in a pleasant tone the lady of the house ignores.

"You!" Helena comes to an abrupt stop at the sight of Cora. She's in her robe, her pale hair loose and hanging around her shoulders. Her eyes, lovely and wide when her husband is around, narrow to slits.

Cora drops her head, not from shame, but to hide the smile creeping onto her face. She's unsuccessful, and the sight of her smirk enrages her stepmother.

"You little *wretch*," Helena snarls, her pretty mouth spitting the words.

From just outside the door that leads into the garden, the others have stopped to listen. Deirdre takes hold of Peter as he attempts to barge back into the kitchen and leap to his sister's defense, and the door swings slightly wider. With her head still bowed, Cora glances up and spots their faces filling the doorway. She winks, then holds a finger to her lips as Deirdre wraps her arms around Peter. Deirdre hugs the boy tightly, willing him to be silent and stay clear of Helena's furor as she pulls them all back and out of sight again. The second Mrs. Cooke won't hesitate to turn her anger on whichever child blunders into her path, even little Peter.

Children in general don't fit with Helena's vision of an ideal life, especially three undisciplined stepchildren. Cora takes a particular sort of pleasure in shattering Helena's expectations. But Cora's campaign of terror against her stepmother has perhaps gone too far this time.

"Mrs. Cooke, would you like a cup of tea?" Mam asks soothingly.

"Tea?" Helena shrieks, pulling her gaze from Cora to glare at the housekeeper. "No, I do not want tea! There are . . . There are . . ."

She makes an unladylike noise deep in her throat, and her face twists as she forces the words past her lips.

"There are *toads* in my closet! Toads in my dresser drawers. There are toads covering my bedroom floor and all my things! Hundreds of them, and this horrid, hateful child put them there!"

"Cora," Mam says on an exhale of breath. "Is this true?" Her voice is heavy with disappointment, knowing already how pointless the question is.

"It was a joke," Cora says, feigning an innocence that neither woman believes. "Toads are harmless."

Helena nearly chokes on her indignation. "Harmless? *Harmless?* Their disgusting bodies are crawling through my shoes! In my bed! They're wriggling in my *undergarments!*"

From their hiding place behind the door, the other children can hear Cora's snort of laughter.

"Cora Eugenia Cooke." Mam's voice is strong now, incensed. "You should be ashamed of yourself! You march up there this instant and clear those toads out of Mrs. Cooke's room, child."

"But—"

"Don't *but* me. Don't you dare. You will catch every last one of those creatures and put them right back in the pond where you got them. Immediately!"

"Yes, ma'am." Cora's reply is subdued. Saoirse Donnelly rarely raises her voice, but when she does, none of them dare contradict her.

Helena sputters, "I hardly think the fate of the toads is the most pressing issue, Mrs. Donnelly. What about my things? What about my *underwear?*"

"Cora, once those toads are back where they belong, you will come straight back here. You're going to spend your day washing, ironing, and folding your new mother's clothing and bedding."

"But—Ow!"

Mam has a way of gripping an ear that makes you think it might pull right off your head.

"Every stitch! Right after you *bathe* yourself, and I don't want to hear another word spoken from your lips. Toads, bath, laundry, in that order. Now, go!"

Cora is on her feet, running from the room before it occurs to Helena that, with all the efficiency of a drill sergeant, Mrs. Donnelly has dealt with the problem and sent the offender scurrying off to do her bidding.

Helena is left with a still-seething anger and no outlet at hand.

"Your father will hear about this, you mark my words!" Helena shrieks after the girl, stomping her foot like a petulant child.

"Aye," Mam agrees, though her tone is markedly calmer than that of her mistress. "Mr. Cooke will be livid over such disrespect."

This brings Helena's attention back to her as Mam sets a cup and saucer on the table and pours. "Have some tea, Mrs. Cooke, won't you?"

"I told you I don't want—"

"I'd wager a shopping trip to the city might be in order, if he's in a mood. A nice apology for his daughter's behavior."

Helena's head tilts, and some of the anger banks in her eyes. "The girl still needs a strap taken to her backside. The devil is in that one."

As harsh as the words are, they've lost their earlier edge.

"Aye, Cora's a handful. Always has been, but she'll settle down. You wait and see. Poor child. Without a mother since she was just a wee lass. She's having trouble adjusting, that's all."

Helena stiffens, but Mam continues before she can launch a rebuttal.

"Your own babes won't ever have to face such hardship, God willing. Being motherless takes such a toll on a child."

Helena sputters into her teacup. "My own?" she says.

"Well, I just assumed. Forgive me if I've overstepped, Mrs. Cooke. It's just you being so young . . ."

Helena's brows draw together, but Mam goes on, pulling the conversation farther from Cora and the toads, inch by inch.

"My own mam was a midwife back in Ireland, you see, and sometimes I forget such matters aren't considered polite conversation, being raised as I was surrounded by women's business. My apologies."

But Helena is studying Mam intently. "And did your mother pass on what she knew, Mrs. Donnelly? About . . . women's business?"

"Oh aye. I was at her side from the time I was a lass. No older than Cora, in fact."

There's a pause, then Helena speaks again.

"Mrs. Donnelly, may I ask you a question in confidence?"

"A question about babes and birthing? Of course. My mam taught me the importance of discretion."

Deirdre squirms in discomfort. They're old enough to know this isn't conversation meant for children's ears, but that won't stop the girls from discussing and dissecting every stolen word among themselves over the coming days. For now, though, everyone remains still and quiet for fear of drawing attention to themselves.

"Not about birth. Not exactly." Helena hesitates. "The opposite, in fact."

"I see," Mam says, sounding remarkably unperturbed. "Well, I suppose that depends on your present state, Mrs. Cooke. Are you currently . . . expecting?"

The words are free of judgment, but Helena recoils in alarm. "No! Thank heavens, I'm not. And I'd like to make sure it stays that way." Her gaze travels upward, perhaps envisioning another child with Cora's temperament. "Can you help me, Mrs. Donnelly?"

Understanding brings a more genuine relaxation to Mam's shoulders.

"There are steps that can be taken," she says, patting Helena's hand reassuringly.

The strands of Kitty's dream loosen, releasing her to drift free for a time, then settle into a more peaceful sleep.

The peace won't last, but then, nothing does.

13

TESSA

How long can it last, this tentative truce the sisters have settled into?

Tessa is afraid to wonder, as if a mere question, not even spoken aloud, is enough to blow down the fragile web of connection.

And perhaps it is. As the two of them walk up the cobbled downtown sidewalk toward the lawyer's office, a brittle silence descends between them.

A smartly dressed receptionist asks their names and instructs them to have a seat, but Jackson Smith steps out of his office before they've lowered themselves into chairs.

"Right this way, ladies." He holds the door, and the corners of his eyes crinkle slightly as he gives them a subdued smile.

Tessa reminds herself her bags are packed and waiting. All she needs to do is get through this. Whatever *this* is.

"First off, I'd like to offer my condolences once again on the loss of your mother. A fine woman," he says as he settles himself behind the large mahogany desk.

Tessa swallows back a sigh. Not that the words aren't sincere. But there's only so much sympathy a person can absorb before it starts to feel as if you're drowning.

"Thank you," Margot murmurs.

Jackson must sense their desire to move things along, but still he hesitates. "Before we begin, I should warn you, some of this information may come as a shock."

Margot's brows shoot up, and she meets Tessa's confused glance with one of her own.

"Jackson, you're starting to worry me," Margot says. "Mom wasn't the type to keep secrets."

The lawyer leans back in his chair, and his face becomes cloudy, hard to read.

"I wish Jane had spoken with you two about this. I advised her to, many times. She just . . . she thought she had time."

The words are delivered with a melancholy air that reminds Tessa this man has suffered a loss as well. How deep a loss is difficult to know.

But that fact alone is enough to remind Tessa that Jane had a life of her own, one that Tessa, at least, wasn't always privy to.

"Maybe it would be best if you cut right to it, Jackson," Margot says.

Still, he stalls. "There's no easy way to say this."

"Then say it the hard way." Margot adds a smile to punctuate the statement, but it's an afterthought and does little to hide her growing impatience.

Jackson takes a deep breath and places both hands flat on the desk in front of him.

"You mother wasn't who you thought she was."

Tessa meets Margot's eyes and, immediately, they're on the same team again. Because Jackson Smith is clearly deluded.

"Mr. Smith—" Margot begins. Tessa doesn't miss the way she takes two steps back from his first name.

"I know how it sounds, so bear with me while I explain," he says, cutting her off.

"I think you should get on with it, then."

"You've only ever known your mother as Jane Shepherd. Jane Ashwood, before that, daughter of William and Beth Ashwood. And for most her life, that's all she knew as well. But as it happens, Jane was adopted."

There's a pause as the words sink in, but they don't come with any clarity.

"Adopted?" Tessa asks flatly.

"Yes."

Margot sits up straighter and scoots forward in her chair. "I'm sorry, Jackson," she says, though she doesn't sound sorry. Not at all. "But that's completely ridiculous. There's absolutely no way Mom was adopted and never told us." She looks to Tessa. "Am I wrong?"

Tessa shakes her head. "I agree."

But Jackson doesn't back down from the statement. "I know it's a lot to take in. Believe me, Jane was just as shaken to learn the truth."

"And when was that?" Margot pushes.

"Just before I met her," Jackson says. "That's what brought her to me, as a matter of fact. It was right after her father passed away."

"What?" Tessa exclaims. "But that was . . ." She studies her sister questioningly.

"Nearly twenty years ago?" Margot fills in. "Our mother never would have kept something like that a secret for this long. It's not possible."

"I know it's hard to believe, but I'm afraid it's true."

There's silence as the two of them try to come to terms with all the implications of what he's saying.

"But why?" Tessa asks finally. "It's a surprise, sure, but there's no shame in being adopted. Why would she hide it all this time?"

And here they come to the heart of the matter.

"It . . . it's complicated."

At that, Margot leans back in her seat and crosses her arms, even as Tessa leans forward to take the reins.

"Mr. Smith, maybe it would be best if you stop yanking our chains. *Clearly* it's complicated or we wouldn't be here. Now say what you have to say or we're leaving. It's as simple as that."

He has the grace to look embarrassed. There's a small amount of satisfaction in that. Tessa almost feels sorry for him.

"I'm making a mess of this," he says with a frown. When he gets no argument, he continues. "After your grandfather passed away, Jane came to me for help sorting through the tangle of arrangements he'd left behind. As you know, William Ashwood was a wealthy man. His wife had died several years before, and Jane was his only heir. She was overwhelmed by the scope of the estate."

As he speaks, the past glimmers into focus. *Overwhelmed* is an apt description of their mom during those years. A more subdued version of the woman she'd been before she lost both her husband and her parents in such a short time.

For a while, Jane's edges had blurred, her colors faded. In time, they'd sharpened again. The heart is a formidable thing, and time a slow but powerful healer. It's easy to forget those days when Jane carried a quiet hurt she tried hard to hide.

"I helped her sort through and sell off much of the property he owned, though she retained a good deal of stocks and bonds. She invested most of the proceeds, and everything on that front is well in hand. It comes to the two of you, split evenly down the middle, along with the cabin on Lake Cormere and the farmhouse. The information for your mother's broker is in the packet of paperwork I'm sending with you. You should contact him as soon as you can."

Jackson passes two manila envelopes across the desk, but neither woman moves to take them.

"None of this is a surprise," Margot says. "How does an adoption have anything to do with . . . with anything? Why even tell us?"

"Because the inheritance from your grandfather is only part of the story. The rest is less straightforward."

"The rest?" Tessa prompts.

"When your grandfather died, his attorney was in possession of both his last will and testament and a letter he'd written to Jane, to be opened upon his death. The original letter is in a safe deposit box along with stock certificates, deeds, and other financial documents, but I've included copies here for you.

"In the letter he explains how he and his wife came to adopt Jane, and why. He also outlines an agreement he entered regarding a second inheritance. One from Jane's birth family. An estate called Fallbrook. Jane chose to honor her father's agreement during her lifetime, but whether you choose to do so is entirely up to the two of you."

Tessa stares at the envelopes still sitting on Jackson's desk. Does she really want to see the contents?

"Yes," screams some inner voice. *"Yes, of course you do! Are you kidding me right now?"*

This is a voice she recognizes all too well. It goads her, guides her, leads her to try new and often reckless things. It's a voice from her childhood, one she never bothered to temper because Margot was always there. Margot's steady counterpoint was Tessa's voice of reason.

When Margot was gone from her life, anxiety had grown in the gap, like weeds through a crack in the sidewalk.

Only after a nervous breakdown and a string of different therapists did Tessa recognize this. When her most perceptive therapist asked, "Tessa, do you not feel like a whole person?" in a quiet, curious voice, Tessa had finally understood.

She forced herself to learn how to temper her impulses. To sit quietly and allow the first rush of intrigue to break over her like a wave, making no sudden movements until the surf receded.

She does so now, but the curiosity doesn't go away.

Does she really want to see the contents of that envelope?

"Yes," a more rational voice responds. *"It pertains to Mom, and to some sort of inheritance. Decisions will have to be made. It's not lurid or unreasonable to be interested."*

Margot leans forward and slides her own envelope across the desk and into her hand. Tessa watches the way her sister's eyes linger on it.

She nearly sighs in relief.

Margot is still her voice of reason.

"Why don't you take the paperwork and read through it in private," Jackson says. "It will answer many of your questions, and you can contact me once you've had time to absorb everything."

Tessa nods as Margot rises. "Thank you," her sister murmurs in a distracted voice, with both hands gripping the fat envelope.

Tessa slides the one marked with her name from the desk and sends Jackson Smith a half-hearted smile before hurrying to catch up to her sister, who can't seem to get out of this man's office fast enough.

"Margot, wait," Tessa calls.

But Margot is already gone, the door swinging closed behind her.

14

It is a difficult thing, Janie, to leave you with this terrible legacy. Your mother, God rest her, would have preferred you never know. In her mind, as in mine, your life began when she carried you through our door, bundled in love and wiped clean of the past.

I cared too much for her, for you, and for the family we made to go against her wishes. And despite enduring these final years without her by my side, my Beth was always with me in my heart, reminding me there was no need to burden you with such unpleasantness. No need to disturb your tidy view of where your story began. To what end?

And yet, as I draw nearer the day my own story will end, I'm troubled by the difference between the values we've instilled in you, Jane, and the choices I've made. For I dare not place the blame for my decisions on your mother's shoulders. She was guided by her heart, but I, I must admit, have been guided by fear.

It's not a pretty tale, as you've seen, but one drenched in heartache and blood. I feared this knowledge would weigh heavily on you. After you found happiness in your own marriage and the birth of your girls, I chose not to mar that happiness with such a stain. After Beth died, then you lost your husband so suddenly only a few months later, I chose not to place further darkness within your sphere.

These were the excuses I used, but I'm old and wise enough now to understand that what I truly feared was the look in your eyes when you realized I was not your father in the way you'd always believed me to be.

It is the most selfish thing I have ever done, to leave this information in such a way that it will come to you only after my death.

All I can do is hope you'll forgive an old man his cowardice, and know that from the first day I laid eyes on you to the last, you were never less than my own precious daughter in every way that mattered. Born to us in the wake of tragedy, you were our miracle. You made me a better man.

That I still fall short is no one's fault but my own.

Your loving father,

William Ashwood

Tessa squeezes her eyes shut and remembers the scent of her grandfather's aftershave. The way he'd ruffle her hair before pulling a stick of cinnamon gum from his pocket and tearing it in half for the two girls to share.

Her mother's voice comes back to her now, words she said when Tessa was navigating the loss of her own father. Jane had lain down next to Tessa after finding her crying in the night. *"It's natural to mourn what you've lost, Tess. But don't forget to hold tight to the good. That you've had a love big enough to cry for is a blessing."*

She didn't understand that as a child, not completely, but she tried. The best memories she sought out and polished, putting them in a place of honor in her heart. Like a curated museum collection she visited whenever she missed him the most.

Hold tight to the good, she thinks. *Hold tight.*

Though Tessa can't know for certain, she'd like to believe Jane forgave Tessa's grandfather his secrets.

She wipes away a stray tear and glances up to see Margot walking toward her. The sisters didn't speak on the drive home and went their separate ways to read the contents of their envelopes in private.

Margot takes a seat on the opposite bench at the picnic table beneath the oak. Tessa studies her face, but her sister's expression is impossible to read.

"Why didn't she tell us?" Margot asks quietly.

Tessa considers her answer before she speaks. "Maybe it was too difficult to talk about. Maybe she decided it didn't matter. Or . . . maybe she intended to, but time passed, building up like a snowdrift, and before she knew what was happening it was too deep to dig out on her own."

And maybe Tessa is ascribing her own failings to their mother, but the last possibility rings truest, to her mind.

Margot stares into the distance. No amount of shared DNA gives Tessa any hints what her sister is thinking.

"We should sell it," Margot says finally. "Leave it in the past, like Mom did."

Tessa's eyes widen at the decisive note in her voice. "Just like that?"

"Why not?" Margot says. "It's not like it meant anything to her. She didn't even know it existed until Granddad died."

"Still . . . it must have meant *something*. Otherwise, why didn't she sell it herself? Granddad died in 2002. It's been seventeen years."

"I don't know, Tessa," Margot says, her words sharpened to points. "Why did she do anything? Why didn't she ever tell us about this?"

The anger takes Tessa by surprise.

"Why are you so upset, Margot?" she asks quietly.

Her sister whips her head around, and Tessa unconsciously leans away from the pain in her expression.

"Upset? I'm not upset. Why should I be? Our mother is dead, and we're left with an ancient house none of us ever laid eyes on and a completely different family history than we always believed. Our grandparents weren't actually our grandparents. Ben is—"

She stops short and visibly struggles to get a handle on her emotions. "I'm not going to talk about Ben. It's none of your business. Besides, you're leaving. You're probably plotting an escape right now."

Tessa draws in a sharp breath. "That's not fair, and you know it. It's not like I wanted—" She stops midsentence, struck by something Margot's said. "You're wrong."

"*I'm* wrong?" Margot replies, gearing up for a shouting match. "What gives you the right to come back here and—"

"Not that," Tessa says, cutting her off. "What you said before. A house no one ever laid eyes on. But you're wrong. Mom *did* lay eyes on it. And we were with her."

Tessa rises from the picnic table, leaving Margot to follow. She ignores her sister's grumbling and heads straight to the living room, to the photo albums they left on the coffee table the night before.

It takes a few moments of thumbing through the plastic-covered pages to find the shot. Tessa still doesn't recall much about the day or the unexpected detour Mom had taken on the way home from Granddad's funeral, but she peers at the photograph, trying to fill in the gaps in her memory.

"Here," Tessa says, angling the album to show Margot. "This has to be the place."

The old house, tilted in the background, looks more menacing than it did when they glanced at the photo the day before, and the sadness in their mother's expression more poignant.

Tessa hasn't yet said the words aloud, hasn't had time to fully comprehend what they mean, but if William Ashwood's letter is true, then the house in the photograph is much more than a moldering pile of rusty nails and rotting boards. More than an unexpected inheritance to sell and collect the proceeds from.

This was the home of his former business partner, Everett Cooke, and his wife and children. And one of those children was their mother.

"This is the house where Mom was born," Tessa says. "This is the house where her family was murdered."

15

With low-level dread snapping at her insides, Tessa stares at the blank screen of her phone. She turned it off last night.

What reason did she have to keep it on? Her mother is gone, and Margot is in the same house with her. She powered it down with a sense of relief. Of escape.

But Margot stormed away after Tessa insisted the photograph was significant, and now she presses the power button and waits, her fingers itching to comb through the internet searching for information about her mother's family. *And her own,* she amends.

William's letter to his daughter told of the ill-fated Cooke family— murdered in their home, many decades ago. The letter said little else of the crime. Surely such a horrifying event would show up in the most basic search, even if it had taken place when her mother was merely a baby. Born in 1949, Jane would have been seventy, had she survived to see her upcoming birthday.

The loss of her mother hits Tessa all over again. It's inconceivable that she can't turn and simply ask Jane what they should do. Why she'd never told them. To hug her neck one last time. Just that.

But it's too late for wishes, and she and Margot are going to have to figure this out on their own. Margot made her opinion clear, and an old photograph won't change her mind, but Tessa can't bring herself to agree to sell a piece of their history without doing more research.

The screen in her hand lights up, but within seconds her stomach plunges. She has barely a moment to register the number of unread emails before a flurry of text messages scrolls across the screen.

Tessa drops bonelessly onto the sofa as her breath abandons her in a rush. Thoughts of a seventy-year-old tragedy are swept away as Tessa is thrust back into her current and equally horrifying reality.

While Tessa was busy burying her head in the sand, another video hit the news. She clicks on a link that Anne forwarded and braces herself for the now familiar shock of seeing the nightmare version of Oliver Barlow, a man she thought she knew.

The darkened screen clears as Oliver backs away and sits on the corner of a bed in what appears to be an anonymous motel room. It could be anywhere. He looks more ragged than ever. The hairs on Tessa's arms stand on end at the hardened, hateful expression in his eyes.

"Hello out there. I won't introduce myself again. I assume I have your attention now."

He shakes his head, and one corner of his mouth inches up, then drops, as if maintaining the smirk is too much effort.

"I have to say, Winters, I'm surprised you haven't found me yet. You found my dad, sure, but I had to tell you where to look. I'm disappointed in you. Slipping in your old age? I'm not exactly a criminal mastermind. Picked up a few tricks in the pen, sure, but what do you expect when you put a man in a cage with a bunch of lowlifes? But I'll tell you something. Every one of those lowlifes had more integrity in their little finger than you've ever known. They had a code, and they lived by it. That's more than I can say for you."

Sitting with his elbows propped on his knees, Oliver looks away from the camera, then rakes a hand across his face.

"I'm tired, Winters," he continues. "Tired of getting my face shoved back in the dirt. My wife left me. Did you know that? Stuck around until the lawsuit played out, but when she realized there wasn't some big payday coming, she took the kids and, poof, she was gone."

His voice is quiet, the anger still there but vibrating on a lower frequency. "Not that they'll miss me. My kids don't even know me, Winters. They were babies when I went in, and by the time I got out, they were damn near grown. I'm just some stranger who showed up in their lives. Somebody they had to call Dad."

He turns to stare directly at the camera.

"Not like Valerie," he says. He doesn't even pretend to smile this time. "You got to choose what kind of daddy you'd be to your girl. Me? I never got a choice. You took my choices, Winters, and never looked back."

Tessa can't catch her breath. Oliver stands and paces in front of the camera.

"I've been waiting for you, Lloyd, but I'm getting sick of it. I wanted a little bit of peace before this was over, but you're dragging it out, so I'll give you a hint. Talk to Tessa Shepherd. She knows. Maybe she'll tell you . . . if you can get her to answer the goddamn phone."

Tessa's skin tightens and she makes a sound like a wounded animal.

"Come and get me, old man. If you don't, I might just have to come to you, and you don't want that."

The phone drops from Tessa's grip as her hands fly to her mouth. She stares at it lying on the rug between her feet as if it's a snake that might strike at any moment. But it's done that already. The venom of Oliver's voice is still coursing through her veins.

"Tessa!" Margot shouts as her feet pound through the house. She careens around the corner, her own phone in her hand. "Tessa, have you seen this?" she asks. She's panting and her eyes are wide. "What the hell is he talking about? *What* do you know?" Margot demands.

"I . . ." She shakes her head, trying to dislodge Oliver's words, but they won't go. *"Talk to Tessa Shepherd. She knows."*

"Nothing!" she says. "I don't know anything, I swear!"

"Well, clearly he thinks you do," Margot insists. They both startle when Tessa's phone rings from its abandoned position on the floor. "And thanks to him, so does the rest of the world," Margot adds.

Tessa's heart is racing like she's run a marathon, but her limbs are frozen in place.

She stares at the phone until the ringing finally stops, sending the unknown caller to a voice mail box that is probably full by now.

Tessa shakes her head. "But I don't know anything. I don't know where he is. I don't know why he's doing this, and I don't know why he'd say something like that."

The phone rings again.

"The press," she whispers.

"Or the police," Margot says. When Tessa stares at her uncomprehendingly, she continues, slowly, as if Tessa is a child. "Oliver Barlow just turned you into a suspect, Tess. A conspirator. Like it or not, the police are going to want answers."

Tessa's stomach drops. She'd reached out to Bonham PD when this whole thing started. She'd offered to help in any way she could and been summarily dismissed. But the truth was, she'd only called as a salve to her own conscience, knowing full well there was nothing she could do.

Now, though, Oliver has thrust her in the middle of a situation she can't control. She moves quickly to the window and checks behind the curtains. Nothing stirs. Everything looks the same, but it's an illusion. Nothing will ever be the same. Their mother is gone, Valerie Winters is gone, and Oliver Barlow has set the world upon her.

"I have to get out of here," Tessa says, as much to herself as to her sister.

"*Excuse* me?" Margot replies. "What are you talking about? You can't just run away from this."

"What choice do I have?" Tessa cries, turning back to face her. "If I stay here, you'll have police and reporters beating down the door, camped out on the lawn."

"I'm a grown woman, Tessa. I think I can deal with some reporters," Margot says.

"No. This isn't your problem," Tessa insists. She pats her pockets, searching for her keys before she remembers they're in her purse, sitting on the kitchen table. Her bags are packed and waiting in the trunk of her car.

"Are you kidding me right now?" Margot says, staring at her with her hands perched on her hips.

"Margot, I can't stay here!" Tessa says. "I don't know anything! There's nothing I can say that will help the police find him, nothing I can say that will bring Valerie back!"

Margot plants her feet and crosses her arms. "So tell them that," she says.

Tessa's eyes slide from her sister's, and she hurries back across the room to scoop her phone off the floor.

"You're being completely irrational," Margot says. "The police are going to want to talk to you. If you don't know anything, you don't. All you have to do is say so."

Tessa stills. "You don't understand. It's not that simple."

Margot laughs, a harsh, electric sound that crackles in the space between them. "Yeah, Tess, actually it is."

The hurt between them shimmers in the air like heat waves. Tessa can feel her mother's presence in every part of this house, feel the nearness of the past closing in on her. It's too much to process, and she doesn't have time.

"I can't stay here," she says, wondering if she repeats the phrase enough, she'll eventually believe it. Judging from Margot's face, she certainly doesn't.

"You're being completely—"

"I can't face him!" Tessa shouts, admitting the shameful truth to both herself and her sister. Her breath is ragged in her chest, and anxiety is clawing at her, seeping through the cracks in her defenses.

Margot's eyes widen, but still she doesn't understand. "Who?" she asks, shaking her head.

"Winters," Tessa says. "Lloyd Winters. I can't face him, Margot. His daughter is dead. *Dead.* And she'd still be alive if it weren't for me."

Tessa can barely manage to stand up beneath the weight of blame she carries on her shoulders. The loss of her mother has already shaken her to her core. If she has to sit in a room across from Lloyd Winters's justifiable accusations, she'll crumble completely. She's barely holding herself together as it is.

"Where are you going to go? Your apartment in New York won't be any better, and you'll be . . ." Margot trails off.

What? Tessa wonders. *Alone?* She's been alone for so long she doesn't know any other way to be.

"Not New York," Tessa concedes, looking frantically around for anything she might have missed. "Somewhere else. Anywhere else. I just need someplace no one will find me until this blows over."

"Blows over? Tessa, do you hear yourself? This isn't going to blow over. At best, you might convince the police you know nothing. At worst? Oliver Barlow has implicated you in conspiracy to murder!"

"I don't know anything!" Tessa cries, hating the pleading tone in her voice.

"Then tell them that," Margot insists, her voice gentler, but still firm. "Don't run from this. Stay."

The irony is so big, so utterly absurd, that Tessa might laugh if she weren't so close to tears. Since the day she walked out the door at eighteen, she'd only ever wanted one thing. It flowed like a hidden underground river beneath every decision she'd made since.

She wanted her sister back.

The only force on earth strong enough to keep her away was Margot's own need to have Tessa out of her life.

Now Margot is asking her to stay. She can practically hear her mother siding with her sister. *"Stay, Tessa. Face this together. You were always stronger together."*

But that's not true. Not anymore.

Maybe it once was, a long time ago, but their dynamic has changed. Tessa isn't the same girl she used to be. She no longer has the confidence it takes to be strong. And Margot is different too.

Maybe it's the loss of their mother, or the cracks in Margot's marriage. But Tessa suspects it's more than that. The Margot she knew, that amenable, agreeable girl, content to follow where Tessa led, didn't survive the fall. The woman who grew in her place is . . . harder. She's brittle where she used to bend. Her soft edges are sharp now. Sharp enough to slice a person in two.

Tessa could hide here. She could draw from Margot's strength, lean on her for support, when Lloyd Winters eviscerates her.

For a moment, she considers what that might look like. The press, tracking her here. The police at the door, just like the night when they were ten. Margot thrust in the middle of a situation she hasn't caused. A situation that's only in her life because Tessa brought it here. Margot forced to deal with the aftermath of Tessa's guilt and anxiety.

Tessa's phone rings in her hand, and they both jump.

"No," Tessa says, stabbing a finger at the button to decline the call before the second ring. "I won't do that to you."

She wants nothing more than to bridge the distance between them, to repair that rift in any way she can, but not like this. Not with the shadow of Oliver Barlow, yet another of Tessa's mistakes, hanging over them.

She walks past her sister, whose expression has morphed into a blank mask of disapproval. Tessa accepts the stab of regret.

She picks up her purse from the kitchen table, then pauses at the sight of the manila envelope. Her fingers run lightly across her name written in bold, black lines.

A piece of their history. A decision to be made.

She slides the envelope quickly into her hand and turns to brush past Margot again, who is standing immobile with her arms crossed in the hallway, watching her behind shuttered eyes.

Tessa walks to the coffee table, then leans over and peels back the plastic from the photo album to carefully pull the picture of their mother from the page. The old house, the one Tessa has begun calling *the murder house* in her mind, tilts crookedly over Jane's shoulder.

Fallbrook.

"Here," she says, holding up the photograph. "This is where I'll go."

It's ridiculous. Utterly absurd. But Tessa grasps onto the idea like a drowning woman.

Margot's affected apathy slips and her jaw drops. "You can't be serious."

But it's the perfect solution, and it's been sitting right in front of them, waiting for Tessa's befuddled brain to catch up.

She slides the photo into the envelope, then tucks the entire thing into her purse and slings it over her shoulder.

"I'll come back," Tessa says, unable to hide the hope hidden behind the words. "When this is all over. We'll decide what to do about Mom's house and . . . and the other thing . . . but I have to do this first."

"This is your idea of dealing with the situation?" Margot asks.

"Please understand," Tessa pleads. "I can't bring this here to you. You have enough to deal with, and I won't be the cause of more problems." Problems that extend far beyond what Margot might imagine. Pushy reporters pale in comparison to psychiatric units and the dark days and nights that necessitate them.

Margot turns away from her, and Tessa walks to the front door. Her hand is on the doorknob when she hesitates. She's got nothing else to lose.

"Margot," she calls. Her sister stops. "Talk to Ben. Please."

She has no right to ask her sister for anything, but she can't help herself.

"You deal with your mess your way, Tessa. Leave me here to deal with mine. That's how we do things, isn't it?"

The words cut to the bone. But after so many years of silence, of empty wishes, and phone calls that never came, Tessa welcomes the pain. She holds it tightly and breathes it in.

Then she walks out the door and shuts it behind her.

Tessa hurries to her car. The address for the murder house is in the paperwork Jackson Smith gave her. She'll plug it into her GPS and let it lead her down a path she's never been on while she hides from a present she can't control.

Her head is filled with the urgency to keep moving. An echo of her own voice repeats, *This is the right thing to do*. If she focuses on that alone, she can almost drown out the other voices. The voices of Margot, of her mother, of Oliver Barlow. Of her guilt and her fears. Of the lost and unknown family waiting to be found, whispering things she doesn't want to hear.

16

KITTY

"'Tis the gravedigger's bell you hear, lass."

Kitty doesn't realize she's whispered the words aloud until Deirdre places a bowl of stew in front of her.

"Speak up, Kitty," her sister says. "I can't understand you when you mumble."

Steam rises from their dinner as Deirdre settles wearily into the chair across from her. The scents of thyme and parsley, fresh from the garden, mingle in the air, the same as they did when Mam made it.

"Do you remember the story of the gravedigger's bell, Dee?" Kitty asks.

The occasional crackle of the fireplace fills the silence. A pause drags on long enough that Kitty wonders if she even spoke aloud.

"We need to bring in more wood," Deirdre says. She doesn't meet Kitty's eyes.

"It was one of Mam's stories. You remember, don't you?" Kitty prods.

Deirdre sets her spoon against her bowl with a clink and picks up a glass of water to take a long drink. She wipes her mouth on her napkin and sets it primly back in her lap, as if they're dining someplace fancy instead of their own worn, comfortable kitchen.

"No," she says finally, then spoons another bite into her mouth.

Kitty watches her sister chew like an old woman and wonders if that's true. Perhaps. Truth and memory are slippery animals that creep around them these days, haunting the shadows, then fading away again. While Kitty seeks to capture them, Deirdre steadfastly refuses to acknowledge their existence.

It's exhausting, helping her sister maintain her ignorance. Kitty sighs and lets the subject drop.

"I should bring in a few more logs," Deirdre says, happy to let her do just that.

"Aiden can do it when he gets in," Kitty replies.

"Who knows what time that will be. I'll take care of it."

"He worries me, wandering every inch of this place day and night the way he does. What if he falls, or . . . I don't know."

"He could fall just as easily here," Deirdre points out. "He can't abide being cooped up, Kitty."

"You're no help at all. We should get some chickens. Maybe a goat or two. Give him something to fill his time. A purpose."

"Let him be," Deirdre says. "No need to mother him."

As if their conversation has conjured him, Aiden enters the kitchen a few moments later. Kitty rises to fill a bowl for her older brother.

"Saved by the bell, you are, Denny," she says.

Kitty stops, stew dripping from the ladle she holds midair over the pot. She said the words, intending to share with Aiden her plan to tie him down with a goat, but once spoken, they cracked open the delicate shell of the very memory she's been searching for.

The words, the taste of Mam's Irish stew. The warm, welcoming kitchen. Time slips and she holds tightly to the thread of the past. Ignoring her siblings, Kitty wanders out the door, takes a seat in her rocking chair, and lets the memories carry her along. Surrounded by moonlight and night air, lines form in the center of Kitty's brow, and she waits and watches as her mind plays the sepia-tinted moments, so precious, back to her.

"Saved by the bell, ye are, lad," Mam's voice says in her soft Irish brogue. "Five more minutes and dinner'd go cold."

Aiden stomps his boots and leaves them by the door, bright with youth and mischief as he joins his waiting family.

"Why?" Kitty asks, always curious.

"Because Mam would have everyone combing the woods if I'm not home in time for supper, little one," Aiden says, ruffling Kitty's hair, and her feathers too. She's growing up, but no one seems to notice.

Aiden steals a piece of bread while Mam's back is turned.

"But why a bell?" Kitty insists. "How can a bell save someone?"

"It's a saying," Aiden says, shaking his black hair from his eyes. "Like a boxing ring, the bell means the round is up and you have time to catch your breath before the other lad starts pounding on you again."

He proclaims the words with the puff-chested confidence of a man-child in the company of females.

"Denny, you silly lad." Saoirse Donnelly's voice is gentle, softening the rebuttal. "'Tis the gravedigger's bell that matters. Have I never told you that tale?"

Young Kitty's eyes grow large and Aiden frowns, though he dares not disagree.

"Sit down, then. Deirdre, you as well, and I'll tell you now." Mam's eyes are bright and the shadows deep, flickering from the firelight of the cookstove. She takes a seat at the head of the table.

"A hundred years ago, in the old country, there was a lass whose life was soft like a down mattress." She glances one by one at the children gathered, drawing them into her confidence.

"'Twas no fault of her own, she'd simply drawn a fine lot at birth. The only child of a rich man, she lived in a fancy house and all was done for her before she had a chance to want, with no reason to believe it would ever be otherwise."

"Sound familiar?" Aiden whispers in Kitty's ear, but Mam shushes him before Kitty can snap back that her hands are as rough as his.

"And so it might have gone forever, with no more to the story, had she chosen wisely, but a woman's heart is a mystery and cannot help but seek the path it shouldn't take. She fell in love with a young lad, more boy than man."

Kitty raises a brow pointedly in Aiden's direction, but he's busy sopping stew with his bread, oblivious.

"Soon they were engaged. Preparations were made, and a wedding was planned in a flurry of excitement. And with each passing day her betrothed heard stakes being driven into the ground, binding him forever to a future with a predetermined shape. Every decision made for him by others who'd already lived their lives. Others who saw no need for excitement or adventure. And his fickle, restless heart began to yearn. Not for the love of a respectable lass, but for the sights and smells of a wider world."

"But didn't she want those things too?" Kitty asks.

Mam's lips turn up slowly, sadly. "Perhaps, love. But no one bothered to ask her, did they?"

She winks at Kitty and goes on with her tale.

"When the morning of her wedding day dawned sunny and clear, the lass woke to find an envelope slipped beneath the crack of her door, her name across the front in a hand she recognized well."

"What did the letter say?" Deirdre asks before Kitty has a chance.

"My love," Mam says. *"Though I've promised to be a husband to you, I canna live with myself if I don't first become a man you could be proud to have on your arm. I'm off to put my mark on the world, or it on me,*

whichever comes first. Do not cry, my dear, for this is not goodbye, but only goodbye for now. I shall return when the winds are right and make you my wife, of that you can be sure."

Aiden gives a low whistle and turns his eyes downward toward his bowl.

Deirdre's mouth falls open before she clamps it shut again, sits back in her chair, and crosses her arms. "Good riddance," she proclaims. "She's better off without him."

Kitty glances between the two of them, wondering about the fuss. "Well, maybe he was telling the truth. He could've come back," she says, but Deirdre rolls her eyes, as if she were so much older and wiser.

"Nay, he took the coward's way," Mam continues, trying to hide her smile at Kitty's consternation. "For the only thing worse than leaving a woman standing at the altar with her heart in her hands is giving her hope that you may someday return. For years and years, she waited, growing pale and thin, sacrificing the bloom of youth to wasted hope. As the days piled up and the years became decades, he did not return, but still she hoped. Still she waited. Until one day, a well-meaning friend suggested that perhaps he *could not* return. Perhaps a mishap had befallen him on his travels and he was gone to be with the angels above. That he was watching over her, wishing for her to move on with her life, to forget him and live again."

"What did she do?" Kitty asks Mam, breathless.

"Well," Mam says, leaning close to Kitty. "She was shaken to the bones of her toes by the very thought. What if her friend was right? What if her young man intended to keep his word, but something had happened to stop him? It was the only explanation, and the more she thought on it, the more convinced she became."

Deirdre snorts, and Kitty's eyes shoot daggers in her direction.

"Our lass was not so young now, and with a head of silver hair and wrinkled, papery skin, but she rose and dressed, and she readied herself for a journey all the same. She was convinced her lost love was waiting to be found, if only she looked in the right place. So, she took the train to the next county over and began to search."

"But if it had been so long, how did she expect to find him?" Kitty asks.

"Well now, the places she was looking were the sort that once you arrive, you won't be leaving anytime soon."

Kitty frowns, and Mam lowers her voice, her eyes dancing at the dark and fanciful tale and her rapt audience. "She was checking the boneyards, child. From one town to the next, she wandered through the cemeteries, up and down the rows of stone markers, reading the names in search of the one that was also carved on her heart."

Kitty's eyes grow wide, then sympathy clouds them and her shoulders droop.

"All over Ireland, as far as the railroad tracks would take her, she made her pilgrimage. Word spread about the silver-haired lady searching for her vanished betrothed, and soon people were whispering behind their hands from the moment she arrived in a new town.

" '*She's come,*' they'd say. '*Come to search the graves for the man who jilted her, the wee barmy thing.*' To escape the unwanted attention she was receiving, our silver lady had begun to undertake her lonesome search in the dead of the night, with only a lantern and the stars to show her the names chiseled upon the stones."

"Wasn't she frightened?" Kitty asks.

"Aye, Kitty, more than likely. But she didn't let that stop her. And so it was that one night many months after she'd left home, and with only the moon as a witness, she came upon a lone figure carrying a shovel and spade. He was the caretaker, you see, and the gravedigger as well, though she didn't know those things when she came face to face with him stepping 'round a dark bend at night.

"She held her lantern high in front of her and swung it wide. *'Get back,'* she cried, fearful of this hulking stranger whose face was half hidden in shadows.

"*'My apologies, madam,'* he said, as politely as you please. *'I didn't mean to startle you. I'm as surprised as you, truth be told. Normally have the place to meself at this hour.'*

"I'd have died right there," Kitty exclaims. "Dead on the spot."

"And you, Dee?" Aiden asks with a grin. "Would your poor heart have exploded with fear?"

"Nay," Deirdre says. "I'd have hit him with a stick and told him not to be sneaking up on women in the dark."

Mam laughs. "No doubt you would have, child, but our lady had nothing to fear from the old caretaker, for he was a gentle soul. He led her to a nearby bench, for he could see how shaken she was. He had heard the rumors about the silver lady who roamed the countryside, searching for something she'd never find. He'd hardly believed them, yet here she was, in the flesh."

Their bowls were empty, and the fire was growing small, but the family gathered around paid it no mind. They were lost in Saoirse's story, sitting in a dark boneyard with a silver lady, an old caretaker, and the stars winking above.

"Once her heart slowed, our lady told the old man of her search. The whole sorry tale poured out of her, from beginning to end. He listened without interruption, and made not a sound, and when she was done, he sat in silence for a moment before he spoke.

"*'I've spent many a year in this place, with only the dead for company. I've seen things you wouldn't believe. But back in the days before time had its way with me, I met a lad, brought into town slung over the back of a horse.*

"*'He'd been set upon by highwaymen, and he was near enough to death's door that the doctor called for the gravedigger before the young man had even drawn his last, so sure was he of the outcome. I was hardly more than a boy myself, so I sat with him while he raved, delirious and half mad. His face was sliced from a bandit's blade, and he'd taken a bullet to his leg. The doctor had been forced to take the leg, and it must have pained him greatly, but the lad didn't speak of these things, only the lass he'd foolishly left behind, waiting for him at the altar.*

"'*He died that day, with words of regret on his tongue. Regret that he could never return and be a man she'd be proud to have on her arm.*'"

Kitty draws in a sharp breath. Aiden is quiet. Even Deirdre looks shaken.

Saoirse Donnelly, with all the tricks of a born storyteller at her fingertips, pauses to let that sink in.

"The caretaker might have expected tears or lamentations from a woman who'd waited so long on a boy who'd never had the chance grow to a man, but instead, she simply stood, though her bones were old and creaky. '*Would you take me to his grave, then, sir?*' she asked.

"'*Of course, my lady,*' was his reply. So with slow steps and her head held high, our silver lady was shown to an unmarked grave. '*We never knew his name,*' the caretaker said, a note of apology in his voice at the simple wooden cross that tilted in the shadow of the moon. '*But this is where he lies. Perhaps you can be at peace now, ma'am.*'

"She knelt at the foot of the grave and placed both hands on the ground in front of her, closing her eyes. The caretaker backed away, thinking to give her some privacy to grieve, but she turned back to him and spoke. '*Tell me about the bell, sir, if you don't mind. I've seen this before in my travels, a bell with a chain that leads to a pipe in the ground.*'

"He pushes back his hat and scratches his head. His eyes drop away from hers. '*Aye, miss. That's the old ways, that is. To keep a body from being buried alive, when the doctor wasn't so sure of himself. If the dead awoke by some miracle happenstance, they could pull the chain, and we'd dig 'em up. Saved by the bell, as it were. But I promise you, ma'am, your lad was gone for good before he was lowered into the ground. Make no mistake. I added*

the bell myself, for his was one of the first graves I dug, and I had a fanci-
ful notion that if he weren't really dead, perhaps he and his lass still had a
chance. But that bell never rang. Sadly, it weren't meant to be."

Kitty wipes tears from her eyes. She always forgets that Mam's tales
never have happy endings.

"He left her then, to say her goodbyes, and walked slowly back
to the lonely, ramshackle cabin at the edge of the graveyard he called
home. There were hours still to go before the break of a new day, but
the pain in his chest for the fate of the woman wouldn't allow him to
rest. He listened instead, ears pricked for any sign of a lady's distress.
But none ever came.

"Time ticked past and he lay in his cot. Tears dried on his weathered cheeks. Then a sound he'd never heard before found his ears. It
echoed in his soul. He sat upright, fear and wonder coursing through
his old veins. It was the gravedigger's bell, clanging in the moonlit
night. Once. Twice. Three times it rang, and he bolted toward the
cabin door.

"He hurried up the hill as quickly as his battered body would take
him and rounded the path to the place he'd left the silver lady mourn-
ing. What he hoped to see, he didn't know. But the sight that greeted
him as the first rays of the sun appeared over the horizon broke his old
heart all over again.

"The lady was lying on her side. Her hands curled peacefully
beneath her head as she lay upon the earth over the unnamed grave.
He moved toward her, inch by inch, but he was a gravedigger by trade,
and he knew what he saw. Her skin was ghostly white, and no breath
came from between her lips. When he touched her neck to be sure, he
found her cold, dead for heaven knew how long."

Then who rang the bell? Kitty wonders, though she can't bring herself
to speak and break the spell the story has cast upon them all.

"There upon his knees, with the body of the woman so still before
him, the caretaker was sure of one thing. He was going to hell for all

his lies. The bones in that grave had never belonged to the lad the silver lady had been searching for. He'd spun the tale hoping to give her some peace at last. So that she could go home now, and live her life in comfort and warmth, not searching to the ends of the earth for a foolish boy who'd never deserved a love so loyal and true."

"He lied?" Deirdre cries. "How dare he lie to her?" She seems to have forgotten she thought the woman a fool.

Mam nods. "He did, indeed. Some would say he lied from compassion, though, Dee. That he lied because a lie told out of kindness is less of a sin than the cruelty of a harsh truth."

"I don't believe that," Deirdre says, crossing her arms again.

Saoirse Donnelly's eyes are melancholy as she studies her daughter. "And my hope for you, child, is that you're never forced to put those fine principles to the test," she says gently.

Kitty wonders what she believes, but it's too tangled to make sense of.

"But what of her betrothed, Mam?" Kitty asks, desperately tugging the loose end she's left to dangle. "Was he truly never heard from again?"

"Well now, Kitty cat, I'm not quite sure how to answer that. Some would say no, that our lady's young man had surely died somewhere along the road that took him away from the promises he'd made. But others, perhaps, would disagree. What I can tell you is that once dawn was fully broken on that fateful morn, the townspeople found not only the cold body of the silver lady they'd all heard so much about, but a second body as well.

"For the caretaker, unable to live with what he'd done, had returned to his cabin, fashioned a noose from an old length of rope, and taken his own life, God rest his poor tortured soul. It was there they found him, with the sun shining through the door and no shadows left to hide behind. An old man with scars on his face from a bandit's blade, and a wooden leg strapped on to replace the one the doctor had taken after he'd been brought to town, slung across the back of a horse, many, many years before."

The memory gently releases Kitty to float back into the present, her eyes glazed and unseeing. She reaches out to hold the images close for a moment longer, but they're fading, as insubstantial as the morning mist.

17

TESSA

The little black rental car hugs the curves of the two-lane road as it winds its way northwest. Tessa concentrates on the road, channeling her erratic thoughts and energy toward the path ahead. It works, and she feels more in control than she has in days. After exiting the highway, each town she's passed has grown increasingly smaller, outnumbered and surrounded by state forests and game lands. Tessa welcomes the isolation.

She stops to get gas and fishes her phone from the bottom of her bag. She turns it on, but stubbornly ignores all notifications and does a quick search for someplace to rent a room for the night. The internet gives her one choice in Snowden, the closest town to the murder house.

Bracknell Lodge.

There's no website, and Google's street view stops without venturing quite so far into the wilds of northern Pennsylvania. Tessa doesn't have high hopes. But the voice that answers the phone is friendly and confirms there's a room available.

"What name should I put this under, dear?" the woman on the other end of the line asks.

"Tessa—" She hesitates. Not Shepherd. Oliver's story is plastered all over the news, and Tessa's name is now too closely associated with it. Her mind immediately goes to Russell, Margot's married name, but she'll forever associate that with Ben. Impersonating Ben's wife is a line she isn't willing to cross.

"Ashwood," she finishes with a silent grimace at the lingering pause. "Tessa Ashwood."

Her credit cards clearly say Tessa Shepherd, but she can only hope her hostess doesn't notice.

When the GPS indicates she's nearing her destination, Tessa slows the car. Snowden is the smallest small town yet.

Houses dot the main street, mostly neat and well kept. A tire swing sways in the breeze, dangling over a soft green lawn.

She passes a park on the left, surrounded by a chain-link fence that encircles plastic playground equipment that used to be red. A small post office sits next to it with a blue-domed letter box out front and an American flag hanging by the door.

Then, the crown jewel of Snowden. A white clapboard church with an impossibly tall and narrow spire that juts into the sky, as if daring the devil to do his worst. There's a cross at the top so high that Tessa leans forward and cranes her neck uncomfortably to see it.

Enthralled by the sight of it looming above, she doesn't spot the scruffy brown dog that darts into the road until it's almost too late. She gasps, jerks the wheel of the car to the right, and slams on the brakes.

It takes a moment for her to catch her breath. The little dog now sits along the edge of the road, watching her. One of its oversized ears stands at attention. The other flops across the top of its head. A little girl with a brown ponytail runs up behind it and stops to stare at Tessa as well.

Tessa forces a smile and raises a hand in a wave, but neither the girl nor the dog respond. Tessa hits a button and her window slides down, allowing a breeze into the car that cools her face.

"Cute dog," she says.

The little girl tilts her head, raises one hand, then extends her middle finger upward, as boldly as the church spire at her back. She grins, then whirls and runs off. The dog sits for a moment longer, tongue hanging from the side of its mouth, then trots after the girl.

"Cute kid," Tessa mumbles under her breath. A small blue truck passes slowly on her left, and she meets the curious glance of the woman in the passenger seat with a wan smile. Tessa rolls her window up and pulls onto the road, watching more carefully this time for stray animals and cocky kids.

At the end of the road, Tessa takes a right and, a short distance later, the GPS declares, "You have arrived at your destination."

Tucked at the back of a driveway lined with maples and oaks sits Bracknell Lodge. The symmetrical brick Georgian facade is softened by trellises heavy with climbing pink roses and a hand-painted wooden sign in the front garden. It brings to mind a girls' boarding school, and the effect is surprisingly charming.

Tessa is greeted at the door by a small woman in her fifties, with thick dark hair pulled back into a bun. She gives the sports car parked in the drive a lingering glance, then turns a curious eye to her guest.

Mrs. Coburn, as she introduces herself, checks Tessa in with little fuss and shows her to her room.

"What brings you to Snowden, Ms. Ashwood?" she asks as she unlocks the door to the guest room.

"Sightseeing," Tessa says. "In fact, maybe you can help me. There's a house nearby. Fallbrook. Do you know it?"

Her hostess's brows slowly rise.

"Oh yes, I know it." The curiosity in her gaze turns to reservation. "If it's historic homes you're interested in, there are quite a few better preserved ones within driving distance. I could get you a pamphlet if you like."

"That won't be necessary, thank you." Tessa rolls her suitcase past the woman into the room and leaves it next to the bed.

"Are you doing research for something, then?" Mrs. Coburn asks, her gaze narrowed. "Some sort of article, or a book?"

Tessa doesn't miss the disapproving note in Mrs. Coburn's voice, which tells her the proprietress is aware of the house's history.

"No," Tessa replies truthfully. "Not exactly."

She doesn't elaborate, but Tessa can see she's not made an ally.

"Well, I doubt there's anyone left around here who'd be much help when it comes to that sort of thing. Ancient history, all that. And the Donnellys keep themselves to themselves. Never a bother to anyone. It'd be a shame to see them disturbed at their age."

Tessa swallows the urge to ask more. It would be pointless. Mrs. Coburn has made it clear how she feels about Tessa's interest in Fallbrook.

"I don't plan to disturb anyone," Tessa says mildly.

"I hope not," Mrs. Coburn adds. "That would be a shame. Now, Ms. Ashwood, breakfast is served at seven a.m. sharp. Will that be a problem?"

Tessa shakes her head with the sense she's been reprimanded by a headmistress.

Once Mrs. Coburn retreats, Tessa glances around the room, debating her next move. Her practical side says now is the time to unpack her laptop and do some of that research she claimed not to be doing.

But the furor over Oliver's latest video will still be burning strong, and she can't face submerging herself in the real world again. Not yet. Not when she's just managed to buy some hard-earned distance. It's cowardly, but there it is.

Instead, Tessa jingles the keys in her hand. There's still time yet before the sun sets. What she needs is to keep moving forward, even if moving forward means coming face to face with the past.

Maybe, just maybe, if she doesn't slow down, she'll have no time for regrets.

18

Tessa misses the turn. Twice.

After the second time, she mutes the irritatingly pleasant voice of the GPS and studies the tangled brush along the side of the gravel road as the car creeps back in the direction she's just come.

Squinting, she spots two faded tracks that snake forward, then turn sharply and disappear behind a wall of greenery. Clearly, Fallbrook doesn't get many visitors.

According to her grandfather, the property isn't entirely unoccupied. At least, it wasn't at the time of his letter. He mentioned a cottage, and a trust with funds for a caretaker's salary.

Tessa has dredged her memories of that afternoon visit. She's short on specifics, but what she does remember is an overwhelming sense of abandonment. No cottage, no caretaker. In fact, she's sure they didn't meet another living soul that day.

The little car bumps slowly along the tracks. Brush and overgrown trees close in on her, branches scraping across the windshield, and she can't shake the sense that she's passing some unseen threshold separating her from the world she knows.

Tessa presses on, as much out of relief to leave that world behind as interest in what might lie ahead.

She's quickly enveloped by a thick stand of towering old-growth trees, as tall and resolute as sleeping guardians. Tessa inches the car forward, eyes on the trail to show her the way.

When the path eventually clears, it happens suddenly, and Tessa stops the car, overwhelmed. Her patchwork memories settle into place, overlapping with the present and filling in some of the missing color and details.

The day was warm, she recalls. Stifling almost. She and Margot were quiet and drowsy on the drive home, their mother distracted. They hadn't expected a detour, and Jane offered no explanations.

Tessa was dozing, her forehead pressed against the window of the car, when the road became bumpy. She awoke groggy after banging her head a few times against the glass. Once she came fully to her senses, she saw the same view that greets her now.

Tucked away in its own private realm, surrounded by forest and secrecy, Fallbrook stands ahead at the end of a long path, seemingly unchanged since that day.

The sun is dropping lower in the sky, sending a diffuse light through the trees and illuminating the peaks of the once-grand home.

Entranced, Tessa drives the car slowly forward, caught in the tendrils of an old spell. For a moment, she sees it as it would have been. Built for strength and beauty in equal measure, this was a home that visitors would never mistake for ordinary.

As she comes closer, her eyes skim over the gables and the intricate railing on the balcony that lines the second story. She searches the shadows of the deep front porch, but nothing and no one stirs.

The engine hums as she pulls up in front of the house, a sound she doesn't notice until she parks and turns off the ignition, and silence falls.

Tessa takes a deep breath and opens the car door.

The house is monstrously large, rising proud and haughty from the ground and reaching high into the air, but up close the strange spell it cast breaks apart. Any illusions that Fallbrook hasn't been ravaged by time and neglect evaporate.

The wide steps that lead up to the front entry list to one side. Decorative carved moldings frame the top of the porch between crumbling columns, but they've broken and fallen away in places. What remains resembles dirty, tattered lace.

Tessa's eyes rove over the deteriorating structure. A good number of shutters are missing. A few cling to their positions by a single corner, tilting crookedly across windows with broken panes of glass. Spiders, untroubled by the rot and mold, have spun an impressive maze of webs between the rafters overhead.

Decay seeps through every nook and cranny, as pervasive as a cancer. The grounds that surround the house are untamed, and vines twine their way between the boards and up the columns and exterior walls, reaching toward the colonies of spiders above.

Bit by bit, the earth is reclaiming this space, feasting on the remains of the Cooke family home. Given enough time, it will swallow every board and nail, digesting it by increments, and leave nothing but the bones behind.

Tessa doesn't try to resist the intangible pull of the double front doors with their chipped and peeling paint. With a careful eye on where she puts her feet, she makes her way up the steps toward the porch. A telling softness in the third step warns her to place her weight on the fourth instead.

The porch groans faintly, but Tessa holds her breath and continues forward. She stretches a hand out to the doorknob. Her fingers brush the surface of the tarnished brass, but just as she touches the cold metal, a hollow thumping fills the air. Tessa draws back as if she's been scalded, but the noise doesn't stop. Instead it grows louder and inexplicably faster, coming from everywhere and nowhere. A rustle of beating wings joins in as a flock of startled birds takes flight from somewhere above.

Tessa glances wildly around. Whatever it is, it's getting closer. Over the heavy beating of her heart, she hears a childlike voice, high and wavering, singing a lullaby.

Ring around the rosies . . . thump thump . . .

Pocket full of posies . . . thump thump thump . . .

Ashes to ashes . . . thump thump thump thump thump . . .

The sound crescendos. Then, as suddenly as it started, it stops and a figure appears at the edge of the house. Tessa gasps and takes an involuntary step backward, but her feet get tangled and she ends up sprawled in the dirt and dried leaves that coat the boards of the porch.

"You're not supposed to be here," the figure says in an indulgent voice, as if a stray cat had wandered in through an open door.

Tessa scrambles backward, but a sharp pain radiates upward from her wrist, cutting short a burgeoning scream and turning it to a gasp.

"You've hurt yourself," the figure states, then steps around the corner of the house and comes toward her. The fading sunlight shows Tessa what she couldn't see through her fear and surprise.

It's an old woman.

An old woman with a softly rounded figure and long white hair plaited into a braid that lies across her shoulder. A pair of reading glasses hangs from a silver chain around her neck. Her face is lined. Her eyes are bright and sympathetic, and she's holding a stick in her hand.

"You look like you've seen a ghost, dear," she says as she approaches the steps. She holds up the stick with an apologetic smile, then tosses it onto the ground next to her. "Sorry about that. An old habit. Scares off any wildlife that might have found a nice place to nest in the big house. Raccoons, mostly, though I haven't seen any for a while. Just the birds up in the rafters these days."

Tessa stares at her, slowly piecing together that the thumping noise was the stick rumbling along the edge of the house and echoing through the empty spaces inside.

"Is it broken, do you think?" the woman asks. "I'd give you a hand up, but at my age I probably wouldn't be much help. We'd both end up sprawled on the floor, and then where would we be?"

Tessa shakes her head. She's having trouble keeping up with the airy twitter of the woman's voice, so unexpected given their surroundings.

"That's all right," Tessa says as she picks herself up off the porch. Gingerly, she bends her wrist back and forth, but the sharp pain has subsided to a dull ache. "It's not broken."

"Well, thank goodness for small mercies," the woman says. "I'm Kitty. And you are?"

Kitty. Not what Tessa would have guessed, but it was oddly fitting for the plump, soft woman standing in front of her. More so than Betty or Doris or Edith would have been.

"Tessa," she answers, dusting off her pants. "Tessa Shepherd."

Kitty doesn't ask what Tessa is doing creeping around the abandoned property, though by rights she should. Tessa and Margot may be the legal owners now, but that doesn't lessen her sense that she's treading someplace she shouldn't.

"My family lives in the caretaker's cottage," Kitty says, gesturing toward one side of the property. Tessa can see nothing but forest, increasingly more shadowed as the sun drops lower. "You're lucky it was me who found you. Deirdre isn't keen on sightseers, though we don't get many willing to venture out here in the middle of nowhere. There's Aiden, too, but he wouldn't hurt a fly."

"Have you lived here long, then?" Tessa asks.

"Oh, all my life," Kitty says. "Mam was the housekeeper at Fallbrook, God rest her. It's the only home I've ever known."

If Tessa had to guess, she'd put Kitty's age somewhere in her eighties, which means she must have known the Cooke family in her childhood. If information is what Tessa is after, Kitty is the stuff of a documentarian's dreams. A firsthand source.

Not that she's making a film, of course. An opening shot of the house from a distance, just as Tessa first saw it, then moving slowly closer, revealing the state of the place by degrees. No music. Only the sound of the wind in the trees, underscoring the desolation.

Force of habit, nothing more.

Still, Tessa chooses her words carefully, as she would during first contact with any potential source.

"I don't suppose you'd be willing to show me around?"

Kitty puts her hands into the pockets of her cardigan and shrugs. It's unsettling, and it takes Tessa a moment to pinpoint why. Despite her obvious age, Kitty carries herself in the loose, unguarded manner of a much younger person.

"Deirdre wouldn't like it," Kitty says as she makes her way up to the porch, avoiding the third step as Tessa had. "But you seem like a nice girl."

She stops and smiles, an open, welcoming smile that immediately makes Tessa feel guilty, like she's hiding something. She is, of course. Hiding something.

"Not much to see, really. Not anymore," Kitty continues as she moves past Tessa toward the big double doors.

She opens one of the doors and pushes it wide. It creaks as it swings, and all thoughts of truth and lies of omission flee Tessa's mind. Even Kitty is forgotten as Tessa is captured once more by whatever old magic this house wields.

Slowly, she steps forward, into the gloom of a glittering past that's long ago lost its shine.

The dying light of the setting sun penetrates only so far through the broken panes of glass, and Tessa's eyes travel upward, from the debris-strewn parquet floor, past the curving spiral staircase, to land upon the domed, colored skylight overhead.

When the sun is at its peak, it must be magnificent.

Her gaze falls, and she wonders to what end? All the colored light in the world can't hide the atrophy of the room below.

"Is it safe?" Tessa asks.

"Safe enough," Kitty answers. "As long as you keep to the first floor and watch your step. I wouldn't trust the stairs, though. Nothing much left up there to see anyhow. The roof has gone in places, and the weather and the birds have finished things off."

Tessa has so many questions, but she doesn't want to offend Kitty, and needs to be careful how she words things.

"So no one has lived here since . . ."

"Not since the old family were all gone. No one much interested in it after, what with the rumors and the stories. But I suppose you'll have heard all that already."

"Some," Tessa says, not untruthfully.

"A shame, really. The place was nice, once. But that was a long time ago. A lifetime. A house dies a slow death without a family to fill it. This one certainly has."

"Kitty," calls a new voice from outside. "Kitty, are you in there?"

The sound of footsteps shuffling along the porch reaches them, and Kitty turns to Tessa and holds a finger up to her mouth before answering, a gesture Tessa takes to mean she shouldn't mention the conversation they've been having.

"In here, Dee," Kitty calls.

A second woman fills the doorway, as tall and thin as Kitty is short and round. She's even older, if Tessa is any judge. There's a wooden cane in her hand, but instead of leaning her weight against it, she holds it up and points the tail end toward Tessa.

"I suppose that fancy car belongs to you, then," she says darkly.

"Yes," Tessa answers. "My name is Tessa. Kitty was just showing me the house."

"I can see that," the woman says. The cane changes direction and points at Kitty. "What have I told you? You can't be letting in every lookie-loo off the street."

Kitty opens her mouth, but before she has a chance to speak, the second woman continues. "This is private property, and you're trespassing. You need to leave." She steps back and holds the door wide, waiting for them to make their exit.

Tessa glances quickly at Kitty, who rolls her eyes. "Deirdre, there's no need to be rude," she says.

But the other woman ignores her. "Come on now, shake a leg. I can't be standing here all day."

Tessa has no desire to upset anyone, least of all an old woman, so she walks back toward the front doors, Kitty dutifully by her side.

Deirdre closes the door firmly behind them, then stands fast, barring them from reentry.

"Go on now," she says, gesturing toward Tessa's car. The sun is almost fully set, and darkness is creeping across the yard.

Kitty sighs. "It was very nice to meet you, Tessa," she says. "I'm sorry our visit was cut short. My sister isn't known for her welcoming manner, I'm afraid."

Deirdre glares at her and folds her arms, but Kitty doesn't apologize. Tessa is reminded of Margot, and the universal language of sisters.

"Thank you," Tessa says, then turns to Deirdre. "Maybe I should introduce myself properly and tell you why I'm here."

"Doesn't matter why you're here." Deirdre dismisses her with a wave of a bony, age-spotted hand. "Whatever it is you want, we're not interested, and we don't speak to the press."

The irony of being mistaken for a reporter and thrown off the property doesn't escape Tessa. Deirdre is already walking away and has made it down the steps into the yard. Kitty follows a few steps behind and sends Tessa an apologetic smile and a wave goodbye.

She needs to explain, and quickly.

"My mother's name is Jane," Tessa calls to their retreating backs. "At least, we thought so. But that wasn't true. Her birth name was Imogene. Imogene Cooke, and she was born in this house."

The two women stop in their tracks. They turn first to one another. Whatever communication silently passes between them Tessa can only wonder at. Then they turn to stare at her.

"My mother was the baby," she says. "The one who survived."

19

"Baby Imogene." The words tumble from Kitty's lips in a whisper of wonder, ending the stunned silence between them. "Imagine that."

As if Tessa's words have flipped a switch, Kitty brightens and her face shines with delight.

But it's Deirdre that Tessa's eyes are drawn to. She's gone still. In a span of seconds, the elder of the sisters has managed to fold and put away whatever emotions Tessa's statement might have brought tumbling down. Even her earlier irritation at finding an uninvited visitor is hidden quickly behind bolted doors.

"My goodness, how lovely," Kitty says. "Dee, this is baby Imogene's daughter. Imagine that."

Deirdre cuts a glance at Kitty, but her eyes come back to Tessa soon enough. She considers the interloper while carefully guarding her thoughts, perhaps searching Tessa's face for some resemblance to the family she would have known as a girl.

Tessa fights an urge to look away, forcing herself to meet the woman's gaze head-on. "My mother died. We buried her yesterday," she says quietly.

"Oh dear." Kitty visibly deflates at the news. "I am so very sorry, Tessa. You've lost your mam. Oh, you poor, poor thing."

She didn't say the words to elicit sympathy, but Kitty closes the gap between them and pulls Tessa into a hug. It's oddly comforting, and Tessa returns the embrace, breathing in Kitty's citrus scent. Her eyes find Deirdre over Kitty's shoulder. She hasn't moved a muscle.

Kitty pulls back, though she keeps Tessa's arm tucked in hers.

Tessa fumbles. Where to start? "My sister and I had no idea about this place. Mom never told us."

"You have a sister?" Kitty asks, brightening a little again. "How lovely. There's that, at least." She pats Tessa's hand and glances back at Deirdre. "Baby Imogene had daughters, Dee. Imagine that."

The light is fading fast. Tessa catches a flicker of something pass across the older woman's expression, but it's gone before she can identify it.

"I assume you have questions, then," Deirdre says. She's grasped the crux of the situation quickly and completely.

"Yes." Tessa can hear the relief in her own voice.

Deirdre nods, then straightens her spine. "We'll do our best to answer those," she says. "But not tonight. Come back tomorrow at a civilized time and you'll have what you're after."

The woman appears resolute. Defiant almost, and Tessa realizes suddenly how this all must seem. The threat she could potentially pose.

Tessa nods. It's getting late, and Deirdre looks older than she did only moments ago.

"Of course," she says.

Content with that, Kitty gives Tessa's shoulders a final squeeze and a small, conspiratorial smile before joining her sister again. The women turn to make their way back toward their home, hidden out of sight in the woods. Tessa walks slowly to her car and places her hand on the door handle.

But she can't let them go without attempting to put their minds at ease.

"I mean you no harm," she calls to their retreating backs.

Deirdre stops and turns, leaning her weight against the cane. Kitty watches the exchange with curiosity and no sign of concern.

"No one ever does," Deirdre says. "But that rarely changes anything. Good night, Tessa."

20

KITTY

The muffled hoot of an owl keeps Kitty company as she nurses the warm cup of milk in the darkness of the front porch. The owl joins her nightly ritual often, and she misses him when he's gone.

Tonight, Aiden has joined her too.

"I think you'll like her," Kitty says. He's been more quiet than usual after hearing about their visitor and her impending return. "There's nothing to worry about. Really."

Aiden shifts in his seat, but it's too dark to see his expression.

"I'm not worried for me, Kitty," he says softly. "Just don't want the woman to feel uncomfortable, that's all."

"Well, that's silly. Why in the world—"

"There are reasons, as you know very well, so don't play dumb."

She pauses, considers her words, then plunges ahead all the same. "Denny, no one blames you. That was only ever in your fool head."

He gives a dry chuckle. "You're a fine one to talk, Kitty cat. There were plenty who did, whether you want to admit it or not. Probably a few old-timers left who still do, for that matter."

"Pshh. Then you're not the only fool left around here. Gossip and idle tongues, that's all there was to it. There was never any doubt who did it. You and Dee think I was too young to know then and I'm too old to remember now, but you're wrong on both counts."

The rocking chair creaks beneath her as Kitty shifts it faster. She can sense his surprise when he turns to stare at her, even if she can't read his expression.

"What exactly *do* you remember, Kitty?" Aiden asks slowly.

"Enough," she tells him. "Enough to know that Lawrence Pynchon was not a good man."

A choked sound comes from behind them, and Kitty turns to find her sister standing in the doorway clutching a shawl around her shoulders. Deirdre's white nightgown faintly glows in the moonlight, and her face is nearly as pale.

"Don't you say his name, Kitty. Not in this house."

Deirdre's voice is hoarse. Kitty wants nothing more than to take the words and stuff them right back into her mouth. She'd eat them raw and choke on their bitterness if she could erase the hurt on her sister's face.

"I'm sorry, Dee," she says, and struggles to rise from the chair, but her old bones betray her and she's not fast enough. Deirdre backs away, into the safety of the cottage and away from the conversation she's stumbled into. She waves her hand in front of her face, as if a wasp is buzzing around her.

"No," she says, cutting off whatever comfort Kitty might try to give. "No, just . . . please. Don't ever say that name."

She turns and hurries back toward her small bedroom, gone in a flurry of nightdress.

"I've upset her," Kitty says. She's always doing that. Lately, it seems she does nothing else but state the obvious and upset her sister.

"She'll be all right." But there's a trace of concern in Aiden's voice that contradicts his words. "You know how she is. Dee shut the door on those days a long time ago, and she doesn't like it when someone jimmies the lock."

Kitty shifts uncomfortably, biting the inside of her lip.

"Does she know?" Aiden asks. She's never been good at hiding her thoughts from him. "That you still see them?"

Kitty shakes her head. "No. It upsets her too much. After last time . . . I try not to bring it up anymore."

Mam saw ghosts too. Kitty remembers, even if Deirdre won't admit it. The conversations with someone unseen while she worked in the garden. Sometimes they made her cry, but Mam was the one who taught Kitty there was nothing to fear from the dead.

"The dead are at peace now, Kitty cat," she said. *"It's the living who struggle."*

"Tomorrow won't be easy for her."

"That's why I think you should be here," Kitty says, urging him again to stay and meet Tessa.

Aiden shoves his hands deep in his pockets and blows out a breath. "I doubt that would help. It'll just bring up more questions. We don't know how much this woman knows or what her plans might be. You heard Dee. She thinks I ought to make myself scarce."

"But why is it up to her?" Kitty presses. "She's not our mother."

"Ach, maybe not, but she was always a bossy one, wasn't she, lass." The honeyed brogue of their youth gets a smile out of her, if a small one.

But it's also a sign he's done with the subject. The dark silhouette of his form rises and moves to stand at the edge of the porch. It'll do no good to say anything else. Aiden lives by his own inscrutable rules.

"I believe I'll take a walk," he says, as if the thought has only just occurred to him. Kitty rolls her eyes and mouths the words along with him as he finishes his pronouncement. "Night air does a body good."

"Be careful out there, please," she says shortly. And, again, wonders why she bothers. It's not as if he's going to set out to *not* be careful, and only her admonishment will keep him safe.

"Always," Aiden replies jauntily, as he always does.

She sighs and watches him go. The walls of the cottage never hold him for long. It's been this way since he returned to them a few years ago, home at last from his travels.

He doesn't speak about the years he spent away, and she doesn't ask, but she wonders sometimes about the things he must have seen and done.

If she could peek at the ledger of Aiden's life, would the sum equal a good man?

Kitty has her opinion, of course, but sometimes she worries she's too close to see the truth of the ones she loves. She wouldn't be the first to suffer that kind of blindness.

And now Imogene's daughter. Not a ghost, but a living, breathing relic of an ancient past. The baby that was never wanted grew up and had babies of her own.

"You were right, Mam," she whispers into the wind, recalling another dark night a long time ago.

Mam is working by the fire, darning socks and mending clothes the children are constantly growing too big for. She sends the girls off to bed and tells them not to stay up too late giggling, but of course they do.

Dee gives in first. She sleeps now, her mouth open, breath raspy, in the bed next to her, but Kitty's mind is too busy to settle down.

A hushed sound travels through the small cottage. A shuffling of feet and a murmur of voices find Kitty's ears, then the rattle of a tea-kettle warming on the stove.

Curious, Kitty slides from the bed. She's quiet when she wants to be. Sneaky, Aiden calls her, though he says it with a wink and a laugh.

She pushes the bedroom door open the slightest bit, just a crack, careful not to push too hard and give herself away. Kitty knows she's eavesdropping, and she feels not the least bit bad about it. No one tells her anything. She's proud of how good she's gotten at listening at cracks in doors.

She expects Aiden and Mam, hopes to hear what he's been doing out so late with his friends, though she doubts he'll share the interesting bits with his mother. Aiden's world, full of boys and plans and futures she can only dream about, is a siren's call she can't resist.

But it's a woman's voice that alternates with Mam's, not Aiden's after all. Kitty tamps her disappointment down, and focuses on the voices, straining to make out words.

". . . desperate, Mrs. Donnelly . . ."

Kitty knows that voice, though she's never heard Helena sound quite like this before. She . . . she's pleading. But for what?

A shiver of excitement courses through Kitty, and she leans forward, pushing the door a bit wider. A fraction of an inch. She doesn't like Helena Cooke. None of them do, though Mam won't hear a word against her.

Whatever has brought her to the cottage, Kitty's sure it's meant to be a secret, and *secret* is her favorite word. A delicious word. One that sounds exactly like what it is. *See-cret*, she thinks, drawing it out in her head in a dramatic whisper.

And she must have it.

"I'm not sure I understand what you're asking, Mrs. Cooke," Mam says. She's using the voice she saves especially for her employers. Kitty hates that voice. It's a small voice, one that makes Saoirse Donnelly less than what she is. A servant's voice, one who knows her place.

". . . not sure how much more clear I can be. I'm begging you. I can't have . . . simply not possible."

Their unexpected guest is growing agitated. The crack is wide enough now that Kitty can put one eye to the door and just make them out. Mrs. Cooke is leaning forward over the table, the one where they share meals and stories. She's sitting in the chair usually reserved for Kitty.

The affront makes Kitty cross, and she turns her ear again, leaning closer. She's determined to discover what has Mrs. Cooke so upset.

"I'm afraid you've misunderstood, ma'am," the housekeeper says. "I don't have the knowledge or experience you're asking for." Saoirse Donnelly stops, and the silence that follows is deafening. Kitty holds her breath, willing them to say more.

"And even if I did, I'm afraid I still wouldn't help you."

Kitty's eyes widen. That was Mam's voice. Her real voice, the one that knows she's not small, the one she never, *ever* uses with the Cookes.

Kitty peeks again, fear and anticipation growing in equal measure.

Mrs. Cooke backs sharply away from the table, and Mam leans forward.

"Please, Mrs. Cooke. Try to understand. A child is a blessing. A gift from God. It's natural to be fearful with your first pregnancy, but you mustn't allow fear to overrule your good sense."

Pregnancy? Kitty feels a hollow pit open inside of her. Mrs. Cooke is going to have a baby? That isn't the kind of secret she ever hoped to know. She would scrub the knowledge from her brain if she could.

She'll never go away if she has a baby, Kitty thinks. *Never, ever.*

And, more than anything, she wants Helena Cooke to go away. Kitty wants everything back the way it was before this woman came to Fallbrook and tipped their lives on end.

Things are different now. Peter has turned quiet as a mouse afraid even to squeak. Cora's single-minded goal is to torture her new stepmother into submission. Ruby and Kitty were never close, but now Ruby is so busy molding herself into Helena's idea of a proper young woman that she no longer has smiles or hugs even for Mam.

But for all their faults, before Helena, they were a family.

Now, Mam is nothing more than a servant.

"Do not presume to lecture me, Mrs. Donnelly," Helena says in her sharpest lady-of-the-manor voice. She no longer bothers to keep her voice down, and pushes away from the table in a flurry of outrage.

"No, ma'am," Mam says quietly, but Kitty doubts Mrs. Cooke hears her. She marches to the door, her nose held impossibly high, then turns back to remind Mam of her place. As if she could forget. As if any of them could forget.

"You will not speak of this, Mrs. Donnelly," Helena Cooke says. "Not unless you wish to find yourself tossed out on the street. Do I make myself clear?"

Mam nods. "Yes, ma'am."

With a slam of the door, Mrs. Cooke is gone.

But she isn't. Not really. Helena Cooke's presence reverberates inside the only two waking souls within the cottage. She'll never be gone.

With one last look at Mam, who has slumped down into a chair at the kitchen table, Kitty pads slowly back to the bed where Deirdre sleeps, blithely unaware, and slides beneath the covers next to her.

Kitty shivers and lets Dee's warmth soak into her skin, but it's not enough to soothe the worry that's awakened in her.

More than seven decades have passed since that night. With stars now winking overhead, Kitty rocks and listens to the owl call to her from the tops of the trees.

As it turned out, Mrs. Cooke didn't go anywhere. It was Cora who was exiled from Fallbrook. Cora, who refused to give her stepmother a moment's peace, no matter how much Mam tried to persuade her. How Deirdre had cried the day her friend was sent away.

And before Cora returned, there was a new daughter. Baby Imogene. A daughter who survived to have daughters of her own. *Imagine that.*

"You were right, Mam," Kitty whispers again. "Children are a blessing."

21

TESSA

The big house, Kitty called it. *The murder house.*
Fallbrook.

Whatever name it goes by, the house, what's left of it, and its elderly caretakers have made an impression on Tessa. She drives back to the bed-and-breakfast on autopilot, replaying the sights and sounds, the *feel* of the place, in her mind.

Questions stack up, and Tessa recognizes the familiar tingle of obsession that comes at the beginning of any new project. She's itching to get to work with her laptop, to ferret out whatever information can be found about the Cooke family, their lives and their deaths.

It's a coping mechanism, a crutch to avoid reality. Easy enough to recognize, but harder to convince herself it's a bad thing. Especially when she made a career out of channeling her obsessions.

But this isn't a story. This is personal.

All the best stories are is the whisper that flits through her mind. Tessa pushes that away. She's not making a film. Those days are done. Possibly for good. After Oliver . . . She shakes her head. Where would she find the nerve?

Tessa turns into the drive for the converted Georgian, and all thoughts of escape vanish like a soap bubble. As if she's conjured the very thing she's running from, she's greeted by an SUV marked with the distinctive brown-and-black logo of the Bonham Police Department.

No.

Tessa's muscles tighten, and the cold, heavy weight of dread settles on her limbs. She sits in the driver's seat of the unmoving car, staring.

No.

What a fool she was, to think she could outrun this. To think, for one second, that a little bit of distance was all it would take to shield her from the man waiting inside.

How did he find her?

Even as the thought occurs to her, she has her answer.

Margot.

She texted her sister the address after she booked the room at Bracknell Lodge, for no other reason than to keep open that delicate line of communication. It was shut down for so long that Tessa can't let it go now.

I could just turn the car around. Drive away, farther this time, faster.

But the thought is fleeting, chased away by the memory of her sister's words. *"You're being completely irrational."*

Tessa puts the car in park. There's no point in running anymore. Margot insisted she needed to face this. Now she's forcing her to.

She makes her way to the door.

The trio of people gathered in the front room fall silent when Tessa enters. Mrs. Coburn, seated in a green brocade wing chair, sits back and folds her arms primly as she stares icy daggers in Tessa's direction.

A second woman, one Tessa's never met, is seated on the edge of the sofa, dressed in nondescript slacks and a white blouse with a badge hooked to her belt. The woman glances up from the small notebook open in her hand and looks Tessa over, her expression giving away nothing.

For a moment Tessa dares to hope she's been granted a reprieve, but that hope dies when she spots the figure of a man leaning against the wall, his arms crossed in front of him.

Lloyd Winters.

He's watching her through a mask of strained indifference, but Tessa isn't fooled. Her gaze flits away from him, searching for anywhere else to land.

Mrs. Coburn is the first to break the silence. "Good evening, Ms. *Ashwood*," she says sharply. "We've been waiting for you."

Tessa steps farther into the room and gingerly shuts the front door behind her.

"These officers and I have been having a little chat. An enlightening experience, to say the least." Tessa's eyes widen at the woman's poisonous tone. "I'll see myself out," Mrs. Coburn says to the female officer, "so you may interrogate Ms. *Shepherd* as you see fit."

Mrs. Coburn's heels click sharply across the floor as she exits the room, leaving no doubt about her feelings regarding her guest, whom she'd apparently be perfectly pleased to see waterboarded among her antique furniture.

"Tessa Shepherd? I'm Detective Joanna Morello with the New York State Police. I believe you know—"

"She knows who I am," Winters barks.

Tessa flinches, but Detective Morello ignores him and continues in a calm, professional tone that Tessa tries to focus on. "Ms. Shepherd, have a seat. I'd like to ask you some questions, if you don't mind."

"Of course," Tessa replies. She walks slowly to the chair that Mrs. Coburn has vacated and perches straight-backed along the edge, her posture unconsciously mirroring the woman studying her. Tessa has been on the other side of a great many interviews, yet she's unaccountably nervous.

The anger coming from Chief Winters in palpable waves doesn't help.

"You are aware of the current . . . *situation* regarding Oliver Barlow, I assume?" the detective begins.

Tessa nods.

"And you're also, no doubt, aware that Oliver Barlow has indicated in the latest video that's been released to the public that you might have some idea of his current whereabouts."

Tessa is shaking her head before the detective has even finished speaking.

"I don't," she says. "I'm not sure why he'd say that, but I truly don't."

Detective Morello stares closely at Tessa, her expression giving away nothing. "Are you absolutely sure about that, Ms. Shepherd? When was the last time you spoke to Mr. Barlow?"

Tessa frowns. "It's been months. Six months, maybe? When he was first released from prison, we spoke more often, but then things got busy at work. I started a new project. He seemed to be settling in okay, and . . . and I just . . ." Even to Tessa's own ears, the words sound like excuses.

She takes a deep breath. "My life revolves around my work, Detective. For a time, that included Oliver. But the sad truth is, I'm not very good at maintaining friendships." Tessa doesn't attempt to defend herself. The causes of her inability to connect to other people may be suited to a therapist's couch, but they have no place in a police interview.

"Oliver attempted to contact me several times in the days leading up to . . ." She glances toward Winters, whose jaw is tense and flexing as he stares down at his boots. "Leading up to the crime," she continues, quickly looking back to Detective Morello. "I didn't take the calls, and he didn't leave any messages. He gave me absolutely no indication he was planning something like this, I swear to you."

Morello's gaze is inscrutable. The silence stretches out, fraught with the emotions emanating from Chief Winters.

"Ms. Shepherd," the detective says, her voice soft but persistent. "A bright young girl is missing and presumed dead. We have no idea what Barlow has done with her body. No idea where he's run to, and no idea what he plans to do next. If you have any information that might aid us in this investigation—"

"I don't," Tessa says with a vehement shake of her head. "Believe me, I wish I did. I would do anything to make this right."

Winters lets out a dry, mirthless laugh. It raises goose bumps on Tessa's arms, and she backs a bit farther into the chair. "It's a little late for that, isn't it, Shepherd?"

Tessa has nothing to say to that. He's right.

"Barlow was right where he belonged before you came sniffing around, shoving your nose into places you had no business being." He pulls his big frame from the wall he's been leaning against, and Tessa can see his fists are clenched at his side.

"Winters," Detective Morello warns in a deceptively calm voice.

Her tone is firm, but still, Tessa's surprised when the big man heeds her admonishment and shoves his hands back into his pockets. Realization dawns on her.

"You're with the state police?" she asks needlessly. The detective has said so several times already, but the implications were lost on Tessa in her agitated state. "Bonham PD isn't taking the lead on the investigation?"

Detective Morello doesn't blink. "The Bonham Police Department is assisting the New York State Police in a supplemental capacity."

Winters's jaw clenches. Tessa has no trouble translating that. Chief Winters and his department have been sidelined. A grieving father whose daughter has been suddenly and violently taken from him. A man used to giving orders and being obeyed. Targeted by his daughter's killer, publicly taunted and jeered. Yet his hands have been officially tied.

They'd have more luck caging a hungry tiger in a cardboard box, Tessa thinks, eyeing the man with a new and elevated level of caution. She has no doubts who he blames for all this.

"Ms. Shepherd, we're also here because your safety may be of some concern. We believe it's in your best interest to be placed under police protection while the investigation of Oliver Barlow's whereabouts is ongoing."

Tessa's gaze swings between the two of them, but Winters is staring determinedly at the wall somewhere above Tessa's head. Whatever the man's agenda, it has nothing at all to do with Tessa's safety.

"I . . . I appreciate your concern, Detective, but I really don't think—"

"He sent another video," Winters interrupts. "They've managed to get an injunction to block the release to the public, but I've seen it. Barlow's coming for you, Shepherd."

Tessa leans backward, but it does little to distance herself from the satisfaction in Chief Winters's voice.

"I don't understand," Tessa says, shaking her head. "Oliver has no reason to come after me. I haven't done anything."

Detective Morello answers softly. "Apparently, he believes otherwise."

"That's crazy," Tessa says. "Besides, even if he's looking for me, there's no way he's going to find me here."

But that thought leads her to the next. A cold chill courses down her skin, leaving goose bumps behind.

"My sister," she says. "You have to warn my sister. Oliver knows where I'm from. If he goes to Linlea, my sister—"

"We've already contacted the police in Linlea," Detective Morello reassures her. "Your sister has been advised of the situation and will also be provided police protection. If Barlow shows up, we'll get him."

Relief floods through Tessa and she grasps the arms of the chair for support. There are too many things to process at once. She scrubs her hands over her face, then glances quickly back up at Morello and Winters.

"What did he say exactly? I want to see the video."

Morello shakes her head. "I'm afraid that won't be possible. But trust me when I tell you, he's become increasingly erratic. We believe the threat he poses to you and your family is very real. I can't overstate how important it is that you take precautions."

"To be honest, Shepherd," Winters says in a harsh, unforgiving voice, "I don't give a damn about your safety. You didn't give a second thought to my daughter's safety when you convinced the world a murderer was harmless, and frankly if he comes after you, that's no more than you—"

"Enough," Morello breaks in.

Winters pulls back the finger he's jabbing toward Tessa's face and blows out a long breath between puffed cheeks. But he doesn't need to finish the sentence. Tessa has no misconceptions about where it was leading.

No more than she deserves.

"I don't want police protection," Tessa says hoarsely. "I can decline, can't I?"

Morello frowns. "I would strongly suggest—"

"No," Tessa says, shaking her head. "Even if he was looking for me, there's no reason for him to look *here*. I'm as safe here as I would be anywhere."

"Ms. Shepherd, I don't think that's—"

"You offered, the woman turned you down, Morello," Winters says harshly. "Maybe she thinks she's got nothing to fear from Barlow. Maybe there's a reason for that."

Tessa glances up in surprise, meeting Winters's piercing gaze head-on for the first time since she walked into the bed-and-breakfast and found the pair of them waiting for her.

"What are you saying?" she asks, her voice so quiet it's almost a whisper.

"There's only one reason you could be so certain that Barlow won't harm you, *Ms. Shepherd*," he says, spitting her name from his lips like it was something foul. "And that's because you're in on this with him."

The accusation runs over her like ice water, chilling her blood.

"You can't seriously believe—"

"No," Detective Morello assures her, glaring over her shoulder at the man. "The state police have thoroughly investigated your interactions with Barlow, and at this time, you're not considered a suspect. Otherwise, you would be coming with me. All we're asking is if you have any ideas, any at all, that might help us apprehend him."

"No," Tessa insists. "There's nothing. When I knew Oliver, he was an inmate with one goal. A new trial. He wanted to prove his innocence and rejoin his family. That's all. And God help me, I believed him. If he'd ever given *any* indication he was capable of something like this, I would have dropped the project immediately."

Tessa risks a glance at Winters.

"I swear to you, I never saw this coming. If I could go back . . ."

Grief breaks through his stony features for the briefest of moments, but it tells Tessa everything she needs to know about how hard he's working to hold himself together.

"Find him," she says softly. Winters's gaze locks on hers. "Find him and make him pay for this."

The flare in the chief's eyes steals her breath.

"I did that once already," he says in a low voice, every word intended to land a blow.

"Then do it again," Tessa says in a tone that echoes his. Words tumble from her mouth without thought of the consequence. "Do it right this time."

Winters moves toward her, quickly coming around the sofa. Detective Morello is on her feet, meeting Winters with a restraining hand before he comes any closer to Tessa. His fists are clenched as tightly as his jaw, and she braces herself for whatever is coming.

But he stops and turns away, wrestling his emotions before he does something he can't take back.

"Why don't you step outside?" Morello says to him. "Get some air."

There's a pause, then Winters nods and walks quickly to the door. He shuts it carefully behind him, with an impressive level of self-control.

Joanna Morello's professionalism slips for just a moment and she sighs, running a hand over her hair.

"I hope you understand why I'm going to decline your offer of police protection," Tessa says. At this point she's probably safer with Oliver than she is anywhere near Lloyd Winters.

"We can keep him away from you," Morello tells her. Tessa's not sure if she's referring to Oliver or Winters, and the concerned glance she throws over her shoulder toward the door says she's not entirely sure either.

"Thank you, but I'll pass."

The detective isn't pleased, that much is clear, but there's nothing remotely pleasing about the situation. Not for any of them.

"If you change your mind, please call me immediately. And if anything, anything at all, occurs to you as far as Barlow's whereabouts—"

"I won't hesitate."

"Then there's nothing more we can do here," she says. The detective stands and Tessa follows her to the door. Morello pauses, then looks back to Tessa.

"I think he blames himself," she says quietly, her hand on the doorknob. "Probably more than he blames you, but you're an easier target."

Tessa doesn't know what to say to that and simply nods. Who the chief blames more . . . it makes no difference in the end.

"We both played our parts. And his daughter paid the price for our mistakes."

Detective Morello nods and surprises her by holding up her hand to shake Tessa's. And then she's gone.

"I've taken the liberty of bringing down your luggage."

Tessa startles. She didn't hear Mrs. Coburn enter the room. She's probably been listening from the kitchen the whole time. It is her house, Tessa reminds herself tiredly. She has no right to complain.

"I don't know why you've come here, and to be honest, I don't much care, but I'll not harbor someone of your ilk under my roof."

Tessa shakes her head. Her emotions are shredded and raw, and too near the surface. "I'm sorry . . . my *ilk*? And what exactly is my ilk, Mrs. Coburn?"

"You're a liar." She says the words as if she's won some sort of prize. "Ashwood isn't your name. *And* you're a person of interest in a police investigation. For *murder*. How you can sleep at night, knowing what damage your little movie has caused, is beyond me, it truly is."

Mrs. Coburn pushes Tessa's suitcase toward her with the toe of her shoe, as if it's something germ-infested she doesn't dare touch.

Tessa sighs and grabs the handle to roll it out the door. As far as how she sleeps at night, one thing is certain. She won't be doing any sleeping under this woman's roof, or anything else for that matter.

If she has any doubts, the slam of the door at her back sets her straight.

22

It's too late to knock on the door of another bed-and-breakfast, even if Snowden had any others. Which it doesn't.

Like a dog with its tail tucked, Tessa points her little black car in the direction of the last town she passed with a population large enough to support a hotel.

The GPS informs her she'll arrive at her destination in thirty-seven minutes. Somehow, the mechanical voice sounds judgmental.

As she navigates the winding, isolated roads that weave through northern Pennsylvania, the forest looms tall around her. Tessa has come face-to-face with Winters and emerged in one piece, but nothing else has changed. Her thoughts slide to Fallbrook. Tessa can't shake a pang of loss for the unfinished business she's leaving in her rearview mirror.

It's not logical. She'll be back in the morning. Yet she can't help feeling like Fallbrook and the mystery of the Cooke family are being pried from her unwilling hands, a gift given, then snatched back before she's had a chance to unwrap it.

But she has more pressing things to worry about.

She hasn't been able to reach Margot.

Tessa dials again. "Margot? Are you okay?" she says when the call is picked up. But all she can hear are broken pieces of Margot's voice. Soon she loses even that.

The text that arrives a few moments later helps to stave off full-blown panic.

Crap signal. Talk soon. Stay safe.

It doesn't sound like her sister has been kidnapped by a murderous lunatic, but she can't relax until she's heard Margot tell her so.

She keeps one eye on the road while she checks the bars on her phone. There's no point attempting a call until her signal improves.

For eighteen years, she and Margot were two halves that made a whole. They turned thirty-six this year, on opposite sides of a mountain that Tessa didn't have the courage to scale. As many years apart as they'd spent together.

She won't let Margot go again. Not now. Not ever.

Tessa is nearing civilization when the bars on her phone light up, first one, then all of them. She could cry in relief, but she takes a deep breath and continues in search of a hotel. She'll check in, settle into a room, and find some semblance of calm before she calls her sister again.

She makes it as far as the parking lot.

With the lights of a Best Western burning behind her, Tessa hits redial and waits.

The call connects immediately to Margot's prerecorded voice mail message. She hangs up and dials again. Same response.

"Margot, I'm worried about you," Tessa says impatiently to her sister's voice mail. "Call me back, even if you're mad. I'll feel better after I hear your voice."

She ends the call, then immediately dials again. This time, Margot picks up.

"Tess?"

"Where are you?" Tessa asks immediately. "Are you safe?"

"—fine—police were—about you—"

126

The few words Tessa can make out are interspersed with bits of static and silence.

"Margot, can you hear me?" Tessa asks, shouting into the phone. Because raising her voice will improve the connection.

There's no response.

"Margot!"

With a few choice words that would horrify her mother, Tessa ends the call and tries again.

Nothing.

She's debating throwing the phone out the window and driving over it a few times when another text comes.

Stop calling. I'm fine. Talk tomorrow.

A low, frustrated growl comes out of her throat, and Tessa tosses the phone into the passenger seat.

She pushes her hair back from her face with both hands and catches the reflection of the hotel lights. There's a room waiting, with a tub, and a minibar, and a bed she's too keyed up to sleep in.

It's the minibar that drags her from the car.

With a stretch and a sigh, she takes her suitcase out of the trunk and walks toward the light.

An annual quilters' convention has her tossing the same suitcase back into the trunk and slamming the lid a few moments later.

"What the hell do quilters need to convene about anyway?" she complains to no one, then recalls the quilt her mother made for her that's folded neatly over her bed in her empty apartment. "Sorry, Mom," she mumbles, sending a quick glance upward.

And now she feels like an ass.

What is she *doing*, sitting in the parking lot of a hotel with no vacancies, growing more frustrated by the minute? She's chasing her tail, running from the still smoldering ruin of her life. Running from everything and everyone.

Even Margot. She finally had a chance to reconnect with the most important person in her life, and she's run to the middle of nowhere just to avoid the conversations they need to have.

She *is* an ass. The world's biggest ass.

Tessa jams the key into the ignition and cranks it harder than she needs to. The engine roars to life.

She should go home.

Not to her empty apartment in Brooklyn. In a burst of clarity, Tessa sees it for what it's always been. A place to sleep between her working hours.

She should go to her real home. To her mom's farmhouse. To her twin sister.

Her hand creeps up and touches the brass key on the chain her mother slipped onto her neck so long ago.

"Let it remind you that you always have a home to come to, no matter how far life takes you."

Tessa hopes that's true. But maybe it's just a string of pretty words. Tessa's not sure she can tell the difference anymore.

23

KITTY

Dreaming. Waking. Kitty's not sure she can tell the difference anymore.

What rest she does manage to get, fitful though it is, ends with the faint and muffled sound of sobbing. Kitty's eyes flutter open and she stares into the dark that fills the space between herself and the ceiling, ears pricked.

She waits.

Nothing.

Was it a dream? A misplaced memory back to plague her, like a child bent on mischief, poking at her with a pointed stick? The possibility isn't so bothersome as the thought that the tears were real, shed in the dead of night with no one to hear but Kitty in her sleep-addled state.

She listens closer.

Still nothing.

With a deep sigh, dredged from the marrow of her bones, she slides from beneath the covers. Sleep won't be back, not for a while yet. Another sacrifice on the altar of age.

She shuffles lightly toward the kitchen, careful not to disturb her siblings. The soft chuff of the refrigerator door would give her away, but no one is awake to hear. Not bothering with a spoon or fork, she breaks off a small portion of cold apple pie to nibble on.

If Deirdre notices, Kitty will just blame it on Aiden.

A flash outside the window catches her eye, and her hand stills, the bit of pie suspended halfway to her mouth. She leans over the sink to peer into the darkness. There it is again.

A visitor? At this hour? It's not Aiden. He returned from his walk long ago. Her eyes move to check the clock on the wall.

The light flickers through the trees, then turns away from the cottage, toward the big house.

Kitty pops the bit of pie in her mouth, licks her sticky fingers, then turns to find her shawl.

With unhurried steps, in her nightgown and slip-on garden shoes, she makes her way down the trail toward Fallbrook. The moon is bright, and subtle shadows filter through the branches overhead, but Kitty could find her way blindfolded.

The forest thins, revealing the familiar sight of the empty house. The only thing out of place is the twin glare of headlights. Another person might be wary, but Kitty is relieved by the undeniably real sound of an engine and the soft thud of a car door. Her ghosts have never shone lights through the woods before, and she's glad to see they haven't taken up the practice.

A distinctly corporeal figure moves in the shadows around the car with no hint of stealth. The trunk opens, and Kitty moves closer.

She's standing next to the car, watching curiously, when Tessa Shepherd closes the trunk, then lets out a piercing scream that startles a gasp from Kitty.

Tessa manages to slap a hand across her mouth and stifle the sound.

"My goodness, you scared me," Kitty says, clutching the shawl near her throat.

"Kitty?" Tessa's panicked breath slows and she lets out a choked sort of laugh. "Jesus, I didn't hear you walk up. What are you doing out here so late?"

"I could ask you the same thing," Kitty points out. "An odd hour for another visit, isn't it?"

The young woman's eyes slide away from hers, and she glances about as if searching for an answer.

"Honestly? I don't know what I'm doing here," Tessa admits, raising her hands, then letting them drop. "I got kicked out of my room at the bed-and-breakfast, and I was in the car, headed for home, but when I should have turned right, I felt myself taking a left."

She meets Kitty's eyes again, her gaze full of unanswered questions.

"Have you ever had that sense that there's someplace you need to be? Like you've forgotten to turn off the stove and your subconscious is telling you to go home and check before you burn the house down?"

Kitty shrugs. "I've never had much need for a subconscious. I have Dee for that. If there's somewhere I'm supposed to be, she's not likely to let me forget it."

One corner of Tessa's mouth lifts. "Sisters."

"Were you staying at Bracknell Lodge?" At Tessa's nod, Kitty's brows draw tightly together. "And Maddie Coburn kicked you out? Why in the world would she do such a thing?"

Tessa's face goes blank in the way Aiden's does when Kitty asks him something he'd rather not answer.

"It's a long story," she says, the words tumbling from her lips in a rush. "I was thinking maybe I'd sleep here . . . If no one would mind, that is."

"Here?" Kitty's eyes widen. She looks Tessa up and down, then turns to look at the crumbling remains of the big house, still illuminated in the glare of headlights. Kitty is used to the place. It's a part of her life in the same way an extra limb might be. There's nothing about it that

scares her, including the occasional ghost, but even *she* can't imagine bunking down beneath what's left of that roof.

"It's crazy, isn't it?" Tessa says, reading the thoughts on her face. "I know. Completely insane. I should just sleep in the car."

Kitty shrugs. "I suppose you own the place now. It's yours to do with as you like, and I doubt the walls are going to cave in overnight. But I can't guarantee you won't wake up covered in spiderwebs and bird poop."

"You're right," Tessa says. "Of course, you're right. I'm sorry. I . . . I get caught up in things, I guess." She shakes her head. "My sister would say I've lost my mind."

"Would you listen?" Kitty asks, genuinely curious.

Tessa smiles, but there's a sadness in it. "Not when I was younger," she says. "But I'm not sure I'm the same person I was then. Our choices . . . they can change us, can't they?"

Kitty tilts her head and studies this woman with the wistful note in her voice.

Imogene's daughter.

Kitty knows that look. It's the look of a person who's lost something and is casting around to find it again. It's the look of a woman who would give everything she owns to speak to her mam one more time.

"What choices have you made that changed you?" Kitty asks gently.

Tessa closes her eyes. A pained expression crosses her face. "It's a long story," she says again, but this time the words are slower. Whatever is hiding behind them has a hold on her, and it won't let go.

"I've got nowhere else to be. Come on," Kitty says, nodding toward the porch, bathed in indirect light. "Let's sit and you can tell me about it."

Tessa hesitates, but Kitty doesn't. She walks toward the steps and lightly brushes off a place for the two of them to sit, then settles herself down with a groan for her aching joints.

She glances up at the younger woman, who hasn't moved, and pats the place beside her. "I won't bite."

This pulls a small smile from Tessa. She gives in and walks around to the driver's side of the car. Quiet overtakes them and darkness follows as she turns off the ignition and kills the lights.

Tessa takes a seat by her side as their eyes slowly adjust to the darkness.

Eventually, Tessa begins to talk and Kitty listens. She's a good listener.

Imogene's daughter tells her about her job as a documentary filmmaker, a life that sounds glamorous and exotic to a woman who's spent her days comfortably ensconced on a patch of earth as familiar as the lines on her own face.

As the tale of Oliver Barlow unfolds, Kitty sits rapt, as she once would for her mam's stories. Tessa's words, though, don't have the buffer of time and distance that her mother's anecdotes of the old country had.

This is no fairy tale.

Her heart aches for the poor, innocent Valerie. And for the heavy burden of guilt that has Tessa straining under its weight. Even for the angry policeman and the pain he's enduring for his sins.

"Back when this started, I told myself I was doing a good thing," Tessa says. "I was fighting for justice for a man the system had wronged. I patted myself on the back when he was released, and let other people do the same."

She stares off into the distance, her face bathed in starlight. "I was so obsessed, so driven. Once I made up my mind, I never considered I might be wrong. That *I* might be one of the bad guys."

She turns and looks at Kitty. "I'd made mistakes before. Lost things because of it. People who mattered. But this time, a girl lost her *life*."

Tessa shakes her head. "Oliver claims he's coming for me, and the police want answers I don't have. But I don't know anything, and the truth is . . . the truth is, I don't trust my own judgment anymore."

She casts a long, searching look over her shoulder to the house at their backs.

"Whatever secrets live here, no matter how terrible, they're no threat to me. Not like what's waiting out there. I just . . . I can't help but feel like this is where I'm *supposed* to be."

Kitty's not sure what to say to that.

Tessa smiles ruefully. "You don't look convinced."

"No," Kitty says, shaking her head. "But . . . well, you might feel differently if you knew the whole story. I'm not sure Fallbrook is a place anyone is supposed to be. It hasn't been for a long time."

She can feel Tessa's eyes on her, her curiosity reaching tentatively into the silence between them. "What happened here, Kitty?" Her voice is soft now. A voice for a church service. But no one would worship at this house.

Kitty searches for a way to answer her question. Images tumble through her head, but they're haphazard. Out of order. The Cooke children and the Donnellys. Mam. The second Mrs. Cooke, forever an outsider. The baby she never wanted.

And Lawrence Pynchon. His arrival was a lit match to a slow-burning fuse, creeping closer to an irrevocable finish.

She thinks too of Deirdre. Then strangely, the sounds of sobbing she'd woken to.

Could it have been?

How to put into words the enormity of it all?

Kitty opens her mouth without any real idea of an answer. The simplicity of what comes from her lips surprises even her.

"A family came to an end."

There's more, of course. So much more, but nothing so important as that.

24

TESSA

There's more. There has to be more, but it's late and Kitty is tired. Tessa insists on walking her home.

"Don't be silly," the older woman says. "I could find my way in my sleep. And you'll only have to walk back on your own."

Tessa holds up the flashlight she retrieved from the trunk of her car.

"Always prepared," she says brightly, though in truth, she's not looking forward to a solitary trek back through the trees, even a short one.

"I wish you'd reconsider." Kitty offered their sofa, but Tessa was unwilling to impose on the elderly siblings. Bad enough to deal with the upset of a new landlord at this point in their lives. She won't add to an awkward situation by forcing herself on them as a houseguest too.

"Don't worry about me," Tessa assures her. "I'm fine sleeping in the car."

But Kitty looks doubtful. "If you're worried about Dee, she won't mind. I know she comes across as standoffish, but she wouldn't want you curled up in that tiny little car of yours. Mam would roll over in her grave at that kind of hospitality."

Tessa is touched by her concern. She leans closer. "Then we probably shouldn't tell either of them," she says in a whisper. "Now let's get you home."

Tessa carefully studies the path through the woods, ranging over it with the beam of her flashlight. She doesn't want to lose her way when she returns without Kitty as a guide.

The woodland sounds are louder here, a bit closer. A bit more real.

"Kitty?" Tessa asks.

"Hmm?"

"Does anything live in these woods that I should look out for?" she asks, despite her earlier bravado.

"Oh no," Kitty says with a wave of her hand. "Nothing to worry about. There's the occasional black bear, of course, but we haven't seen one in a few years."

Tessa's eyes widen and her gaze swivels toward Kitty. Her foot catches on a root, and she stumbles but manages to right herself without falling on her face or dropping the light.

Kitty places a hand on Tessa's arm to steady her. "Careful there."

"Bears?" Tessa strives for a casual tone with questionable success.

"Oh no, not right now," Kitty says. "We'd have seen tracks and other signs if there was one near, but not a whisper of any lately. And Aiden would know. Sometimes I think he only came home because he missed these woods so much."

"Is Aiden older or younger?" Tessa asks. Anything to move the subject past bears.

"He's the oldest, then Deirdre, then me. But Aiden joined the merchant marines when he was younger. Traveled all over. Broke Mam's heart when he left. I still have the postcards. I don't know how this place can hold much appeal after the things he's seen, but I guess you're never too old to come home."

Her mother's brass key sits warm against Tessa's chest. She unconsciously reaches up to touch it.

"Here we are," Kitty says, and Tessa glances around them. Tucked into a clearing and bathed in moonlight sits a little stone house with ivy climbing the walls.

"Oh," Tessa says. "This is lovely." She's not sure what she expected, but this little cottage could have been transported straight from the pages of a children's picture book.

In the stories, a house like this invariably has a witch living in it. But Tessa has always had a soft spot for the witch. Obviously, tossing children into an oven is bad, but Hansel and Gretel's parents should have taught them not to eat other people's houses, even when they're made of cake. It's rude.

"Are you sure you won't sleep here, Tessa?" Kitty asks.

"No, thank you," she says, holding back a smile. "But it's a kind offer."

The cottage hardly looks big enough to hold three people, much less an unexpected guest.

"Okay, but wait a minute before you go back. I have something for you."

Unbidden, Tessa conjures an image of an old woman offering a glossy red apple, polished to a shine. Kitty's figure moves up the steps, then disappears behind a heavy wooden door with cast iron fittings.

Tessa yawns. Exhaustion is catching up with her. Even the seats in her car sound welcoming right now.

Kitty reemerges from the storybook cottage. Somewhat to Tessa's disappointment, there's no sign of a poisoned apple. But then, Tessa's no Snow White. Instead, Kitty offers her a blanket, which Tessa accepts with grateful thanks.

Anything less would be rude.

25

Something skitters across her path on the way back to Fallbrook, but Tessa isn't frightened by small, skittery things.

"They're more afraid of you than you are of them," her dad would say. Which is fine and good, until she's up against something, or someone, with no fear of her at all. Someone with nothing left to lose.

What then, Dad?

Fallbrook stands as silent and still as Tessa left it, outlined against the night sky. A painting with nothing but blues and blacks, and a few touches of moonlit silver.

A familiar frisson of anticipation travels up her spine. Tessa gives herself over to it, gladly letting it blot out thoughts of Oliver and things she can't change.

The night has a chill, but with Kitty's blanket draped across her shoulders Tessa barely notices.

The beam of her flashlight seeks out the double front doors.

She should get some rest. Shut and safely lock her car doors, then curl up and find whatever sleep she can manage. But curiosity is something Tessa is powerless against, and she has long since stopped trying to fight it.

The door creaks as she pushes it open.

More skittering, but Tessa's steps are slow and light. She doesn't want to frighten anything that's taken shelter inside these walls. She's the interloper here.

Tessa walks as far as she'd come with Kitty earlier in the day and takes her time seeking out the nooks and crannies that she barely had a chance to register before. Old furniture, pieces too big to move, sit hidden and lumpy beneath dusty sheets.

She walks farther, her beam traveling up the curved staircase, then down again to darkened doorways that line both sides of the room, tempting her to discover what waits down those hallways and around corners she hasn't yet seen.

But Tessa isn't quite foolish enough to attempt a full exploration of the house, alone, with only a flashlight. She just wants a sip, a taste to slake her before she closes her eyes. Something, anything, to think about other than the problems she created.

She stops and listens, but there's nothing to hear except her own heartbeat, steady in her chest.

She grasps one corner of a sheet draped over the nearest bulky mass and pulls. Slowly at first, then faster, it slides to the floor with a hiss of fabric over fabric.

Her flashlight illuminates a settee with carved wooden trim that curves over the back, framing a heavy red brocade upholstery. There's a rip in one cushion, but otherwise it's in reasonably good condition, considering the circumstances.

Tessa drops onto the seat and turns her light outward, seeing the house from a new perspective. What would the place have been like when it was alive with the energy a family brings?

She closes her eyes, pulling Kitty's blanket more tightly around her, and tries to imagine it. The still silence of the house is contagious. That sense of bated breath. Of waiting.

For the first time in days, her swirling thoughts settle. She considers the Donnellys, distant in their cabin. Kitty with her kindness. Deirdre prickly and reserved. Their older brother, Aiden, a mystery as of yet, who left to see the world as a young man, then found his way back. A circle completed.

Family. Home.

Tessa's eyes are heavy. Her own family is small now, with Margot at the center whether she chooses to be or not. Her sister, whose first thought when learning about this place was to sell it.

"Leave it in the past, just like Mom did."

But sitting here, with so many questions still unanswered, she's not sure she can agree to that. For the Donnellys, this isn't the past, this is their home. Their lives.

And if Tessa is sure of one thing, it's that she's done playing around with other people's lives.

———

An incessant booming pulls Tessa, cramped and disoriented, from the sleep she fought against for so long.

Wings beat in darkness. The booming surrounds her, filling her with dread. A giant stumbling closer through the woods. An angry mob beating drums and chanting. *"Burn the witch! Burn the witch!"*

She bolts upright, struggling against the confusion of waking in a strange place. Her eyes are drawn to a dimming half circle of light that shines on the bottom steps of a curving staircase, and everything comes flooding back.

She jumps from the settee and the blanket falls around her.

Again, the booming comes, but now that she's free of her dreams, it's more an insistent pounding, and it's coming from the front doors.

Accompanying the noise is an angry voice shouting her name.

"Tessa! Tessa, I know you're in there."

Tessa stumbles to the door, but it doesn't move when she pulls on it. She pulls harder, refusing to panic when it still won't open.

"Just a minute," she shouts as she fumbles around in the dark. "It's stuck."

Tessa grips the large brass door handle with both hands and braces herself. With a giant heave, she yanks. It gives way, and Margot, apparently shoving from the other side, falls into the room.

Her sister catches herself and leans her hands against her knees. Her head swings around and she sends Tessa a dark look from beneath the curls that have fallen into her face.

"Tell me something, Tess." Margot's words are deceptively quiet after making such a ruckus. "Have you *actually* lost your mind?"

Tessa gives her a small smile. The sight of her sister, angry or not, lights up a vacant space inside her.

"If I'd known you were coming, I'd have tidied up," she says.

Margot blows the hair out of her face and straightens, glancing around. Even in shadows, Tessa can read the way her posture stiffens. "The only reason this place is still standing is because there's a hundred years of spiderwebs holding it together," she says.

"How did you know I was here?" Tessa walks to where the flashlight emits a weakened beam and scoops it up. It must have slid from her grip when she'd fallen asleep, but the batteries are low now.

"I called ahead and rented a room at the B&B where you were *supposed* to be staying," Margot says distractedly. She reaches out and takes the flashlight from Tessa's hands. "When I checked in, the owner told me the room was free because she'd had a last-minute cancellation."

"Cancellation? That old bat kicked me out, then rented my room to you?"

Margot shrugs. "I guess she liked me more."

Tessa rolls her eyes. "I guess she would. Sending the police after me didn't help her opinion much."

"Oh, I heard all about it. She's not exactly a fan, so I didn't mention that you're my sister. I assumed you'd driven back to a larger town and rented a room, because that's what a sane person would do, so I went to bed, planning to catch up with you in the morning."

Margot walks slowly around the room, shining the dim light into dusty corners and shaking her head in disgust.

"So why drive all the way out here?" Tessa asks.

Margot sighs and turns the light on her. "Because, Tess. I woke up in the middle of the night and sat up in my soft, warm, *clean* bed, and suddenly remembered that you're *not* sane. You're a complete lunatic, especially when you have some idiotic new project stuck in your head."

Tessa squints and holds up a hand to block the light Margot's shining in her eyes. "This isn't a project. Not like you're thinking."

"Oh yeah? Then why am I completely unsurprised to find you here? You could have at least slept in the car, Tessa. Why in God's name are you camping out inside this horror show?"

Oddly defensive, Tessa glances around. "It's not *that* bad."

Margot raises an eyebrow. Okay, so it's pretty bad. She considers admitting she planned to stay in the car and fell asleep by accident, but that probably won't help her case.

"It's not like—" Tessa stops short, realizing something glaringly important she's overlooked. "Wait, you're supposed to be under police protection. What are you *doing* here, Margot?"

But her sister is shaking her head, one finger raised to block that line of discussion before it has a chance to start.

"No," she says. "No way. You don't get to lecture me on my choices, not when you're hanging out in a haunted house, alone, while a murderer with a grudge is making threats against you. Where's *your* protective detail, huh?"

"That's different."

"It's not different."

"Okay," Tessa concedes. "So it's not different, but that doesn't answer the question."

Margot raises her hands, then lets them drop. "What did you expect me to do, Tess? Hang out at Mom's and knit while a policeman stood guard?"

"But what about—" She stops.

Margot glances at her sharply, then fills in what Tessa didn't say. "What about Ben? I'll deal with Ben when I'm ready and not a minute before. You won't make me, Ben won't make me, and Oliver Barlow certainly won't make me."

It's not her place to get in between her sister and her husband, but she already put herself there, then carelessly drove this wedge between them.

"Margot," Tessa says softly. "Ben loves you."

Margot turns away from her. "Love isn't always enough. You and I both know that."

Tessa did know. Year after year of silence taught her well.

"Tessa, this place . . . staying here . . ." Margot lets out a deep sigh. "It's insane, even for you. It's a rathole. It's falling down around your ears. There's clearly no electricity. I don't even want to think about plumbing, and the cell signal is absolute shit. You've probably got fleas already, and you'll be lucky if that's the worst of it. Bubonic plague comes to mind."

Tessa opens her mouth to tell her she didn't intend to stay, but she's not entirely sure that's true. It doesn't matter, though. Margot isn't done.

"I saw the look on your face when you found that photograph. I won't bother trying to talk you out of this, but you're not staying here by yourself."

Tessa's mouth falls open, but a small ray of hope flickers to life, and her shock gives way to the tentative beginnings of a smile.

"Stop smirking. This doesn't mean I don't still think you're crazy, and it doesn't mean I'm speaking to you."

By now the darkness outside has begun to lighten with the coming dawn, and Tessa's eyes have adjusted to the low light filtering into the room.

"Be nice, or I won't share my fleas with you." Tessa can just make out the twitch of Margot's mouth as she tries not to laugh, and it feels like a gift.

26

Life with Margot, as Tessa comes to think of it over the next few hours, has some drawbacks.

For one, her sister has no intention of letting her go back to sleep.

"There's too much to do, starting with a list. I'll drive into Snowden later and pick up some cleaning supplies and something non-flea-ridden to sleep on."

The flashlight finally sputters out just after dawn, but by that time, Margot has enough light that she doesn't even break stride.

"And batteries," she mumbles, scribbling on a shopping list that keeps getting longer.

"We're not moving in. This is temporary," Tessa points out, but Margot waves her off.

"I hate to admit it, but staying here might not be the worst thing. We could get rooms someplace farther away, but someone is bound to recognize you."

"Me? No," Tessa objects, but Margot gives her a look over the top of the notepad she pulled from her purse.

"You haven't seen the news, then. This has blown up, and you're right at the middle of it."

"But . . ."

"There are only so many facts they can rehash, Tess, and you're a big question mark. You haven't made a statement, no one knows where you are, and there's speculation about your motives."

"My motives?" Tessa whispers.

Margot lowers the notepad and studies her reaction. "If the press can't find you, Barlow can't either," she says almost gently. "Speculation is the price for that."

Tessa frowns. She's accepted that there will be repercussions for her actions, but the idea that she's suspected in conjunction with Oliver nauseates her.

She glances around, searching for her phone, then remembers tossing it into the passenger seat of her car the night before.

"I need to get some air," she says, not quite able to meet her sister's eyes.

Margot watches her go without comment.

The sun has risen fully in the sky now, and when Tessa opens the front door, she finds someone has been there. A thermos sits on the edge of the porch with a note tucked beneath it.

Tessa picks it up and reads the message written in a thin, spidery scrawl.

> *I don't know how you like your coffee, so I've taken a chance on a bit of cream and sugar. Come by the cottage when you're ready. The least we can do is offer breakfast and a chance to freshen up.*
>
> *We'll answer your questions as best we can.*
> *Bring your friend.*

The note isn't signed, but Tessa knows who wrote it. She calls out to Margot that there's coffee on the porch, then walks to her car and retrieves her phone.

No signal.

It's Pennsylvania, not the Gobi Desert. Surely there's a cell tower somewhere nearby. She holds the phone above her head, but nothing changes. Tessa glances around, searching for higher ground. A morning mist lingers in the air, and she sees a hill to the left of where she stands, about a hundred yards away. Behind it, the forest waits, partially shrouded in fog.

Tessa wanders in that direction, one eye on the bars on her phone. She wanted a place to hide, and she found it. Fallbrook may have been forgotten somewhere in the last century, but the world continues to spin, and it's spinning a narrative that makes her uneasy.

She trudges up the gentle slope until she crests the hill. Tessa marvels for a moment at the sight. Fallbrook in the morning has a new palette. Gray and white, with bits of green hidden within the mist.

It's breathtaking.

Tessa's phone vibrates in her hand as the outside world at last connects. She shivers, and regrets leaving Kitty's blanket behind, but opens the screen of the little device, determined to discover the state of the world she's temporarily left behind.

Anne has forwarded links to several news articles, and Tessa scans the headlines.

Barlow Hints at Filmmaker's Complicity

Shepherd Drops from Public Eye

What Does Tessa Shepherd Know?

Text messages roll past, many from Anne, which range from panic to frustration and back to panic again.

Tessa clicks on one to reply.

Out of town, lying low. Will catch up soon.

She should check her email, but another text catches her eye, nearly buried in the rest.

It's from Ben.

Margot is gone. Neither of you answering phones. You owe me, Tessa, and I'm calling it in. Need to know she's safe. Call me back!

Guilt, her new constant companion, churns in Tessa's belly. She does owe Ben, owes him more than she could ever repay, and if he's leveraging that, something he's never done before, he's no doubt sick with worry.

She taps the contact on the screen and holds the phone to her ear as it dials.

Ben picks up before the first ring has finished.

"Tessa, Jesus Christ, where are you? Is Margot with you?"

His voice is a sharp and tangled mass of accusation and concern. She's known him for most of her life, and she's never heard him like this.

"She's here. She's safe," Tessa says. "She drove up last night, but the reception is terrible and—"

"Drove up *where?*" he demands, cutting her off. "First the police show up, then Margot comes home from Jane's and throws things in a bag, and the next thing I know she's gone. Barlow is after you, Tessa. I don't want her in the middle of this mess. Goddammit, put her on the phone."

"Ben, I can't," Tessa says. "I'm outside and—"

"Tessa, I put a lot on the line for you, out of friendship and because I care about you and because I knew, whether your sister wanted to admit it or not, that she did too, but *I swear to God, if you don't put my wife on the phone*—"

Tessa can hear the desperation in his voice. She turns, knowing the signal won't hold until she gets back to the house, but she has to try.

She gasps and takes a step backward. Ben is shouting now, but Tessa drops the phone from her ear, struck by the hurt and pain on Margot's face.

Her sister is standing only feet away, arms crossed, with fresh betrayal in her eyes.

Tessa holds the phone out toward her.

"Talk to him," she pleads, but Margot shakes her head, refusing.

Tessa's shoulders drop and she raises the phone jerkily back to her ear, unsure what to do now.

"Ben, I have to—"

But he's still talking, quickly, desperately.

"—if that's really what she wants, I won't fight it, but a divorce won't change how I feel. I just want to know she's safe, Tessa. I need to hear her voice."

Tessa's eyes widen and she stares at Margot, her sister's face set in a hard, unforgiving lines.

Divorce?

"Ben, she's safe, I swear," Tessa says hoarsely into the phone. "I'm sorry, I have to—"

Margot closes the distance between them and holds out a hand. Tessa gives the phone over willingly, but instead of speaking to her husband, Margot ends the call without a word.

She turns and walks away, and this time, she's walking away from more than just Tessa.

There was once a time the three of them were inseparable. Margot, Tessa, and Ben. Now they're shattered and separate, scattered like the broken shards of an old clay pot.

27

KITTY

Bits and pieces of a broken lullaby rattle around in Kitty's head. She doesn't mind. When the words are missing, she hums the melody until the next piece falls into place.

"For goodness' sake, would you stop that racket," Deirdre snaps.

Kitty hums louder, and Deirdre sighs in a great, dramatic puff of breath.

"Oh, quit," Kitty says. "You're acting like someone put the weight of the world onto a saddle, then strapped it to your back. It's only breakfast."

Deirdre places a lid onto a pan of sausages with a clatter and glares at her. "Breakfast for someone who could sell our home from underneath us. Have you considered that?"

"Of course I have," Kitty says. "But I don't think Tessa would do that."

"And you've managed to gain this deep insight into her character how, exactly? And what about her sister? Honestly, your silly optimism is irritating."

"Optimism never hurt anything," Kitty says. "We don't know their plans yet. There's no need to get in a twist about something that might not happen."

Deirdre opens her mouth to argue, but a knock on the door interrupts and her jaw clamps shut. She turns back to the sausages. "Your guest has arrived."

Even Deirdre's black mood can't dampen Kitty's spirits. She has an idea, a beautiful idea, one that came as she woke this morning, bursting upon her like the sun through thunderclouds.

Kitty reaches the door with a bright smile on her face and opens it wide. Tessa is standing on the porch, holding the borrowed blanket folded neatly in her hands. A few steps behind is another woman, a woman with a striking resemblance to Tessa, if one were to look past the riot of blonde curls.

It brings to mind the paper dolls Kitty had as a child. Indistinguishable from one another, they came with a choice of clothing and hairstyles to fold over the top, held by paper tabs. The tabs eventually wore out and fell away, so Kitty had chosen her favorite looks and painstakingly glued them in place.

"Kitty, this is my sister, Margot," Tessa says, glancing over her shoulder to make the introduction. The other woman smiles at Kitty, but pointedly ignores Tessa.

"It's nice to meet you," Kitty says. "Please, come in."

The two women are awkwardly polite as they're welcomed into the cottage, but it's impossible to miss the tension that crackles between them.

They've argued, the poor things. Kitty knows what it's like to have a sister. She recognizes the signs.

"The bathroom is that way if you'd like to freshen up," she offers, giving them the chance to separate for a bit. Tessa nods gratefully.

Deirdre transfers dishes to the long table, and Margot asks quiet questions about how long they've lived here, and the arrangement they had with William Ashwood.

"He asked us to keep an eye on the place in exchange for staying on at the cottage," Deirdre says as she seats herself across from Margot at the table. Kitty can see she's choosing her words carefully. "It was a godsend, really. Mam was alive then. We would have been forced to move away, otherwise, and Mam find another position elsewhere. But this had always been our home, and we were grateful for the offer. He was a good man. A kind man."

Margot nods, though she doesn't smile. "And he made financial arrangements for you? A trust, as I understand."

Deirdre stiffens, but nods. "He did. A salary to be paid monthly." She fingers the napkin in her hand, balling it up, then smoothing it out, only to repeat the action.

"And when my grandfather died?" Margot asks.

Deirdre sits up straighter and meets Margot's eyes calmly. "We received a letter from a lawyer a few months after he passed. Imogene . . . Jane, I should say. Your mother. She inherited the property, as you know. The letter informed us she had no plans to change the arrangements her adoptive father had made."

Margot nods again, her expression serious, but she says nothing more as Tessa returns.

"Did you ever hear any more from her? My mother, I mean?" Tessa asks as she takes a seat next to her sister. They don't look at one another.

Deirdre shakes her head. "Not once, aside from that letter, but she was true to her word, and the deposits have continued to this day. What happens now will be in your hands, of course."

Tessa glances at her sister as Kitty passes around a basket of fresh cinnamon rolls, but Margot barely acknowledges her.

"Forgive my saying so," Margot says, looking from Kitty to Deirdre and back again, "but Fallbrook is obviously in a state of extreme disrepair. Was there no money set aside in the trust for upkeep on the house?"

Kitty doesn't miss the way Deirdre's shoulders square in defensiveness, but her sister's voice is mild when she answers Margot's question.

"Mr. Ashwood made his wishes clear. He wanted no effort or expense put toward maintaining the house. I believe his exact words to our mother were, *'Let it rot, Mrs. Donnelly.'*"

Margot frowns.

"We've done as he asked," Deirdre says.

Margot shakes her head slowly. "I'm sorry, but surely I'm not the only one who finds it odd that Granddad would employ caretakers, employ them for life, no less, for a property he had no wish to be taken care of."

Deirdre lays her fork carefully down on the edge of her plate and meets Margot's gaze head-on. "I've always assumed his feelings about Fallbrook were due to the unfortunate events that took place there, the same events that left Imogene orphaned. It wasn't my place to question his motives, and Imogene—Jane—never altered his instructions."

Margot leans back from the table, her hands folded neatly in her lap, but her brows are knit together.

Tessa clears her throat. "About that," she says, breaking the tense silence that's fallen among them.

Deirdre's posture becomes stiffer, if possible. As brittle as a dead tree fighting a gust of winter wind. She knows what's coming.

"Granddad's letter was very vague," Tessa says, almost apologetically. "And in the confusion of the last few days, we haven't had a chance to do any research on the history of Fallbrook or what happened here." She trails off, glancing at Kitty for support. Kitty gives her a small smile.

Deirdre remains silent.

"You did say we'd answer her questions," Kitty reminds her gently.

Deirdre closes her eyes and pulls in a long breath. When she lets it out, it's with an air of resignation.

"Ask then," she says. "But understand, Kitty and I were quite young. I was fifteen. Kitty even younger."

She glances at her sister. The moment is brief, but Kitty is shaken by a quick flash of something behind Dee's eyes. Something that looks unsettlingly like fear.

"And now we're old," Deirdre continues. "It's not something we discuss if at all possible, and there is a very real possibility that our memories are faulty after all this time."

Kitty's eyes narrow slightly. There's nothing wrong with Deirdre's memory.

Tessa nods. "I understand, and I don't want to cause you undue stress. It's just that we know so little. Whatever information you can share will help us in the decisions we still have to make."

Deirdre looks down at her hands, her fingers tightly laced together in her lap. "Go on, then," she says.

Margot remains quiet, but Tessa sits forward in her chair, leaning her elbows on the table.

"Maybe you could start by telling us about the family? What were they like? Before . . ." Her voice is careful and quiet. As unimposing as it's possible to be, given the probing nature of what she's asking.

Deirdre's eyes stay on her hands. She rubs the palm of the left with her right thumb, and Kitty wonders if her arthritis is acting up or if she simply needs something to occupy her.

"Mr. Cooke needed a wife," Deirdre says finally. "The children . . . they were quite unmanageable, to be honest. The girls, Ruby and Cora, and Peter, their little brother." Dee's voice wavers, and Kitty places a hand on her sister's arm and squeezes, oh so lightly. A show of support, a reminder that she's not alone.

Deirdre looks up and meets Tessa's gaze. "Their mother died in childbirth, you see, when Peter was born. Mam was the closest thing to a mother he'd ever known. We shouldn't have been surprised when

Mr. Cooke married again, but I don't believe anyone saw it coming. Perhaps Mam did. I never asked."

Deirdre stops, shifts in her seat, but forges ahead. "There were a great many changes at Fallbrook after the arrival of the second Mrs. Cooke. Helena was her name. She was young. Pretty. I've never been sure why she married a man with three children. She wasn't the maternal type. But Mr. Cooke was wealthy. That makes up for all manner of inconveniences."

"Helena would have been our grandmother, then?" Tessa asks. "Our biological grandmother?"

Deirdre's mouth tightens. "Yes." The one-word response seems an eternity in coming.

"You were close in age with the Cooke children?" Tessa asks.

Deirdre nods. "We were very close. Ruby was older, of course. Only a year behind our brother, Aiden. And Peter, he was like a little brother to us all, the baby of the group. Until baby Imogene came along."

Deirdre stands suddenly and takes her plate to the counter, where she sets it next to the sink. She's barely touched her food.

"Cora was my age." Deirdre stops to stare out of the kitchen window, lost in some long-ago memory. Kitty's heart squeezes tightly and she has trouble drawing a breath. It's a difficult thing, to watch Dee remember Cora, when she's tried so hard to forget her.

"We were best friends," Deirdre says softly. "The best of friends."

Something foul overtakes Kitty, and she remembers suddenly what it felt like to be a child, powerless to mend the things that hurt. "I hated Cora," she says, then pulls in a sharp breath, as surprised by the admission as anyone. Deirdre turns to face her, eyes wide with shock. "I've never told you that, have I?"

Deirdre stares blankly, uncomprehending.

"Oh yes," Kitty continues. "It's been long enough now, I suppose I can admit that. Cora . . . Cora had everything, but it wasn't enough. She wanted more. She wanted what I had."

Kitty shrugs, then turns back to the women seated across from them. "But even I didn't hate her as much as Mrs. Cooke did. Cora was the reason . . ."

She stops and turns back to her sister, a question on her face. Deirdre shakes off Kitty's revelation, then walks swiftly back to the table and takes her seat again.

"Before Mrs. Cooke came, we all attended school in town together," she says, taking over for Kitty. "It was a small school, as Snowden was a small town. Smaller even than it is now. But Helena felt the children, Cora in particular, would benefit from a more disciplined approach to their education."

Her mouth tightens again.

"For a time, Cora was sent away to a boarding school, but that didn't last. She returned home in disgrace. But Helena Cooke was a persistent woman when she set her mind on something. A tutor was hired."

Kitty holds her breath. How she wishes Aiden had stayed at the cottage this morning. She begged, but he insisted his presence would only complicate things. Deirdre took his side.

"His name was Lawrence Pynchon." Deirdre's words are strong and clear. Only Kitty knows what it costs her to speak his name.

"His name was Lawrence Pynchon, and less than a year later, without warning or apparent reason, he murdered them all."

Deirdre's eyes are facing forward, focused on some point on the wall above Tessa and Margot's heads. She pulls in a shaky breath.

"If you'll excuse me, I . . ." Deirdre trails off, then pushes quickly back, her chair scraping against the floor. She turns and walks toward the front door, shoulders straight, but her arms are crossed protectively in front of her.

The three women who remain watch her go. No one moves to stop her.

Tessa is the first to speak.

"Kitty, I'm so sorry to drag up such terrible memories," she says. "This must be difficult for both of you."

"Yes," Kitty mumbles, her eyes still on the door that her sister closed behind her. "We don't speak about it."

"I think we've imposed on them enough for today, Tess," Margot says quietly. It's the first time she's spoken directly to her sister since they arrived.

Kitty's eyes swivel back to the pair. They're rising from the table. Soon they'll disappear out the door.

"Please don't go yet." She reaches a hand across the table.

"We should give Deirdre some space—" Tessa begins.

"No, no. You don't understand," Kitty says.

Tessa and Margot exchange a look, and Kitty wishes she were better at this. She searches for the right words, but there's no good way to say it.

"You don't understand," she says again. "Deirdre . . . well, my sister is lying."

28

TESSA

"My sister is lying."

Tessa stares at the plump, grandmotherly woman seated in front of her. They should be discussing recipes and sewing patterns, not the annihilation of a family.

"Kitty, what are you saying?" Tessa asks carefully.

The old woman shakes her head, and her voice drops to a low whisper. "She's lying," she says. "Not only the things she said, but the things she didn't. Mam used to tell us that a lie of omission is still a lie."

She says the words as much to herself as to Tessa and Margot, as if her sister is a series of puzzle pieces she can't quite fit together.

"I think we should go," Margot says.

Tessa is on the verge of agreement, but Kitty isn't done.

"There's something important you need to understand. Lawrence Pynchon . . . he tutored all of us. All but Aiden, who was done with school by then. He was a charming man. Handsome. Sophisticated in a way we'd never seen. Fifteen sounds so young, doesn't it? A child still, but those are the years when a girl's heart first tests its wings, searching for a chance to fly."

Kitty trails off, lost in another time. Another place. The silence stretches long enough that Tessa looks again to Margot, who's studying Kitty intently.

"Are you saying . . . Deirdre . . . ?" Margot asks.

Kitty comes back from wherever she's wandered and meets their searching faces.

"Dee was in love with him," she says sadly. "She was in love for the first, maybe the only, time in her life. Something happened in those days before it all went terribly wrong. Something happened, and if I could just clear away the fog, I think I could see it. It's there, hiding right beneath the surface. If only . . ."

Tessa frowns. "Kitty, if that's true, if Deirdre was really in love with a man who turned out to be a murderer, then these memories must be even more painful than we could have imagined. We—" She stops and glances at Margot. "*I* have no business dragging this up. I don't want to cause either of you more pain."

Kitty gives her a small, sad smile. "It's not that simple," she says. "If that's all it was, I'd never speak of it again. But there's something else you need to know."

She leans forward, a new urgency coursing through her. "Lawrence Pynchon was killed in prison, before he had a chance to go to trial. He was attacked. Beaten by the other inmates. He never regained consciousness."

Tessa shakes her head, struggling to understand.

"Without a trial, it was never proven once and for all that he was the killer. Without a trial, there were whispers. Gossip. Terrible things said behind cupped hands that couldn't be washed away by the truth."

"But surely," Tessa says. "If there was enough evidence to arrest the man . . ." But Tessa trails off. She thinks suddenly of Oliver. Of the evidence planted by Winters's men. She shakes her head. Oliver *was* guilty, she tells herself.

"Someone still planted evidence to make sure he was convicted," a small voice whispers.

"Do you believe he did it?" Margot asks.

"Of course he did," Kitty says without hesitation. "There was no one else who could have. There were other reasons too. Something about the way they found him with the bodies . . . I remember something . . ." Kitty shakes her head, dismissing whatever the something is that she can't recall. "The point is, without a trial, there was room, too much room, for questions. For doubt and for gossip."

"What kind of gossip, Kitty?" Tessa asks.

Kitty's face grows as hard as Deirdre's had been at times. "The kind that won't go away. The kind that pushed Aiden to join the merchant marines to escape. For years, decades, he was gone from here, unable to come back without people whispering behind his back, saying the most evil things."

A light dawns and a connection falls into place. Tessa finally begins to understand.

Kitty meets her eyes. "They said it could have been Aiden. They could never be sure. It was ridiculous. He'd walked into town that day. He wasn't even here, but people made a game of twisting the facts. It drove him away, but it's followed him, a cloud he can't escape, all these years."

A thousand questions churn in Tessa's head, flitting past in a way that makes her itch for a notepad and pen.

Every project begins with questions. The right questions, the wrong questions, the questions you don't know yet to ask. Finding those answers, then stringing them together into a coherent and compelling narrative, *that* is the obsession.

This isn't a project, she tells herself. Firmly. Definitively. But it feels like a lie.

"Ms. Shepherd," Kitty says. The formality makes Tessa wary. "You said you make films. I know nothing about that, and it's a great deal to ask, but I'd like you to consider making a film about Fallbrook. About what really happened. Set the record straight. Prove Aiden's innocence once and for all. We're old now. All of us. But maybe, if you could do that, then he could smile and show his face without looking over his shoulder. Please."

Tessa stares at the woman's earnest face, and a great weight settles on her. Somehow, she knew this was coming. It was inevitable.

I can't do this, she thinks. *I can't.* For so many reasons. A million reasons, and one very specific one.

A young woman is dead because Tessa was determined to prove another man's innocence.

I can't.

She opens her mouth to tell Kitty so, but a movement in her peripheral vision catches her eye. She turns and sees Deirdre standing quietly by the door. Her eyes are enormous and full of horror. One hand is pressed to her mouth as if she's going to be sick, and her skin has gone a terrible shade of gray.

"Deirdre," Kitty says, the word both an apology and a plea. "I'm sorry, I should have told you. But can't you see? He needs this. We all need this."

Deirdre shakes her head and backs up several paces. "Oh, Kitty, what have you done?"

29

"That went well."

Tessa sighs. She forgot how lethal Margot's sarcasm can be when she's angry. She says nothing as the two of them walk back through the woods toward the big house.

Deirdre didn't throw them out. Not exactly. But both women understood they'd stayed past their welcome. Kitty walked them to the door, full of apologies and hope.

"You know you can't give her what she wants, right?"

"Yes," Tessa says.

"There's enough on your plate with the last man you claimed was innocent. It's hardly the right time to take on another cause."

"I know that."

"I can't believe you'd even consider it. The police still haven't found Barlow. This is crazy."

"I really wish you'd stop calling me crazy," Tessa says softly.

Her sister isn't aware of the two weeks Tessa spent in a psychiatric hospital in upstate New York. Jane never knew either. Ben was her only visitor, and she'd begged him not to tell them. He'd done as she asked.

This doesn't seem like the best time to point out that terms like *crazy* and *insane* are offensive. Tessa prefers generalized anxiety and panic disorder, with a side of medication, thank you very much.

"You need to focus on helping the police find Oliver, Tessa. Until he's behind bars, that's the *only* thing you need to focus on."

Tessa stops and glares at Margot, her hands coming defensively to her hips.

"I'd appreciate it if you could stop telling me what I *need* to do, Margot. I've told the police the same thing I told you. There's nothing else I *can* do. I don't know anything."

Margot glares back and crosses her arms.

"Well, there's got to be some reason he claims you do, and instead of trying to figure it out, you're about to dive headfirst into a new film."

"I am *not*—" Tessa stops and pauses to take a breath. She forces her voice into an even tone before she continues quietly. "I'm not starting a new project. I told you that. Just like I told you I can't find Oliver."

"There's a reason he mentioned you, Tess. Didn't you hear the video? *'Ask Tessa Shepherd. She knows.'* You know him better than anyone."

Better than anyone.

Tessa thought she did. Once. How could she have been so wrong? A part of her, even now, insists that she *wasn't* wrong. The Oliver Barlow who sat across from her in Merrivale Correctional simply wasn't capable of committing those terrible acts he was sent to prison for.

But if that was true, then somewhere along the way, amid the injustice and the broken promises and the devastating losses, a good man had turned bad. If that was true, then good and bad—right and wrong— they lost all meaning.

Tessa can't accept that. She can't accept a world where right and wrong don't matter. A good person wouldn't have taken out his rage on an innocent woman, no matter how much injustice the world served up.

"No, Margot. I thought I knew him. I spent hours with the man researching that series. We talked about *everything*. But it turns out, I didn't know him at all. I have hours and hours of recordings, days' worth, and they're nothing but lies. He was playing me. I fell for it, and

I have to figure out a way to live with that. Now, I love you. I always have, and I'm grateful you've allowed me back into your life, even under these circumstances, but I've got to tell you, you're not helping right now."

Tessa shoves her hands into her pockets and turns toward Fallbrook, trying to rein in her emotions before she says something she can't take back.

"How do you expect me to help you when you won't bother to help yourself?" Margot calls. Tessa grimaces, but doesn't pause. "Maybe it's time to look again, this time with the knowledge that he was lying. You weren't looking for that the first time."

Tessa whips around, disbelief etched on her face. "Of course I was! I was looking at nothing but that! I didn't go into that prison with my mind already made up, Margot. I was looking at everything he said, and God help me, he convinced me. Trust me, there's nothing there. Nothing but lies. Very convincing lies. It won't help anything."

But Margot's face is stubbornly set and she refuses to back down. "So what?" she says, lifting her hands, palms upward, then letting them drop. "So what if it doesn't? At least you'll know you've done everything you can."

"I know that already."

"You're running away from this, like you always do."

"I didn't run from you, Margot! You pushed me out!" Tessa's composure is slipping with every jab.

Her sister's lips thin, and she crosses her arms again. "Fine." She spits out the word in a way that says it's anything but fine. "Don't do it, then. Bury your head in the sand and move on to the next tragedy."

Tessa's throat tightens. How did they get here?

"There's nothing there," she says quietly.

"How do you know if you don't look again?"

"Why do you care?" Tessa shouts, unable to bear the badgering any longer.

"Because he's coming after you next, you idiot!" Margot advances on her. Tessa stands her ground, refusing to back up. "And *you*"—Margot shoves Tessa with both hands. She stumbles backward a step, but Margot closes the distance—"and all the bullshit that comes *with* you"—she shoves Tessa again—"are all that I have left!"

The two of them stand, staring at each other, their breath coming in short, heavy gasps. Like a sudden rain shower, realization dampens Tessa's frustration.

Margot's not angry. She's scared.

"Fine," Tessa says lightly. "I'll listen to the tapes."

Margot had shoved her.

"Better yet," she says, "you listen to the tapes, since you're so convinced. Then maybe you'll believe me."

"Fine," Margot says, with a tilt of her head and one eyebrow raised. She turns to walk back to the big house, keeping a few paces in front of Tessa.

"Fine," Tessa mumbles, but she doesn't kid herself. If that was a battle of wills, she was the loser.

30

Margot is heading back to Bracknell Lodge to shower and grab a change of clothes. Tessa writes down Anne's email address for her.

"She'll forward you the files from the Barlow interviews," she says, keeping her word, despite reservations.

The idea of anyone, especially Margot, viewing those files sets off butterflies in her stomach.

The scenes that made it into the documentary focused on Gwen Morley's murder and the aftermath, but the raw footage includes so much more. Tessa had built a relationship with Oliver over time, something that never could have happened without mutual trust.

You can't ask a person to let down their guard, then open themselves up in front of a camera unless you're willing to do the same.

Margot has no idea what she's asking.

It's sadly ironic that sharing intensely personal thoughts with an inmate at Merrivale Correctional left Tessa feeling less vulnerable than the thought of sharing the same footage with her twin sister.

But if it helps Margot feel she's doing something proactive, Tessa won't stand in her way. Her sister is worried about her, and Tessa understands all too well the helplessness that comes with that kind of worry.

In return, Margot brandishes a small handheld vacuum cleaner she's retrieved from the trunk of her car. "Try to find the least repellent place to set up camp," she says as she pushes it into Tessa's hands.

Tessa stares at the little vacuum, then back at her sister, dumbfounded. "You want me to clean up *that* place"—she gestures to the crumbling house at their backs—"with *this*?"

But Margot only rolls her eyes. "It's the best I've got." She opens her car door. "I'll be back later. Try to stay out of trouble, please."

Tessa clamps her mouth shut on a retort as Margot turns the car around and heads off.

31

KITTY

Kitty follows two steps behind her sister. "I'm sorry, I should have talked to you first, I know. But I don't understand why you're so upset."

Dee slams the dresser drawer and glares at Kitty standing in the doorway. Her lips have thinned to an angry slash, and she elbows past her.

"Don't be this way," Kitty pleads. "It only makes sense. She makes movies. She could tell the real story about what happened, for the whole world to see."

Deirdre turns on her. "What do we care about the world, Kitty? The world's forgotten about us. Forgotten Fallbrook. Why couldn't you leave it alone?"

"You're the one who's forgotten, Dee. You've spent your life pretending it never happened, but it did. And all that pretending . . . it's changed you."

Deirdre stares at her, openmouthed, then shakes her head. "You have no idea what you're talking about."

Kitty moves toward her, holds out her hand. "It's never gone away, Dee. It lives here with us, even if we don't talk about it."

Deirdre looks at her outstretched hand. For a moment, Kitty thinks she'll turn and walk away, but finally she places her age-spotted hand in Kitty's and squeezes lightly. The anger in her expression fades, replaced by a bone-deep sadness.

"I know, Kitty. I know that. But this is where it belongs. Here, with us. Not out there for other people to pick apart and examine. To be discussed and debated as entertainment for strangers."

Kitty places her other hand over the top of her sister's. "Tessa's not a stranger. She's Imogene's daughter. And this belongs to her too."

Deirdre sighs.

"Aiden deserves the truth to be told," Kitty says. "Tessa can give him that."

Deirdre pulls her hand away and blows out a short breath. "Aiden, is it?" She shakes her head and walks to the door. "Aiden isn't the one who wants this, Kitty, and somewhere inside, you know that."

A chill sweeps over her at Deirdre's words. "What are you saying?"

Deirdre opens the front door. One hand rests on the knob as she turns back to her sister.

"I'm saying . . ." She stops and pulls in a long breath. "Nothing. I don't know what I'm saying."

But a seed of doubt has been planted, and it begins to grow.

"You don't believe Aiden . . . ?" Kitty trails off, unable to voice the rest. "He has nothing to hide."

Deirdre doesn't answer right away. She looks up toward the sky, like she's waiting for the right response to drop down from the heavens.

Kitty holds her breath.

"No," Deirdre says at last. "Of course not. Aiden has nothing to hide."

But the words have the mechanical echo of a lie. An old, worn-out lie, one she's told herself too many times to believe anymore.

Deirdre shuts the door softly behind her without meeting her sister's eyes.

The cottage is silent, but Kitty's mind is anything but. Her ears are ringing as if a series of bombs is exploding in the distance. They're coming closer, louder, and shaking the foundations of her simple, well-constructed beliefs.

She reaches blindly for the sofa and drops down on the cushion before her legs give out.

Not Aiden. It's not possible.

Kitty shakes her head, but she can't dislodge the look on Deirdre's face. It was sympathy. Sympathy for the poor, stupid girl who lives in a make-believe world.

32

TESSA

With her sister gone, and nothing to occupy her other than the hand-held vacuum, Tessa's mind finds its way back to the Cooke murders and Kitty's impossible request.

She told Margot she had no intention of starting a new project. She didn't lie.

So *why* is she brainstorming ways to overcome the obstacles? Finding financial backers with her reputation in tatters will be impossible. She doesn't have her crew or any equipment. She has only one willing participant. She doesn't even know the whole story.

And all that pales in comparison to the sickness she feels at the thought of Valerie Winters.

Tessa simply doesn't have the confidence to make another film. Not now. Maybe not ever.

And still, she can't let it go.

There *is* a story here, she can feel it. A story big enough to save her career, if that's what she wants. But *is* that what she wants? Does she even have the right to want that?

She wanders around the house for a while, peeking into doors and waving away cobwebs that cling to her face and hair, but the stillness and silence of Fallbrook only magnify the growing list of questions forming in her head.

She opens a door to a room that might have once been a parlor. There are no windows, and no holes in the roof or floor, so the outdoors has been slower to invade the space. The wood in one spot does feel soft beneath her feet, but there's no sign of bird droppings. Peeling wallpaper lines the room. Pink roses on a faded white background.

"Least repellent, here we are," Tessa says aloud. She glances around, wishing for a broom and a pail of hot, soapy water.

She could trek back to the caretaker's cottage and impose on the Donnellys' hospitality for a loan of some cleaning supplies, but she's certain she's the last person Deirdre wants to see again so soon.

Kitty would happily lend her what she needs, but she'll have questions in her eyes that Tessa doesn't have answers for yet.

She runs her fingers over the curve of a faded pink rose.

Since the day Tessa left Linlea, there's only been one place where her footing was sure, and that was her work. Perhaps the biggest question of all . . . *Does she have the courage to believe in herself again?*

Tessa turns and walks swiftly out of the house, heading to her car. After digging around in the glove compartment for a moment, she returns to the rose room.

She pauses. With one arm crossed, and the elbow of her other arm resting on it, she taps her lips with the permanent black marker. Her eyes are glazed, her attention turned inward.

Where to start?

Then Tessa pulls the lid off the marker with a pop and tucks it into the pocket of her pants. She walks to the center of the wall and begins to write.

She starts with the word *Imogene*, draws a circle around it, then straight lines fanning outward.

The thick black marker squeaks as it transforms Tessa's thoughts into bold, definitive lines, her favorite brand of therapy.

When she runs out of room, Tessa drags a heavy wooden chair across the floor and starts on the empty space above.

By the time she stops for a break, the wall is covered with Tessa's version of a makeshift storyboard. A central section is taken up with the names of the Cooke family, and the Donnellys are directly next to them. Questions cover the rest of the space, some underlined, some circled, some with curvy arrows pointing back to other questions or to the names in the center of the wall.

The handheld vacuum is completely forgotten.

She steps back and surveys her handiwork.

Her eyes are drawn to one name in particular near the center of the wall. If this was a new project, which of course, it's not . . . But if it was, the next person Tessa would want to talk to is Aiden Donnelly.

But if this was a new project, Tessa would have done extensive online research already. Many of the questions she's laid out here she'd have answers to. Even the most basic details of the crime are still a mystery.

Her forehead wrinkles. She'd give a lot of money for a halfway decent internet connection right now. Unfortunately, the best she has available is the hill outside where she made the call to Ben.

The thought of Ben has Tessa biting her lip. She told Margot she wouldn't call him again, but only after her sister promised, grudgingly, to let him know she was safe. Tessa reminded her of that promise before Margot left for Bracknell Lodge. She can only hope Margot will hold up her end of the bargain.

Tessa fishes the cap to the marker out of her pocket and clicks it back into place.

She has a date with a phone on a hill.

Tessa blinks against the bright sun as she emerges from Fallbrook, a bear coming out of her den in the spring. She stretches and pulls her phone from her pocket.

Her eyes are on the device in her hand as she walks toward the hill at the edge of the trees, but the bars remain stubbornly unlit, even as she comes to the top.

"Come on," she says, raising the phone higher in the air.

Movement at the edge of the forest catches her eye. Her limbs freeze and she studies the tree line intently, her hand still holding the phone uselessly in the air.

She scans the shadows, then lets out a breath she didn't know she was holding when she spots someone wearing a bright yellow shirt or jacket moving through the trees.

Aiden Donnelly? Could it be?

Whoever it is, it's not a bear. Bears don't wear yellow, outside of children's storybooks.

Her thoughts circle back to the questions outlined on the parlor wall and Aiden's name scrawled there. She could introduce herself. It's not unreasonable. She's sort of his new landlord, in a way, although the word sounds uncomfortable to her ear. Landlord. A lord of land. Tessa's not a lord of anything.

She shouldn't be thinking what she's thinking. According to Kitty, there are rumors the man could be a mass murderer. Even if it is just gossip, she still has no business wandering into the woods in search of someone she's never met.

Yet her legs are already moving, quickly crossing the distance between herself and the place she watched the yellow jacket disappear into the trees.

"*Crazy,*" Margot's voice whispers in her mind.

But Margot handed her a baby vacuum to clean an abandoned house.

"And she thinks *I'm* the crazy one," Tessa mumbles under her breath as she follows a stranger into the woods.

33

KITTY

Doors to the past opening inside her. Doors that have always been there, down a labyrinth of darkened passageways. And what creeps out of those doors can't be pushed back in.

Aiden. Young, beautiful Aiden, who spent his days caring for the horses in the barn. Pruning trees and repairing the fence. Helping a new mother give birth to a litter of pups.

Aiden, angry and scared.

No. No, that's not right.

It was Mrs. Cooke who was angry. Always angry after the night at the cottage. Mam grew careful around her. They all did, walking on eggshells to avoid her sharp tongue.

"It's unacceptable, Everett," Kitty overhears, listening at the library doors. "They're lazy and disrespectful, the lot of them. I don't see why we can't replace them with a better class of people."

"Helena, we've discussed this. Saoirse Donnelly has been with us since the children were small. They're fond of her, and I cannot fault her work. Aiden is a hardworking young man and dependable, a quality not so easily replaced. I will not dismiss them simply because you have some inane prejudice against the Irish. Not without cause."

Kitty hurries away when footsteps approach, fearing Helena's wrath if she's discovered.

But the second Mrs. Cooke is patient. She wants rid of the woman at the center of her household, a woman who knows more than she should.

That wish is second only to her desire to rid herself of her youngest stepdaughter.

Everett Cooke withstands his wife's insistence that the Donnellys must go because the Donnellys are useful. Cora, on the other hand, is growing more impossible as the months wear on. She can't seem to help herself, and spends most of her time refusing to do anything her stepmother asks, then running off into the woods every chance she gets.

Mam despairs of her.

"Poor child," she calls her. "Poor lost child."

A time comes when the library doors are always closed. Helena's voice is muffled and Everett's responses too low to make out, even with an ear pressed to the door.

But when those doors finally open, a decision has been made.

Cora's bags are packed and a car is waiting to take her away. She'll attend a boarding school, they say. She's fourteen now, a young lady. She'll be sent to a fine school, where her insolence won't be tolerated and she'll be molded into an acceptable young lady.

"Please don't go, Cora," Peter cries, holding her tightly at the waist. But Cora's usual bravado has deserted her. Where Helena's presence made her reckless, it dampened her little brother's spirit, leaving him silent and fearful.

"Don't cry, Petey," she says, holding the boy tightly. "I'll be back soon, and I'll write you every day. I promise."

Deirdre holds his hand as the car drives away, but the little boy isn't the only one with tears. Deirdre puts on a brave face, but her cheeks are wet with sorrow.

Helena won that battle, but the war is far from over. Cora is true to her word, and in less than a year, the boarding school has sent her back. But Fallbrook changed while Cora was away, or perhaps the changes were in her. Either way, the world she returns to no longer seems to fit her, if it ever did.

Despite Helena's reservations, the second Mrs. Cooke has become a mother after all. Baby Imogene is born.

But the biggest change, one with consequences no one could dream of, comes in the form of a private tutor and a battered violin case.

Lawrence Pynchon isn't the only person to answer the advertisement Helena places for a private tutor, but he is the last. It's easy to see how he managed to win her over, and it has little to do with the music lessons he offered to include.

"Your children are in good hands, Mrs. Cooke," he says in a smooth baritone as he leans at the waist to kiss Helena's hand upon accepting the job.

"Stepchildren," she corrects.

"Of course."

The smile he gives her is conspiratorial, punctuated by a wink that brings a bright flush to the apples of her pale cheeks.

If ever there was a snake in the Cookes' garden, it was Lawrence Pynchon, violin in hand.

Even Deirdre, practical, no-nonsense Deirdre, is taken in. Everett Cooke, perhaps in an attempt to compensate for his wife's disposition toward the family that keeps his home running smoothly, hires Mr. Pynchon to tutor not just his own children but the Donnellys as well.

Kitty longs to go back to the village school, but Deirdre watches the man with an undisguised adoration that leaves Kitty cold and resentful.

"You don't understand," Deirdre says when Cora teases her about her obvious infatuation. "You'll always have opportunities, because your father is rich."

Cora tries to laugh that off. "Mr. Pynchon is chock-full of opportunity, all right. The opportunity to flatter his way into my stepmother's bed. I wish he'd pied piper her right off a cliff."

Deirdre's eyes flash and Kitty watches, shocked, as she turns away from her oldest friend in anger for the first time in the girls' lives.

"Deirdre," Cora calls. "I'm sorry. Come back."

But she doesn't.

———

"Come back," Kitty calls softly as the fog steals the image of her sister's retreating back. She fights through the mist, searching for her way home. Her eyes open, and she's seated in the cottage again, as she has been all along.

But she's not alone.

"You're not looking in the right places," Peter says sadly from one corner of the room.

"You only see what you want to see," Cora says from the other corner.

"There's more," Ruby says by her side. She leans closer and cups a hand around her mouth to whisper in Kitty's ear. "You know there's more. Don't be scared."

"I don't want to," Kitty says, but Ruby takes her hand and leads her back through the fog, leads her to a door Kitty doesn't want to open.

"Go on," Ruby whispers. "You've been here before. The dead can't hurt you anymore."

Click. Click. Click.

Heels upon the hallway floor.

Click. Click. Click.

Heels moving quickly to the library door. Mrs. Cooke's heels, while Kitty's world teeters delicately in the balance.

The latch is pressed and the door swings wide.

"Your daughter has gone too far."

Mr. Cooke doesn't look up from the ledger open in front of him.

"Helena, please refrain from dramatics. What has Cora done?"

"Not that daughter. This one." Helena's voice is brimming with something like glee.

Everett Cooke glances upward, his eyes grazing the tops of his glasses, and studies the pair in front of him. His second wife is gripping the forearm of his eldest daughter.

"Ruby?" he asks. He removes his glasses and massages the bridge of his nose. "What seems to be the problem?"

"Tell him," Helena prods. "Go on."

"Papa, I . . ." Her face is clouded with worry, and she glances back and forth between Helena and her father. Finally, she pulls her arm from her stepmother's grip and stands up straighter.

"Papa, I'm not a child any longer," she says with only the slightest hint of a waver in her voice.

Everett Cooke sits back slowly in his chair.

"I can see that, Ruby."

"I've made a decision. It's my life, and I have a right to make decisions about my own future."

Helena scoffs. "I would hardly call what you were up to an intelligent decision, Ruby Cooke. Not with that . . . that—"

"Don't talk about him that way," Ruby says sharply.

"Young lady—"

Mr. Cooke raises his voice to be heard over the two of them. "Perhaps one of you would be so good as to tell me what's going on here before this degenerates into a shouting match."

"She—"

"I—"

He holds up his hand for silence when they both try to speak at once. "No, no. That won't do. Ruby, you may begin."

His wife stiffens at the perceived slight, but Everett Cooke doesn't seem to notice.

Ruby takes a deep breath and clasps her hands together. She spares her stepmother hardly a glance before she takes two steps closer to her father's desk.

"Papa . . . I'm in love." Ruby's voice contains all the breathless hope and naivety that should always accompany those words.

"*Love?*" Helena barks out a high-pitched laugh, one full of derision. "My dear, I assure you that what I saw had nothing to do with love, and if he's managed to convince you it does, then you still have a great deal to learn about the ways of the world."

"This has *nothing* to do with you," Ruby hisses. "You're not my mother."

"Consider yourself lucky, dear, because if I were I'd lock you in your room and throw away the key. You're certainly not capable of protecting your virtue on your own."

"My virtue? Since when do you give a damn about my virtue? All you care about is spending Papa's money and worrying about what people might say. I'll tell you what they say, *dear* stepmother. They say you're a gold-digging, coldhearted bi—"

"Ruby, that's enough." Everett Cooke doesn't raise his voice. He doesn't have to. The words pin his daughter where she stands. Anger colors her face and neck, but she lowers her eyes to hide her temper.

"I'm seventeen, Papa. I'm old enough to decide for myself, and I intend to marry him."

Everett Cooke narrows his eyes and stares at the top of his daughter's head.

"Ruby, you've yet to tell me exactly who it is you're determined to marry. I believe that might be pertinent information to share at this point, don't you?"

Ruby looks up at him, her face full of wishes and worry.

"Aiden, Papa. Aiden and I are in love."

He says nothing, and the silence that fills the room is broken only by the ticking of the grandfather clock.

"Do you realize how ridiculous you sound?" Helena finally says. "You're the daughter of a prominent man, Ruby. You can't simply run off and marry the stable boy."

But Everett holds up his hand again for silence. He leans forward and rests his elbows on the desk. One hand comes up to massage his temple.

"Where is the boy now?" Everett asks. His voice is mild, revealing nothing of his thoughts.

"I sent him away after I caught them embracing," Helena says. "He nearly refused to go, in the most outrageous display of disrespect. I did try to warn you these people couldn't be trusted, Everett. Now look where we are."

Ruby opens her mouth to refute her stepmother's claims, but Everett speaks before she has the chance.

"One hour, Ruby. The stable boy who wishes to marry my daughter has one hour to present himself before me, and until that time, I do not intend to discuss the matter further."

He picks up his glasses and hooks them back upon his ears. Neither his wife nor his daughter moves. After a moment, he raises his gaze.

"Go on, then. Both of you."

———

Kitty's heart is beating heavily in her chest. She's having trouble catching her breath. "Aiden and . . . Ruby?" she whispers. The figure seated to her right smiles sadly.

"I did love him," Ruby says. "And he loved me. But hatred grows best in a place where love dies, Kitty."

She holds out her hand, but Kitty's seen enough. Too much. She pulls away, stands, and turns her back.

"Be brave," Peter says in his sweet, clear voice.

"You only see what you want to see," Cora repeats.

"No." Kitty shakes her head, but Ruby is back by her side, and this time there are tears on her cheeks.

"Forgive me, Kitty," she says, then reaches toward her. Kitty's eyes flutter closed, and the fog is thick. She waves her hands, trying to push it away from her nose and mouth, but it won't go.

Fear overtakes her, and she's choking. She can't breathe. Kitty opens her eyes as the library doors are opening again.

Ruby's face beams, and Aiden stands next to her in his worn, stained work clothes. He grips her hand in his, a united front in a world he's only seen from the outside. Until now.

Everett Cooke claps him on the shoulder and holds out a hand for Aiden to shake, as one man does to another.

"I come from nothing," Mr. Cooke says. "I do not believe a man's station at birth determines his worth. I've watched you grow into an honest, hardworking young man. I'm confident that, given the right opportunities, you can make something of yourself."

Aiden almost smiles, then schools his expression back to one of deference. "Thank you, sir," he says. "I won't let you down."

Mr. Cooke glances at Ruby. Another sort of man might embrace his daughter upon granting approval for her to be wed, but Everett Cooke isn't given to displays of emotion.

He gives the pair a nod. "See that you don't."

Ruby and Aiden leave the library together, and the joy on their faces is clear for anyone to see. Even Mr. Cooke, as indecipherable as ever, has an air of satisfaction about him.

Only Helena, seated in a chair and forgotten, seethes with indignation.

She stares at the place where the pair of lovers disappeared, and the venom in her gaze reaches across time and death and memory. Kitty gasps, stumbling backward.

A crash brings her back to the present, back to the cottage and a broken lamp at her feet.

She studies the pieces scattered across the floor, dismayed at how quickly a thing can be broken. How delicate an illusion happiness can be.

At how quickly a person can become lost, without moving a single step.

34

TESSA

She could get lost in here.

Tessa is deep in the forest before the thought occurs to her. Strangely, it doesn't concern her as much as it should. The wind is wistful and soft. The birds are calling, heedless of the woman wandering below them.

There is a path, she's relieved to see, though it's strewn with fallen leaves and branches and dotted with moss-covered rocks. She follows it deeper, letting curiosity lead her on.

Water trickles into her consciousness. By the time she registers what she's hearing, the music of a brook has been playing for a while, growing more distinct as she gets closer.

There's no sign of Aiden Donnelly and the yellow jacket, if in fact it was Aiden she saw. Tessa can't be sure, and she's lost the urgency to find him, abandoned it somewhere along the way.

If she looks behind her, will she see that urgency scattered like bread crumbs, marking her path?

She doesn't look, content to keep her eyes forward. Eventually, the forest thins. A small stream lies in front of her, and the path curves to follow beside it. Clear, cool water tumbles over the rocks in the streambed.

She lifts her gaze and spots an old wooden bridge that curves up and over the water a little farther ahead. Beyond the bridge, even deeper into the woods, a flash of yellow catches her eye.

Slowly Tessa makes her way across. She doesn't call out, but makes no effort to hide her presence.

The yellow, it turns out, isn't a jacket at all, but a knitted cardigan the color of freshly churned butter.

"Hello," Tessa says softly as she approaches.

Deirdre Donnelly is kneeling, facing Tessa's direction. There's a basket on the ground at her side.

"Ms. Shepherd," she says. The greeting isn't warm, but neither is it contemptuous. The elder Donnelly sister sounds resigned.

"This is a beautiful spot," Tessa says.

Deirdre nods, and continues her task without looking up. She's carefully removing moss and undergrowth from a section of ground.

Tessa takes one step closer and sees that there are cut roses in her basket. She stops, not wishing to intrude on whatever pursuit has brought the woman all this way.

Deirdre doesn't seem inclined to talk. Tessa should feel awkward, but the peacefulness of their surroundings enchants her. The low-level anxiety she normally carries, one even medication can't eliminate entirely, is silent for once, and the lack of it leaves her feeling serene.

"Have you made things right with your sister?" Deirdre asks, surprising Tessa out of her contentment. Deirdre's hands don't slow, but her sharp eyes study Tessa while she works.

Tessa's gaze slides past hers, and she curls her arms protectively around her middle.

"As right as they can be, I suppose," she says. "For now."

Deirdre doesn't respond. She simply watches her.

Tessa's interviewed hundreds of people. She's familiar with the urge to fill silence with explanations. It's an old trick that shouldn't work on her, but her guard is down and she feels inexplicably safe here, a million miles from the real world.

"Margot and I . . . we . . . we've been estranged for a long time. Only our mother's death brought us back together."

"You were close once?" Deirdre continues with her task. Her voice is unconcerned, as if the answer makes no difference, but Tessa can't help feeling it's a test.

"Yes," she says. Whether that means she's passed or failed, Tessa can't know, but it is the truth. Anything less would be wrong in a place like this.

Deirdre leans back on her heels and brushes scraps of green and brown from her pants legs. She reaches for a handful of roses from her basket. Pink roses, like the wallpaper peeling inside Fallbrook.

"What does it take to break the bond between sisters?" she asks as she lays roses on the section of ground she's cleared. "Only something monumental, I would think."

Against her will, Tessa goes back there, the place her dreams insist on taking her. The stars overhead, the feel of lake water drying on her skin in the cool night breeze.

And the panicked realization of what's about to happen. Reaching, always reaching. The feel of Margot's skin sliding through her palm, fingers fumbling as her sister is ripped away, taken by gravity and an inescapable fate.

"An accident," Tessa says. Her words are sparse but heavy with everything that's come before them. "My fault."

The familiar shame and helplessness the memories bring wash over her.

"She survived, but . . . she asked me to leave."

Deirdre peers at Tessa, her head tilted slightly to one side. One eyebrow rises above the other. "So you left?" she asks.

It's a simple question. An obvious one. But it dawns on Tessa that it's one she never asked herself. Of course she left. Margot was broken.

In pain. Damaged in a way Tessa could neither understand nor fix, and the only thing her sister asked—no, not asked, demanded—was that Tessa go.

Margot excised her from her life.

There was never any question of choice. Tessa had no choice.

Did she?

The skepticism in Deirdre's eyes says differently. The thought leaves Tessa breathless.

The old woman stands, then leans down slowly to pick up her basket. She walks a few steps to her right and sets the basket down again.

With a sigh, she lowers herself back into a kneeling position. "Getting old is hell," she mutters. "But I suppose it's better than the alternative."

She leans forward and begins clearing the earth in the new place she's chosen.

With a start, Tessa realizes what Deirdre is doing. She looks around with fresh eyes, taking in a wider view of her surroundings. They're standing in a small clearing. The gentle melody of the brook sings softly in the distance. Branches and leaves frame a circle of blue sky overhead, and there's an overwhelming sense of tranquility.

Tessa moves a step closer. She can see clearly what to look for now that she understands.

Deirdre is tending graves.

Growth patterns on the earth mark the differences, and Deirdre's hands work at a section at the head of each plot, uncovering a rectangular marker that lies flush upon the ground.

"This is where the family was laid to rest?" she asks.

Deirdre nods. "Mr. Ashwood," she says, "your grandfather, was Mr. Cooke's business partner. There was no family to speak of on either side. None who cared to make themselves known, at least. Money might have brought a few distant relations out of the woodwork, but the Cooke estate was held in trust for your mother."

Deirdre's hands are slow but steady as she clears away the unobtrusive headstone.

"Burying them on the property was his decision, but Mam agreed. Placing them in a town cemetery would invite the morbid to come and gawk. She chose this place. It was one of her favorites. And I think she chose well. The gravestones were paid for by the trust."

Deirdre stops to massage one hand gently with the other.

"Would you like me to—"

"No," Deirdre says, waving her away, though not unkindly. "This has always been my duty, though I don't come here as often as I should. One day, perhaps, it will be yours. That depends on what you and your sister decide. Until then, I can manage."

She places another handful of roses on the ground, then runs a hand gently along the marker of the grave.

With a sigh, Deirdre struggles to her feet. Tessa is tempted to offer her support but suspects she'd be waved away again.

For the first time since she's arrived, Deirdre turns her attention fully on Tessa. She pulls the edges of her sweater tightly around her bony frame.

"There's something you need to know about Kitty, Ms. Shepherd." Her tone is stern, reminiscent of the woman Tessa has come to expect.

"My sister lives in a world of her own creation. It's not her fault, I suppose. My mother encouraged her when she was younger. It was harmless, I thought. A shared fantasy that helped them both to cope. But age has loosened her hold on reality."

Tessa frowns, unsure where this is leading.

Deirdre raises a hand and gestures for Tessa to come closer. Tessa hesitates, but after a moment, she does, careful where she places her feet. She doesn't want to tread upon anything she shouldn't.

Closing the distance between them, Tessa stops at Deirdre's side. The older woman is less fearsome up close, her eyes full of knowledge and regret.

"Look," she says, pointing a hand toward the gravestone at their feet.

Tessa's eyes widen as understanding crashes down upon her, upending the peace she's gathered in this quiet, lovely place and scattering it on the breeze. Disbelieving, her gaze combs across the markers Deirdre has cleared and the ones she hasn't.

There are six. Tessa does the math. Five members of the Cooke family. And the grave they stand in front of.

Aiden Donnelly.

Tessa stares. Her eyes read over the inscription, followed by the dates of his birth and death. A great many things become clear at once, and just as many new questions arise.

"He died . . ." Tessa looks to the grave closest.

Ruby Cooke. Beloved daughter.

Ruby was born on March 3, 1933. Her date of death was May 22, 1950.

"He died before the year was out," Deirdre says.

September 1950. He'd only just turned eighteen.

"But Kitty said . . . the merchant marines. I don't understand. Was there an accident?"

Deirdre shakes her head, a deep furrow in her brow. "No," she says.

"But . . ."

Tessa trails off when the older woman grimaces. Her eyes flutter closed and Tessa notes the blue tint of her paper-thin eyelids. She sways slightly on her feet, and Tessa reaches to support her, alarmed.

"I'm sorry," Deirdre says. "I think I need to rest. Would you mind walking me back?"

"Of course," Tessa murmurs, alarmed by how pale the other woman has become. Tessa hooks her free hand beneath the handle of the basket of roses, and the pair of them slowly make their way back to the path through the woods.

Tessa doesn't press her, but she can't stop the runaway train of her thoughts. After a moment, Deirdre speaks, though she doesn't loosen her hold on Tessa's arm.

"There were no merchant marines," she says. "Aiden never left here."

Tessa studies her, but Deirdre keeps her eyes determinedly forward.

"It broke Mam's heart when he died. Kitty's too. I'm not sure who started it. Mam, most likely. A game of pretend, born out of grief and despair. Then there were postcards, with cheerful messages written in Mam's hand. They were never postmarked, but neither of them mentioned that. In their minds, at least, Aiden lived on."

Tessa tries to imagine it. Deirdre as a girl, a bystander as her mother and her sister shared a fantasy that didn't allow her to grieve for the brother she lost.

"That must have been so hard for you," she says. Deirdre glances at her, surprised, then shrugs.

"It made them happy, and I tried not to hold that against them. I even played along. It may not have been real, but for Mam and Kitty, together in their shared delusion, it *felt* real. I suppose that was enough."

She sighs.

"After Mam passed, talk of Aiden died with her. I didn't have the heart to play their game anymore. Not with Mam gone. Kitty and I were grown women by then, but Mam . . . she lived a great many years after Aiden died, but I don't think she ever really recovered from his death. It was a relief when Kitty let him go. Enough time passed and the stories about Aiden and his grand adventures faded and began to feel like childhood dreams."

Deirdre stops. They're nearing the edge of the forest now, and Tessa can see the point ahead where the path will take them out. Fallbrook, and the Donnellys' fairy-book cottage wait on the other side of those trees.

"Nearly a year ago," Deirdre continues, "and much to my surprise, Aiden returned."

Tessa frowns. She considers the implications of everything Deirdre is saying and all that she's not.

"Has there been an official diagnosis?" Tessa asks carefully.

Deirdre gives her a half smile, one that seems to say Tessa will understand one day. When the time comes.

"No," she says. "To what end? I've learned to play along again, and Kitty's happy. At least, she was."

"Until I showed up," Tessa says, completing the sentence.

Deirdre nods. "Yes."

There's no judgment in the word, no sense that Deirdre blames Tessa for something she couldn't have known or predicted, but Tessa feels the responsibility settle on her shoulders all the same.

"Mam suffered with dementia, too, in her last few years. I recognized the signs in Kitty when they began. Stories about our brother are one thing, but when she started to see more than just Aiden, I had to face the truth."

"I'm so sorry," Tessa says. "That must be a terrible burden."

Deirdre waves off the sympathy. "There are worse things. Kitty mostly remembers what she wants, and I let her. At this point, my one goal is to protect my sister from her own failing mind."

"And now she wants me to make a movie to prove her brother innocent of a crime that no one believes he committed."

Deirdre raises her brows again. "You misunderstand," she says. "Aiden's death was no accident. He took his own life."

Tessa pulls in a sharp breath. Deirdre watches as her words sink in.

"By that time, Lawrence Pynchon had died in jail," she continues quietly. "The police were convinced they'd gotten their man. And even if they hadn't, no one was going to continue investigating a crime in which all the possible suspects were dead. But that didn't stop the locals from speculating."

"So Kitty wants his name cleared for good reason," Tessa says.

"Oh yes. I, on the other hand, can think of no bigger disaster than an attempt to prove Aiden's innocence. People said he killed himself because he couldn't live with what he'd done."

"Are you saying . . . ?" Tessa can barely fathom it. Aiden was her brother.

"I'm saying I believe they were right."

Deirdre drops her hand from Tessa's arm. She's recovered some of her strength, and her color has returned to normal. She walks a few steps forward, then turns back to speak again.

"My brother is dead, Ms. Shepherd. He has been for a long time. Truth and lies make no difference to him. The world has forgotten he existed. But for Kitty . . . I think the truth might destroy her."

35

Tessa stares at the black marks she made on the parlor wall. Little lines, scribbles, that add up to nothing. Questions she has no business asking.

A useless exercise in futility.

She's wasting her time. She's wasting Margot's time. Worse, she's waltzed into the lives of two elderly women who lived through a horrifically traumatic event and stirred up painful memories best left dead and buried.

Tessa stands on the chair she scooted next to the wall when she was still telling herself she wasn't planning to make a documentary about Fallbrook.

She was lying. The story is a lifeline, one she's desperate to hold on to. Margot had Ben. Margot had Mom. Tessa, alone in the city, had only her work.

Without it, there's nothing left, and in that empty space, the anxiety will grow unchecked. Meds help to keep it at bay. Therapy has taught her coping skills. But Tessa never forgets. She can't. It's a patient little monster, waiting and watching for her to drop her guard.

She can feel it now, the panic she's been fighting since she clicked on the link to Oliver's first video. Since she opened the door to find

Margot at her apartment. Since watching her mother lowered into the ground.

Tessa grabs one peeling corner of faded wallpaper. With a sweeping slash of her hand, she rips it from the wall.

Little worries will grow, until they take up so much space in her head there's no room left for rational thought. An article about faulty engineering will leave her unable to drive across bridges without breaking into a trembling sweat. A recall on one type of produce, and she can't purchase food that might have been shipped on the same truck. Statistics about pedestrian fatalities will keep her locked into one city block.

Eventually, her world will shrink to the space of her apartment. Four walls. Four silent walls. No television, no internet. The risk of hearing about world leaders edging closer to a renewed nuclear arms race, endangering even the tiny space she has left, is too great.

She grabs another curling edge of the ancient rose paper and yanks, tearing across the space with her arm.

The fear will grow bigger. It will grow vicious, gnashing teeth, and Tessa will grow smaller, until finally, desperate and alone, she'll crawl out of the bathroom where she's been hiding in the tub and find her phone. She'll dial the number for the one person who can make her feel real again.

But Margot won't answer.

Tessa rips down the roses with both hands now. She rips, and she rips again, until the ground around the chair is littered with piles of moldy, shredded paper.

She stands, her chest heaving, and stares at the barren, termite-eaten boards she's exposed.

Tessa's hands come to her mouth, pressing to hold back the fear, and her face crumples. She slides downward into a heap.

Panic is building like a cyclone, bringing her thoughts around to the same place in ever-widening circles.

She's afraid. She's afraid of emptiness. She's afraid of fear. She's afraid of fear eating away at her life, the way it did before.

Somewhere inside the swirling chaos, Tessa forces her arms up to protect herself.

Time passes, but she doesn't know how much. Minutes? Hours? A lifetime?

Tears fall, and Tessa shakes, and a little voice, a voice that might be her own, struggles to be heard.

"Breathe," the voice says. *"Deep, deep breaths from the center. In and out."*

One. Two. Three.

"I am afraid." The words form on her lips in a weak, shaky whisper. "But I am not in danger."

Breathe again, between the choking sobs.

Once. Twice. Three times.

"Fighting feeds the fear. Accept the fear. This too will pass."

Breathe. Breathe. Breathe.

"I am afraid, but I am not in danger."

Tessa knows where this can lead but pushes back, hard, at the thought.

Once before, she went all the way down, a descent that spiraled out of control, free-falling faster than she ever had before. She didn't understand what was happening. She had no room for understanding, no room for anything except the fear. It was everywhere, in every thought. It overtook her senses until there was nothing else left.

Almost nothing. There, in the abyss, she had one last hope. Margot.

Somehow, in the midst of her panic, she managed to reach her phone. With shaking hands, and a desperation she never felt before, she reached out to her sister.

The call rang and it rang. There was no one at the other end of the line. Her phone fell from her hand and clattered on the bathroom floor, lying useless as Tessa fell farther into the darkness.

In real time, less than an hour passed after she dropped her phone. In Tessa's mind, the minutes turned to lifetimes.

They were the bleakest moments of her life.

And then the phone rang. Tessa grasped it for the lifeline it was, and Ben's voice was there, a connection to her past, to her present, to her everything.

"Tessa?" he asked.

She doesn't know if he could make out any of the words that tumbled from her lips between the sobs and the pounding, pulsing anxiety. She doesn't know where he told Margot he was going.

But she knows he was at her door before the night was through.

She holds tight to the thought of Ben, who dropped everything and came to help her when she needed him.

"Fighting feeds the fear. Accept the fear. This too shall pass."

Her last real descent was so long ago. She had bad days, of course, but none so bad as that. She collected the clear days like badges of honor. Thirty days, one year, ten. She holds those numbers tightly, as if they can protect her, but they can't.

But this time, Tessa is prepared. She won't let the fear take her all the way down. She fights against it with all the weapons she's collected since that terrible day. She repeats the words, breathes deeply between them. More time passes. More breaths.

She channels her thoughts to calm. She rides the waves of anxiety until, at last, they begin to recede.

Weak now, as exhausted as if she's run for miles, Tessa sits with her arms around her knees, her head resting on top of them. She's shaky, she's wrung out, but the worst of the storm has passed, and she begins to feel a little bit like herself again. Her edges are slowly coming back into focus.

She opens her eyes, surveys the damage spread around her.

Once rational thought returns, Tessa can see what she refused to see before.

Margot's right. Tessa shouldn't be here. This place belongs in the past. It doesn't have to be sold—they can simply walk away and leave all the arrangements in place, just like Mom did.

The ground will eventually swallow Fallbrook whole, and Kitty and Deirdre can live out the remainder of their lives on money from the trust.

Tessa forces herself to her feet. She sways a bit on shaky legs, and places a hand against the wall for support.

She won't hide any longer.

It's time to deal head-on with the consequences of the mistakes she's made, no matter what that brings.

Tessa walks to the door of the parlor. She places a hand on the doorknob and throws one last look over her shoulder.

It's time to leave this place.

Tessa turns back to the door, rotates the knob, and pulls.

Nothing happens.

She frowns and places both hands on the doorknob, bracing her legs like she did when the front door was stuck.

She pulls again.

Still nothing.

Finally, she stops, staring with wide eyes at the barrier between herself and the outside world.

She doesn't want to believe it. It makes no sense.

But she can't hide from the facts.

The door to the parlor isn't stuck.

Someone has locked her inside.

36

KITTY

Kitty is trapped, locked inside her own head with the terrible, unwanted suspicions.

"You can't trust her, you know." Aiden is skipping rocks across the brown-and-green surface of the pond.

"Don't talk like that," Kitty says. "She's our sister."

Aiden shrugs. "That doesn't mean she can't lie. Dee can lie with the best of them, Kitty."

She frowns. She hates it when he's like this. It makes her feel disloyal, pulled in two directions at once, with no way to please anyone.

"That's not fair," Kitty whispers. "You never told me about Ruby."

Aiden turns to her, surprise widening his eyes.

"You knew about Ruby," he says. "Everyone knew! I loved her as long as I can remember." He turns back to the pond and sends another rock flying. His voice is soft when he continues. "It was the best day of my life when I realized she felt the same."

"That's not the way I remember it," Kitty scoffs, angry for his sake, even if he can't dredge up any anger for himself.

"It was, Kitty cat. It was beautiful. While it lasted."

She stands, dumping the rocks she's been collecting for him on the ground as she does.

"And how long was that, Aiden? Twenty-four hours? Forty-eight?"

He doesn't look at her. Instead, he tosses his last rock into the pond. It sinks to the bottom with a hollow plunk.

"Don't blame Ruby. It wasn't her fault."

"Whose fault was it, then?" Kitty shouts.

He turns to look at her, and his whole being seems stitched together with sadness and grief.

"We both know the answer to that, even if you don't want to see it, Kitty. It was mine."

Her heart breaks all over again, and hearts are one of the few things Aiden can't mend.

"No," Kitty whispers, shaking her head. "That's not true. It's not. I remember."

"It is true." He takes her hand in his. "But Kitty, you need to understand, it's not me that Deirdre lies for."

Kitty's throat feels thick and dry. She struggles to swallow against the awful, bitter taste in her mouth.

"She's protecting me," Kitty whispers. "She thinks you did it. She's thinks I can't handle the truth."

He studies her, then sighs. "Do you really believe that? Can you think of a single time I gave Dee, or anyone, a reason to suspect I had something like that living inside of me?"

The puppies. The scruffy little mama dog, who gave birth to one too many pups to care for. It was Aiden who massaged his tiny body when he was born not breathing. Aiden who cared for him and kept him warm. Aiden who bottle-fed him when his brothers and sisters pushed him out of the way.

"No," she says. "No."

It was Aiden who stood, ostracized, in Everett Cooke's study, accused of a crime he'd never have committed. It was Aiden who was betrayed.

As if he can read her thoughts, he says again, "Ruby's not to blame, Kitty. Ruby was never to blame."

But the memory is close and it's raw. It hurts to recall, hurts like it was only yesterday.

———

A taste of wild blueberries lingers on her tongue. The basket in her hand is full, and Peter's is too, despite the vast quantities they picked that never made it past their mouths. He'd found her. She was upset by one thing or another, and he begged her to join him in the woods.

As usual, he's lifted her mood, and she'd like to return the favor.

Peter is six now, and he seems happier since the return of his sister from boarding school, but he's still too quiet by half.

"Are you getting along with Mr. Pynchon okay?" she asks, though the man's name sticks like a bone in her throat.

Peter shrugs. "He doesn't pay much attention to me," he says. "I think he likes Ruby a lot, though."

Kitty doesn't voice her thoughts on that. Not to Peter. But she too has seen the way the new tutor looks at Ruby, with her glossy auburn hair and the curve of her hips.

"Mam will make us a pie with these, Pete," Kitty says instead, nudging his shoulder with hers. "Maybe even two."

He smiles, but it falls from his face when he turns away, like it was there for her benefit alone. Kitty feels an overwhelming need to hug him tight, to pull a true smile from his face, one that lights him up all the way to his eyes.

Does she have some sense how gravely things are about to change?

The two of them emerge from the woods near the back of Fallbrook, and the sounds of raised voices reach her ears. One voice, to be exact.

Peter and Kitty come around the side of the house and stop short at the scene in front of them. Helena isn't angry. She's triumphant. A gorgon holding the stone head of the vanquished high in the air.

Her voice is the one that rings out, sharp and clear and cold, from her place at the top of the porch steps.

"Don't think for a moment that I won't send the police after you if you or your family choose to help yourself to any more of the silver, Mrs. Donnelly."

Kitty's eyes find Mam, whose shoulders are hunched. In her entire life, Kitty can't recall seeing her cry, yet tears are coursing down her plump cheeks. Aiden stands with an arm protectively around her shoulders, the two of them with a pain in their eyes that Kitty has difficulty comprehending.

"Go on, now. You heard Mr. Cooke. You have until tonight, and not a minute more, and you should be grateful for that. I suggest you don't waste time."

Kitty's eyes flash to Helena, who is stiffly mirroring their stance with her arm around Ruby's shoulders. Ruby's face is blank and drawn. She looks more like a beautiful statue than a human girl.

She appears to take no comfort in her stepmother's embrace.

Deirdre emerges from the front door of Fallbrook, looking confused and disoriented.

She's been in the upstairs parlor, the one that was converted to a schoolroom with the addition of Lawrence Pynchon to the household. Kitty can tell from the distracted, love-addled expression in her eyes. She's come from a music lesson. With *him*.

Helena gives Deirdre an openly scornful glance when she appears behind her.

"You too, girl," she says. "You'd best hurry and catch up. There's no place for you here anymore."

Deirdre lowers her gaze, but not before a searching glance in Ruby's direction. Ruby doesn't meet her eyes.

Peter bolts suddenly from Kitty's side, around the corner of the porch to stand in the yard between the two groups of people.

"What's happening?" he shouts. He turns to stare at Mam's and Aiden's retreating backs, but they don't turn around, even though they must hear him. Mam's shoulders hunch even lower than before, as if she's taken an unexpected blow.

"Come along, Peter," Helena says. She turns Ruby back toward the front door of Fallbrook, and Ruby goes where she leads.

Peter doesn't move.

"Peter, I said come along," Helena repeats, her voice sharper now. "This doesn't concern you."

Deirdre hurries down the steps, ignored by Helena now that she's been dismissed. She kneels in front of Peter and hugs him tightly, then whispers something in his ear that Kitty can't hear.

"I said now, Peter," Helena barks.

From somewhere inside, the baby begins to cry. Awake from her nap, little Imogene has woken into a world that's turned on its head.

Deirdre touches her forehead to Peter's and nods through tears, then she stands and ushers him toward his stepmother's waiting form.

Reluctantly he goes, but not before one last, longing glance over his shoulder.

Deirdre forces a smile, but Kitty knows her face. She won't be able to hold back the sobs for much longer.

Frozen in place, Kitty can't wrap her mind around what's just happened.

Only when the front door of Fallbrook shuts resoundingly, with the finality of a church bell tolling at a funeral service, and Deirdre turns to follow Aiden and Mam, does Kitty find her voice.

"Dee," she shouts, running after her. "What's happened? What's going on?"

She grabs her by the hands, but Deirdre's given in to the sobs, and it's hard to make sense of what she says. It takes a long time for Kitty to piece together what's taken place.

"Mrs. Cooke accused Aiden of stealing," Deirdre says, through tears and snot.

"No," Kitty says. "Aiden would never."

But Deirdre is shaking her head. "He admitted he had them," she cries. "He says he found them and was returning them. The candlesticks. The silver ones from the dining room that belonged to the first Mrs. Cooke."

Kitty goes cold.

"And it might have been okay. Mr. Cooke might have been talked around, but . . . but . . ."

"But what?" she demands. But Deirdre's sobs are shaking her chest, and her words are hard to decipher.

"It was Ruby," Dee finally says. "Ruby burst into the library, and she said Aiden did it. Aiden took the candlesticks, and . . . and . . . Mr. Cooke is throwing us out. We have to leave, Kitty."

From somewhere inside the house, Lawrence Pynchon's violin begins to play, and Deirdre gives herself over fully to the tears. Kitty can do nothing but hold her while she cries.

Her family.

Kitty is numb, her nerve endings burned away. Her family is being thrown out of their home.

———

Aiden tosses a final rock into the pond. The biggest one, saved for last. It lands with a plunk. He brushes his hands against his pants before he sighs and takes a seat next to her on the grass. "Who was she crying for, Kitty?" Aiden asks by her side.

"For you," Kitty insists. "For us. For all of us."

"Are you sure about that?"

Kitty doesn't know what to say. Doesn't know what Aiden's trying to say.

Except that she does know. Deep down, she knows.

"Not for him," she whispers. "She wouldn't cry for him."

Aiden gives her a sad smile. "Fifteen sounds so young, doesn't it? A child still, but those are the years when a girl's heart first tests its wings, searching for a chance to fly."

Kitty shakes her head, denying the words that have a haunting ring of familiarity.

"But Pynchon didn't love her back," she whispers. "He was a flirt, but there was only one girl who really caught his eye."

"Only one girl," Aiden agrees. "Ruby. And I was in the way of that. Until those candlesticks went missing."

Kitty frowns, cocking her head to one side. She can imagine Lawrence Pynchon stealing the first Mrs. Cooke's silver. Can even imagine him planting them somewhere Aiden would be blamed. But . . .

"What has that got to do with Dee?" she asks her brother.

Aiden shrugs. "Maybe nothing," he says. "Or maybe a great deal. I believe Dee knows I didn't take those candlesticks, Kitty. And I think she knows who did."

Kitty shakes her head. "What are you saying?"

"What if, with one word, Deirdre could have prevented everything? It would have been Pynchon who was sent packing, branded as a thief. Just a word. But she didn't."

He's leading her by the hand, one step at a time, toward a new version of the truth, one Kitty doesn't want to see. But even with her eyes squeezed tight, she must follow the sound of his footsteps where they lead.

37

TESSA

Tessa raises her head at the echo of footsteps.

She stares at the door for a beat, then jumps up and pounds her fists against it.

"Help!" she cries, beating harder and faster. "Help me! I'm locked in!"

The sounds stop, and Tessa listens until they start again. Heavy footfalls are coming her way.

Too late it occurs to her that Margot's footsteps wouldn't sound like that. Nor the Donnelly sisters, with their light, shuffling gaits.

And Aiden Donnelly died seventy years ago. If he's wandering around Fallbrook, he's not wearing work boots.

Tessa backs away from the door, her heart beating almost as loudly as her fists were beating on the door.

Oliver.

He's come for her. She thought she was safe here. Thought he couldn't find her.

But she was wrong.

Tessa rakes her eyes around the room, searching frantically for anything she can use as a weapon. She has nothing but a phone with no signal and a black marker that's nearly out of ink.

The slow steps are coming closer. She quickly debates the effectiveness of stabbing a person in the eye with a marker, then spots the chair next to the wall.

Tessa runs for it, grabs it by the back, and swings it around. Her pulse jumps in her throat. The doorknob is rattling, turning back and forth.

It's too late to shove the chair under the door, and that only works in movies anyway, so she picks it up and holds it in front of her with the legs pointing out.

Her arms strain under the weight, but it's the best she's got.

There's a click and the lock disengages.

With a creak, the door swings open. Tessa grips her chair like a novice lion tamer in her first day on the job.

"Shepherd," a deep voice says. "What are you planning to do with that?"

The chair drops from Tessa's grip with a heavy thud.

"Winters," she says with an exhale of pent-up breath. Her pulse is still racing. "Jesus, you scared me."

He leans against the doorjamb and slides one hand in his pocket. His face is lined with exhaustion.

He looks old.

Another person might comment on the state of the room, or Tessa herself. She's filthy and disheveled, her clothing has been slept in, and she has tear streaks running through the dirt and dust on her face.

Lloyd Winters isn't interested in any of that. His face is twisted, mouth taut, like there's a bad taste in his mouth he can't rid himself of.

"I need your help, Shepherd," he says, forcing the words past his lips before he chokes on them. The disdain on his face tells her everything she needs to know regarding his feelings about that. "Unless you're too busy playing around in your little haunted house."

———

Tessa has cleaned up as best she can with facial wipes from her suitcase, which was still packed in the trunk of the car.

Winters waits impatiently on the front porch. She can feel his eyes on her but needs the time and space to prepare herself for whatever has brought him to find her.

She joins him on the porch. They don't sit. This isn't a social call. Winters stands with his shoulder against one of the columns that frames the steps and stares outward. Tessa leans her back against the other and watches him.

He doesn't meet her eyes.

"How did you find me?" she asks.

He shrugs. "It wasn't hard. I knew you weren't in New York or at your mother's house, so I went back to Bracknell Lodge. The owner told me you were gone but mentioned you had an interest in this place."

Mrs. Coburn. So much for lying low.

"I guess I'm lucky she hasn't ratted me out to the media yet," Tessa says with a sigh.

He squints and stares straight ahead.

"It's not luck," he admits. "I asked her not to."

Tessa's not sure what to say to that. Winters didn't intervene out of concern for Tessa's well-being.

"Why are you here?" she asks.

"Barlow. What else?" he says.

"Oliver's not here, Chief, and I don't think you expected him to be. So why don't you tell me why you're really here?"

He continues to stare off into the distance, and Tessa fights the urge to insist he look her in the face. The truth is, she doesn't want to see the accusation she's sure to find in his eyes.

"Barlow's leading us on a wild-goose chase," he says.

"Us?" The question is out of her mouth before Tessa has a chance to pull it back.

Winters clenches his teeth, and the muscle in his jaw works.

"The state police," he amends. "He's playing games. Sending them to places that have nothing to do with Valerie. Once they arrive, he's long gone."

Tessa frowns. "What kind of places?"

Winters sighs. "I don't know. Places that mean something to him." He looks uncomfortable, and Tessa can sense there's more he's not saying.

"Mean something how?"

He shoves his hands in his pockets. "Places he feels like he lost something," the chief of police finally admits. "He sent us to Albany. To a law office. That's where his mother was when she died. She was leaving a meeting with a lawyer."

Tessa stands up straighter.

Nisha Singh. Tessa knows her. She took Oliver's case pro bono after the family ran out of money. Nisha is intelligent and tireless, a woman Tessa has a great deal of respect for.

"My God, is she okay?"

Winters turns to look at her, confused for a moment.

"Who?"

"Ms. Singh," Tessa says.

He looks at her like a bug he'd like to stomp beneath his feet. "The lawyer? She's fine, Shepherd. Doesn't even work in the building anymore. It wasn't about her. It was about his mother. He left a note for us in the emergency panel of the elevator where she was standing when the aneurysm burst."

Tessa lets out a deep breath. Donna Barlow's death was heart-breaking for everyone who knew her, and it took a terrible toll on Oliver.

Until the day she died, she stood by his innocence. Tessa is almost glad she's not here to see what's become of her son.

"Then it was the trucking company his father was fired from."

"What?" Tessa exclaims. "When did that happen?"

"Six months ago, about," Winters says. "Apparently he hit the bottle pretty hard after his wife died. You can't drive a truck with a DUI on your record. They let him go."

Six months ago? How did Tessa not know that? But six months ago she'd been hip deep in the last documentary, working long hours. Losing herself in someone else's story. Just like she always has.

If Oliver reached out, she didn't take the call. She'd told herself she'd get back to him.

But that was one more lie. She didn't get back to him. She moved on and left Oliver in the past. A project done. On to the next tragedy, just like Margot said.

"The point is, Barlow's taking the state police on a sightseeing trip through his past. By the time they show up, he's long gone. We need to get in front of him. It's time to stop playing his stupid games. That's where you come in."

He turns, pinning her with his hard gaze.

Tessa hesitates. All that's happened sits heavily between them. "What exactly are you asking?"

"You know his history. You know the moments in his life that stand out to him. You know more about Barlow and what makes him tick than any of the family he has left. I need to find my daughter, Shepherd. I need to bring her home to her mother. And I need him to pay."

Tessa doesn't kid herself. This man is not her friend. He's not her ally. He doesn't wish her well. He might even wish her harm, if he didn't have a use for her.

"Okay," she hears herself say. "I don't know if it will help, but I'll do what I can."

Winters gives her a short nod. He doesn't owe her any thanks, and doesn't bother to give any, but Tessa can't miss the flash of relief in his eyes, however brief.

Tessa explains that Margot is already in Snowden and plans to watch the footage of the Barlow interviews.

"If there's anything I can give you, it'll be in those tapes. We could watch them together. If Mrs. Coburn is willing to let me back into her house."

"I'll persuade her," Winters says.

They take separate cars and agree to meet at Bracknell Lodge.

Tessa watches Fallbrook grow smaller in her rearview mirror, an aging sentinel of a tragic past.

But the past isn't where her focus needs to be right now. It's time for Tessa to fight through her fear and face the monsters of the present.

38

KITTY

Kitty stands on the path to Fallbrook, the forest at her back, and watches Tessa's car pull away. She carries a bundle of sandwiches wrapped in butcher paper and a thermos of lemonade.

Deirdre stops beside her.

"She's leaving," Kitty says to her sister. "Imogene's daughter is leaving, Dee. What if she never comes back?"

The brake lights of the car wink as it disappears around the turn.

"That's not our choice to make, Kitty," Deirdre says.

Kitty turns to glare at her. "How can you be so calm? Tessa was our chance!"

Deirdre carefully avoids her sister's eyes. She turns instead to look back at the cottage.

"I should get those roses pruned," she says. "I've been putting it off, but it needs to be done."

"Forget the roses!" Kitty shouts. "This was our chance to tell the world what happened here. Don't you understand?"

Deirdre whips her head around and glares. "What I understand and what you understand are two very different things, Kitty," she says coldly.

Kitty laughs, a harsh sound that rarely passes her lips. "That, at least, is one true thing you've said today."

Deirdre crosses her arms and stares. Her face is nothing but stony planes and harsh, unforgiving lines. "What exactly does that mean?"

"You know what it means," Kitty says softly. "You're lying. You lied to Tessa, and you're lying to me. Who took those candlesticks, Dee?"

Deirdre backs up a step, as if Kitty has struck her. "What?" she whispers.

"You heard me. I know it wasn't Aiden, and so do you. Who are you protecting?"

"I don't know what you're talking about," Deirdre murmurs. "You're getting things mixed up."

"I'm not. The silver candlesticks. The ones that belonged to the first Mrs. Cooke. How did they end up with Aiden, Deirdre? Someone had to put them there."

"Where is this coming from?" Deirdre's breath is shallow and ragged. "Why are you dragging this up? This is exactly why I don't want anyone digging around to film some ridiculous movie. Talk like this only upsets things. Let it lie, Kitty."

"Why? Because it's easier for you if no one knows the truth? Pynchon planted those candlesticks on Aiden, didn't he?" Kitty whispers. "Did Helena pay him to do it? Or was it his idea?"

Deirdre doesn't answer. She looks heartsick and pale. Miserable.

"Lawrence Pynchon didn't love you, Dee. He never loved you."

Deirdre's face goes still. Kitty regrets the hurtful nature of the words, but they're the truth. After all this time, her sister needs to face the truth.

"He treated you the same way he treated all the women in that house, young or old. All except Ruby. He paid special attention to Ruby. Even I could see that. Those candlesticks . . . they were an easy way to get Aiden out of the picture, weren't they?"

Deirdre has backed up even farther from Kitty. Her face is turned away, and there are tears forming in the bottom of her eyes. Her shoulders are shaking. She's gripping her arms around her bony frame, bracing herself as if against a storm.

Deirdre was never a beauty, not in the way Ruby was. But her heart was no less tender. Her love no less worthy.

"How long have you known who really stole them?" Kitty asks. "From the beginning?"

Deirdre swallows hard, still desperately holding on to words she's not willing to let free.

She shakes her head instead. "No," she whispers. "No. Not for certain. But I suspected."

Kitty has the urge to hug her sister, to hold her tightly until the pain goes away, but Deirdre wouldn't welcome it. Not right now.

"Why didn't you say anything?" Kitty asks quietly.

Deirdre's eyes are dark and bottomless when they meet hers. Her voice trembles when she speaks. "Because the hardest thing in the world is to see the worst parts of the people you love, Kitty. So don't lecture me about what I understand and what I don't. Don't you dare."

39

TESSA

Tessa doesn't dare let her mind wander to all that could go wrong. She stays focused on the tangible goal in front of her and pulls her car to a stop next to Chief Winters's battered old truck.

She steps out and the pair of them walk toward the door of Bracknell Lodge together.

"Let me do the talking," Winters says. "She's no fan of yours."

No thanks to you, Tessa thinks, but she holds her tongue.

Mrs. Coburn's face brightens at the sight of Winters but immediately grows cold when she spots Tessa behind him.

She stands silent while Chief Winters explains the situation.

"Mrs. Russell isn't here," Mrs. Coburn informs them. "She left a little while ago."

Winters glances back at Tessa.

"When she returns, we'd like to use the television in her guest room to screen some video footage. Official police business. And Ms. Shepherd is vital to that process."

Mrs. Coburn's nose wrinkles as if she's suddenly smelled something that's gone bad. Tessa fights an urge to roll her eyes.

"Whatever you need, Chief Winters," Mrs. Coburn says finally, making it clear that he's the only reason Tessa would ever be allowed in her establishment again. "But I can't let you into Mrs. Russell's room without her permission. You understand."

Now she gets a conscience.

"Of course," Winters says as Tessa fishes her phone from her pocket. The bars indicate that, for once, she has reception, and she opens the screen to place a call to Margot.

"I had no idea Mrs. Russell was your sister," Mrs. Coburn says, addressing Tessa directly for the first time since they've arrived. She sniffs. "She seemed so respectable."

Tessa bites her tongue and smiles. "I understand," she says sweetly.

Mrs. Coburn raises her nose and turns back toward Winters. Apparently, Tessa's been dismissed. "I really have no idea when Mrs. Russell will return, Chief."

The cloying way the woman keeps saying the word *Chief* is grating on her. She glances down at her phone to call her sister.

"She and her husband only left about twenty minutes ago."

Tessa's head comes up.

"Ben was here?" she asks.

Mrs. Coburn nods. "Such a polite man."

If Ben is here, Margot must have called him, asked him to come. Her heart leaps. They'll patch things up.

Tessa scrolls through her contacts, presses "Call," and holds her phone against her ear as Winters and Mrs. Coburn continue their conversation without her.

It rings, but no one answers. If Margot has gone back to Fallbrook, she'll have no reception. Tessa waits, listening for the recorded message before she can leave a voice mail.

The message starts, and the sound of Margot's voice fills her ear, but Tessa pulls the phone away. Her stomach drops. Something is wrong.

Quickly she hangs up the phone without speaking and dials the number again.

She listens.

"Shh," she says to Mrs. Coburn, interrupting whatever flattery the woman is shoveling up to Winters.

Offended, Mrs. Coburn glares at her. "That's incredibly rude, Ms.—"

"Shh!" Tessa says again, this time more forcefully. "Listen."

The phone is ringing in Tessa's ear. Margot still doesn't answer, but there's an echo of a ringtone coming from somewhere else in the house.

"Do you hear that?"

Winters stares at Tessa, putting the pieces together faster than she'd have given him credit for. "Mrs. Coburn, I need you to open Margot Russell's room," he says, his voice suddenly official and insistent.

The landlady pulls back a bit. "Chief, I've already told you, I can't—"

Tessa doesn't hear what he says next. She's running down the hallway toward the guest rooms. The call ends and she quickly redials.

First door, second door . . . there. The third door on the right.

Margot's phone is ringing inside that room.

Tessa pounds on the door with as much force as she used earlier when she'd been locked in at Fallbrook.

"Margot! Are you in there? Margot!"

Winters and Mrs. Coburn are hurrying up the hall behind her. The landlady has a set of keys dangling from her hands.

"This is most irregular, Chief," she says, her eyes wide with confusion. "Just because a guest forgets their phone in their room is no reason—"

"Open the door," Winters says, his words one step below a shout.

Taken aback, Mrs. Coburn turns quickly to do as he asks. Her good opinion of him has clearly dropped a notch or two, while Tessa's has come up.

The woman fumbles with the key in the lock and finally turns the handle to the door, opening it upon a tidy room with an open suitcase sitting on the bed.

Nothing appears out of place.

Nothing except that Margot is gone, her car is gone, and there, in the center of the bed, is her phone.

It's not right.

Tessa rushes in and opens the door to the bathroom. It's empty. She walks quickly around and checks the closet. Nothing more than a few wooden hangers.

Winters moves to the bed and picks up her sister's cell phone.

A terrible thought has taken hold of Tessa. It grips her by the throat and she's struggling to draw a breath.

"What did he look like, Mrs. Coburn?" Tessa forces out. "The man with my sister."

Mrs. Coburn shakes her head and stumbles over an answer. "Oh, uh . . . I don't know."

"What did he look like?" she shouts.

"He . . . he was tall. Tall and thin. Hair a little on the long side . . ."

She trails off as a voice begins to speak from the phone Winters is holding in his hands.

A voice Tessa would recognize anywhere. She flies across the room and rips the phone from his hand. The video continues to play.

The face on the screen of her sister's phone belongs to Oliver Barlow.

40

"Your sister didn't want to tell me where you were, Tessa. I don't think she believed me when I told her what good pals we are, but I finally persuaded her. I had to promise not to hurt you, though. I hope you can help me keep that promise. Because I don't want to hurt you."

Her own safety is the least of Tessa's concerns as she watches the video Oliver has left on her sister's phone.

"I'm recording this to set the record straight. Just in case your sister tries something on our way to you. You wouldn't do that, now, would you?" The camera pans to Margot's strained face standing next to Oliver as he films the pair of them. She shakes her head, her expression set in tense lines. Tessa is certain Margot isn't standing there willingly. Oliver must have a weapon, must have made threats to keep her with him.

"I've promised I won't hurt you, and I'll keep my word . . . *if* your sister behaves. We'll see you soon, Tessa. We'll have a nice chat. Catch up, like old friends. And if your sister and I don't make it there, you'll know who's to blame. Right, Margot?"

Tessa sits in the passenger seat of Winters's truck as it speeds back toward Fallbrook and replays the images in her mind. Oliver was following Margot. And now he has her. The thought of losing Margot, really losing her, is so big, so utterly foreign, that Tessa can't look at it straight on. It's like trying to stare into the sun.

So she averts her eyes and looks in every direction but that one. If not, she'll go blind.

Tessa holds her phone in her hand, watching the bars that indicate her signal disappearing one by one.

"No," Winters says. "Don't call the police."

"You *are* the police."

"He wants me too," Winters says. "That's what this is all about. Me. And you."

"But why now? Why like this?" Tessa asks. She just needs somewhere else to focus her thoughts.

Winters's jaw is tight, and for a moment she thinks he's not going to answer.

"I don't know what he wants from you, but he wanted me to admit, publicly, what I'd done."

"What you'd done? What are you talking about? Is this about the evidence?"

The tainted evidence. It was the turning point in the case. While researching the documentary, Tessa had tracked down the teenagers who'd discovered Gwen Morley's car hidden in the woods, miles from where her body was discovered. They weren't teenagers anymore, but young men who'd once been tangentially involved in the most infamous murder in Bonham's history.

The boys drank for years on that story. In a town like Bonham, the tales were rehashed and retold, distorted and exaggerated, until they had only the vaguest resemblance to what actually happened.

But it didn't matter that their stories had been stretched beyond recognition. The revelation was in the pictures.

One of the boys had been carrying a camera during the search. He claimed he'd taken it with him that day because he worked on the school newspaper and he took it everywhere, but Tessa suspected the teenagers were hoping for a more gruesome subject.

In the end, their motivation made no difference. The shots they took of Gwen's car before the police arrived were never shared with authorities, for fear they'd get themselves in trouble. Instead, they sat forgotten on a shelf in a childhood bedroom while the boy who'd taken them moved on with his life.

While everyone moved on with their lives.

Everyone except Oliver Barlow, who spent his days in a cell inside the walls of Merrivale Correctional Facility.

Those pictures, mentioned offhand during Tessa's interview with the boy turned man, clearly showed the back floorboard of Gwen Morley's Pontiac hatchback.

And there was no sign of the T-shirt that belonged to Oliver, which would miraculously appear in the official police photographs. That article of clothing, along with eyewitness accounts that claimed Oliver had made a drunken pass at Gwen earlier that night at a local bar wearing that same T-shirt, had swayed the jury to convict. The shirt was ripped and sweat-stained and had trace amounts of Gwen Morley's blood on it. Oliver claimed he had no idea how it got there, but the jury took one look at that shirt and imagined Gwen Morley struggling for her life.

Gwen's body had already been found when the Bonham Police Department conducted a voluntary search of Barlow's house the day before the discovery of Gwen's car. With his brothers alibied, Oliver was the first and the only suspect they focused on. It didn't matter that no other evidence was found or that there was no sign of Oliver's DNA on Gwen's body. Someone was determined that at least one of the Barlows was going to pay, one way or another.

The photographs proved that someone placed that evidence there. The only question was who, exactly, had made that choice.

The officers maintained throughout Oliver's new trial that neither of them placed the evidence. That it was there when they arrived, and they bagged it and tagged it in good faith.

But the photographs put everything in doubt. Enough doubt that Oliver was granted a new trial. With the T-shirt evidence excluded, he walked out of prison a free man.

It was never determined exactly how the shirt came to be in Gwen's car, nor how it came to have traces of Gwen's blood on it. Tessa couldn't prove who'd placed it there, if anyone. Perhaps the boys had moved it for some reason prior to taking the photographs? Anyone could have discovered Gwen's car prior to the police, just as the boys with the camera had, including the killer. Winters and his men had plausible deniability.

"Was it you?" Tessa asks now.

Winters keeps his eyes on the road, and there's only a slight pause before he shakes his head sharply. "No. I never found out who put it there, but it wasn't done on my instructions."

"But Oliver wanted you to say it was?"

He shakes his head again. "No. He wasn't interested in the shirt. He was talking about Billy Tyson."

Tessa stares. "Who the hell is Billy Tyson?"

She can see the tension in every line of his profile, the stiff way he holds his spine and his shoulders. But he finally answers the question.

"Billy Tyson was a serial rapist. He was arrested in 2005 after he was linked to the murder of a high school girl in Albany. He was going away for a long time. Once they had him, he offered up confessions to other crimes in exchange for a reduced sentence."

Tessa's stomach drops.

"Gwen Morley?" she asks, knowing already what the answer is going to be.

Winters nods. "Among others."

"That was two years after Oliver was sentenced," Tessa says, unable to keep the shocked condemnation out of her words.

Winters glances in Tessa's direction, but quickly pulls his eyes back on the road.

"Some of the stuff he confessed to was credible, but most of it was fantasy. Crimes he couldn't have committed because he wasn't even in the state at the time. High-profile cases. Some unsolved. Some not."

"When did you find out?" Tessa asks. She's not interested in his personal justifications.

Winters sighs. "I got a call while Tyson was in custody. I made the decision not to pursue it."

The only DNA found on Gwen's body never matched Oliver. The prosecution got around that by claiming Oliver's motive was jealousy. He stalked her, followed her as she left the bar with an unidentified male. Watched them while they were together. All he wanted was a chance with her but seeing Gwen with another man pushed him over the edge.

It was a weak argument that wouldn't have stood up in court if not for the T-shirt found in Gwen's car.

"You dismissed it?" Tessa says. "Just like that? You had a DNA profile, Winters. Didn't you compare it to Tyson?"

He looks like he might argue, and for a minute, Tessa hopes he does. She needs something other than Margot to focus on, and Winters's blatant abuse of authority is as good a target as any.

After a moment, he shakes his head. "No. We had our man. Even if the DNA had matched Tyson, it wouldn't have proven anything except that she left the bar with him. We knew there was an unidentified man. So what if it was Tyson? Barlow killed the Morley girl, and he was locked up. Exactly where he should be. Or so I believed. I didn't want to hear anything that would throw that into doubt. I buried it, never put the profile in the system."

His confession leaves Tessa with a desperate sense of loss. Oliver served fourteen years for Gwen Morley's murder. He might have served even more.

And for a dozen of those years, Winters knew there was another potential suspect, one who'd confessed to the crime, and he simply chose to ignore it.

A dozen years of a man's life, wasted, all because of another man's pride.

"Barlow said an ex-con got in touch with him a few weeks ago. An old cellmate of Tyson's. He'd seen the news reports about Barlow's lawsuit. Seen that Barlow lost the case."

Tessa had seen those same reports. The state of New York offered Oliver and his family two hundred fifty thousand dollars in reparations for wrongful conviction.

He sued for more. Thirty million dollars more.

His suit centered around the claim that the Bonham Police Department deliberately and knowingly pursued a prosecution against him without just cause.

The lawsuit was ongoing for months, and extensive interviews were conducted by the attorney general's office. Everyone even slightly involved in the case was held up to examination.

Oliver's lawyers had a solid case. And none of it made any difference.

In the end, the judge ruled that despite evidentiary screwups, there was no clear indication that the general thrust against Oliver was made in bad faith. He would not be receiving a thirty-million-dollar payout, but instead the smaller sum the state had already offered.

Tessa doubted it even covered his legal fees.

She saw the news reports too. And she saw his name on her phone when he called her not long after the decision. But Tessa was in the middle of wrapping up the final edits on her latest project.

She told herself she'd call him back. But she never did.

"The former cellmate passed on the claims Tyson had made to Barlow when they spoke. He told him how Tyson had laughed at the cops who couldn't sort the real stuff from the fake. How he'd laughed about another man taking the rap for Gwen Morley's rape and murder, even after he'd confessed."

Winters looks back at Tessa.

"A week later, Barlow called me and told me I had half an hour to record a video confession admitting I knew about Tyson. He said I'd regret it if I didn't."

She stares at him, an old man whose arrogance set all this in motion. The anger, the pure unfiltered anger Oliver must be carrying around, is breathtaking to consider.

And now he has her sister.

41

They're drawing closer to Fallbrook. Tessa can feel the seconds ticking away, each one an eternity.

She checks her phone, watches as another of the bars disappears. Another minute and she'll lose signal entirely.

Her thumb hovers. Soon she'll lose her chance.

"Don't," Winters warns, the word rough and forceful.

Tessa scrolls, then hits "Call."

"Not the police," she tells him, holding the phone to her ear. "I have to call her husband. He needs to know."

Winters is shaking his head, sure she's making a mistake, but Tessa can't live with herself if she doesn't at least try. Ben might not forgive her for dragging Margot into this mess. Tessa won't forgive herself, but he still deserves to know.

Winters doesn't slow the truck. Tessa hears the phone ring once, then the sound of a voice. Ben's voice, then the call drops.

"Damn," she mutters, feeling the panic pulsing at the edges of her every thought. "Damn, damn, damn!"

The bars are gone. She's got no signal.

Quickly, Tessa opens her text messages and types out words to her brother-in-law. She doesn't even know what she's typing, and he probably won't get the message anyway, but it's the best she can do.

She hits "Send" and hopes, somehow, some way, the message reaches him.

The turn for the old house is in front of them, and Winters slows the truck, then pulls onto the side of the road.

"What are you doing?" Tessa demands. They're so close. She needs to see her sister. Needs to see with her own eyes that Margot is safe.

Tessa can't give in to the thought that she might be anything else. It would leave her curled into a fetal position on the floor of Winters's truck.

Winters doesn't answer. He reaches down to the holster at his hip and pulls out a black pistol. He checks the slide, lets it fall back with a heavy metallic click, then tucks the gun back in place.

Tension ratchets up in every muscle of her body.

"What are you going to do with that?" she asks, her voice barely above a whisper.

The man who meets Tessa's gaze isn't a police officer anymore. He's a father who has had something precious stolen from him.

"Whatever I have to do."

Tessa's mantra begins to repeat in her mind. But it won't help her this time.

She *is* afraid. And this time, there *is* danger.

But she can't give in to the swirling chaos of fear. Margot needs her.

The truck moves forward again, creeping slowly into the woods. Winters scans the trees around them, but Tessa keeps her eyes firmly forward, desperate to see her sister.

Finally, the forest thins, and bits of sunlight dapple the ground in front of them. Tessa leans forward in her seat, gripping the dashboard and peering through the windshield.

The path opens, and Fallbrook stands in the distance, the same way it did when Tessa left it. It's too far away to make out anything other than the small white shape of Margot's car parked in front of the big house.

Did Tessa pass the car on the road when she was following Winters back into Snowden? Wouldn't she have noticed her sister, hands in a white-knuckled grip on the steering wheel, as a man on the run from the authorities, possibly holding a gun, forced her to drive where he directed her to go?

It's a useless question. If Tessa did pass them, she didn't notice. She can blame herself for that later. Right now, she focuses on what's in front of her.

"Can't you go any faster?" Tessa asks.

Winters has slowed the truck to a crawl. He doesn't answer.

They creep closer.

A distinctive sound rings out, and Tessa lets out a short scream. Winters slams on the brakes, and Tessa, already balanced on the front part of the seat, tumbles forward, catching herself before she falls onto the floorboards.

Her eyes swivel to the house, and there, on the balcony of the second floor, behind the crumbling railing, stands Oliver Barlow. He's holding a rifle in his hands.

Despite that, relief floods through Tessa, nearly bringing her to her knees.

Margot is standing by his side.

"He aimed for the ground in front of us," Winters says. With one hand on his gun, and the other on the handle of the door, his eyes remain fixed on Oliver.

"Stay in the truck," he says, then opens his door.

But Tessa can't allow Winters to steer the direction of this thing. Maybe once he had the objectivity to handle a situation like this. But Tessa saw the hot hatred in his eyes. Lloyd Winters is a man who's lost his only child.

She throws open the passenger-side door and nearly falls in her haste to head Winters off.

"Ollie," she calls loudly, keeping her hands above her head and earning a glare from Winters. "Ollie, I'm here. We did what you asked. No cops."

She's not planning her words but letting them tumble from her mouth. She prays she doesn't say the wrong thing.

"He's a cop," Oliver says, gesturing from the balcony above them to the man at Tessa's side. His voice is distant, too distant. She needs to get closer.

She risks a glance at Winters. His right hand is splayed, too near his waistband for Tessa's comfort.

"Not after this," she yells. *Just keep him talking.* "He'll be forced out. Once people know what he's done, he'll never have a badge again."

"Is that supposed to make me feel better, Tessa?" Oliver shouts. Tessa keeps her hands up and takes a few slow steps forward.

She's close enough now to see him more clearly. He doesn't look angry. Not in the way she'd expect a man holding another person at gunpoint to be.

If anything, he looks tired.

Tessa drinks in the sight of Margot, and her pulse jumps.

Her sister's wide eyes are focused on the railing in front of her, and she's backed as far away from the edge as she can while Oliver grips her by the arm.

She's frozen in fear.

Not of the man next to her. Not of the gun in his hand.

Margot is terrified of heights.

Eyes firmly on her sister, Tessa takes a few more steps forward.

"That's far enough," Ollie shouts, adjusting the rifle to point in Tessa's direction.

She stops, hardly daring to move a muscle. "Why are you doing this, Ollie?" she asks, fighting for a casual tone.

Something moves in Tessa's peripheral vision, and Oliver swivels the barrel of the gun to point to Winters this time. He's standing a few paces behind her, staring holes into Barlow's form. Glancing at him, Tessa sees in Winters all the anger she expected to see in Oliver. The police chief is a tightly coiled spring, his fingers twitching with the urge to get to Barlow.

"We're both here. Winters stole your life, and I abandoned you after you got it back. We're right here, right in front of you," Tessa says. Anything, anything to keep him talking. If Winters has his way, he'll rush the house, gun blazing. There's no predicting what might happen after that.

Margot is holding on by a thread. Tessa has only one goal. To get her sister's feet safely on solid ground. Nothing else matters. Not Barlow or the injustices he's been dealt. Not Valerie Winters. And, least of all, Lloyd Winters's desire for blood.

Margot. Feet. Ground.

Tessa's new mantra.

"But Ollie, my sister has nothing to do with any of this. You know that."

He grips Margot's arm tighter. Tessa's hands clench as Margot's face blanches and she struggles to move farther back. Ollie won't let her.

"You wouldn't take my calls, Tessa," he says, sounding exhausted, as if that should excuse kidnapping her twin sister. "I thought you were my friend."

Margot whimpers, and Tessa can feel the heat of Winters's impatience growing at her back.

"I'm sorry, Ollie. I've been a terrible friend. I know that." She holds her palms out wider.

"I was never anything but a story to you, was I? I made you famous, and you had no more use for me after that."

"I'm sorry," she says again. "So sorry, Oliver. And you're right. I did the story, then I closed the book and moved on. I wasn't there for you when you needed me. Let me fix that."

He barks out a harsh laugh. "Fix it? How are you gonna do that, Tessa? Are you going to bring my mother back from the dead? Are you going to turn back time and stop my father from putting a gun in his mouth?"

Tessa's jaw drops.

"They didn't release that little piece of information to the press, did they? They took everything from me, Tessa. Everything! You don't know how that feels. How it feels to lose the only thing in your life that matters. Until now."

He's panting and Tessa can't take her eyes off the barrel of the gun. How much more pressure would it take for Oliver to squeeze the trigger? How much more pressure can one man handle?

"You're right, Oliver," she says. "You're right about everything. What they did to you . . . what *we* did to you . . . it was wrong. I'm not a good friend. I'm not a good sister either. I'm not good at sticking it out when things get hard."

He stares at her. He still has Margot by the arm, but he's listening.

"Look at her, Ollie. Really look." Tessa's voice is calm, a calm she's manufactured from some unknown reservoir of desperation. "You remember, don't you? I told you about my sister, Margot. About the fall. Look at her face. She's petrified, Oliver, and not of you. Let her come down. You don't have to come down with her. I'll take her place if you want, but let my sister come down from there."

Time stops. Tessa watches, her heart in her throat, and for the briefest of moments, she thinks it's going to work.

Then the sound of an engine roaring up behind them pulls everyone's attention to the path that leads to the road.

Oliver raises the gun, and Margot begins to cry.

Tessa panics.

"No!" she cries. "No, Oliver, it's not the police, it's not! It's her husband, Ollie! Don't shoot!"

But he's raised the rifle to his shoulder. He's taking aim.

"No! Look at me!"

Ben's SUV is still barreling toward them. Tessa runs toward it, waving her arms at Ben.

"Stop!" she shouts. "Stop!"

But he doesn't stop. Not until the rifle rings out and bullets puncture Ben's front tires. The SUV swerves dangerously near Tessa and skids to a stop, its passenger side facing Fallbrook.

Tessa runs around the vehicle to Ben, who's already climbing out of the driver's side.

"Ben, no!" She grabs hold of his arm. He barely looks at her, his eyes trained on his wife.

"Let go of me," he growls and shakes her off.

She steps in front of him, trying to hold him back, as another shot rings out. The bullet hits the ground just yards away from them. Tessa and Ben both duck and take cover behind the passenger's side of the vehicle.

"Stay back!" Oliver shouts.

More shots fire, but they're different. Closer.

Tessa peeks over the hood of the SUV and sees Winters aiming in the direction of the balcony, pulling the trigger and taking large steps backward all the while.

Oliver ducks instinctively, but Margot is frozen in place. To Tessa's surprise, he reaches up for her hand and pulls her down next to him.

Winters is still firing.

"No!" Tessa shouts, running out from behind the cover of Ben's car. "Winters, don't shoot!"

Oliver is crouched in front of Margot, making the pair of them small.

Winters ignores Tessa and throws himself behind the wheel of his truck, then slams the door.

"What are you doing?" Tessa shouts as she pounds on his driver's-side window, but Winters doesn't look at her. His face is set in hard, determined lines, and he throws the truck into gear as Oliver's rifle comes up again.

Bullets slice through the air, spraying the ground around them. They puncture the hood of the moving truck. One of them shatters the windshield, but Tessa can only watch, aghast, as Lloyd Winters guns the vehicle and heads straight for Fallbrook.

Ben runs past her, and Tessa's frozen legs finally move. But neither of them can outrun a vehicle with the gas pedal on the floor.

Tessa watches in horror as Winters's truck slams into the corner of the front porch, annihilating one of the already crumbling columns and coming to rest against the other.

The entire house seems to shudder, then, in slow motion, to creak and groan. Something crashes inside the house, and the engine steams and hisses. The balcony floor that Oliver and Margot are standing on begins to tilt and slide.

"No!" Tessa shouts again, running full speed for the house.

Realizing what's about to happen, Oliver runs to the far side of the failing balcony and grasps the edge of the roof, struggles for a moment, and pulls himself up.

But Margot, Margot hesitates, and the floor beneath her continues to tilt and pull away from the exterior of the house.

"Hold on, Margot!" Tessa hears Ben shout.

Somewhere, somehow, his voice must have penetrated the haze of terror that has Margot in its grip. Seconds before the balcony tears away from the main house, she launches herself toward the gabled roof and wraps her hands around a decorative corbel.

The balcony gives way. Margot's feet dangle. Twenty feet of air separates her from the pile of rotting boards jutting out at odd angles below.

"Oliver!" Tessa shouts, running in Margot's direction. "Oliver, she's falling. Grab her hands, Ollie, please!"

Tessa struggles to clamber over the pile of deteriorated porch and balcony, her feet sliding from beneath her.

One of Margot's hands slips and falls away. The corbel begins to pull away from the house.

"Margot, just hold on!" Ben shouts, but his voice is coming from the wrong direction. Tessa looks wildly around. He's running away.

"Ben!" she shouts, but a cry from her sister pulls her attention back to the roof.

Suddenly, the corbel moves again, separating itself from the house by a good six inches. Margot screams. She's going to fall. She's going to fall, and Tessa can't stop it this time either.

Tessa crawls over boards and old plaster and nails, cutting her hands and opening a large gash on her leg, but she doesn't feel anything.

The corbel gives way.

But Margot stays where she is, screaming and sobbing, her legs swinging in the air. Oliver has one of her arms gripped in his, grasping it all the way to her elbow.

His face is straining, but he has her.

"Pull her up, Ollie," Tessa yells. "Please!"

Tessa's heart is in her throat. She can't move, she can't help. All she can do is hope he'll do the right thing.

He reaches out his other hand and, somehow, Margot finds the presence of mind to grasp it. He begins to pull her up, and Tessa thinks that maybe, just maybe, when this is all over, she might be able to breathe again.

Margot's arms are on the roof now, her shoulders even with the eave.

And a shot rings out.

Oliver scrambles backward, and Margot struggles to hold on. Her hands are slipping again.

Tessa whips her head around.

Winters. Winters is lining up to shoot again.

"Get out of the way!" Ben shouts. But he doesn't need to bother. Tessa is already moving, throwing her body over the pile of boards and barreling in Winters's direction.

"That's my sister, you son of a bitch," she shouts. "Don't fucking shoot!"

Winters doesn't even glance at her. He doesn't break his stance either, legs spread, arms outstretched, with both eyes open, aiming for Oliver Barlow on the rooftop.

The sound of an engine fills the air, and another crash happens at Tessa's back. She doesn't have time to look. She has to get to Winters.

She's closing the distance between them, but she's not fast enough to stop the pull of his trigger finger. If he shoots Barlow, Margot will fall. If Margot falls, Margot could die. Tessa can't let that happen.

But that's exactly what is happening, right in front of her, and she's helpless to stop it.

And suddenly, she's not alone.

Tessa is so focused on Winters she doesn't register the figure that appears at his back. Not until an old woman's cane cuts through the air, faster and harder than it should be possible for a woman in her eighties to swing it.

But swing it she does.

Deirdre Donnelly's cane smacks into Lloyd Winters's face with a loud crack. He never sees it coming. The gun falls to the ground at his feet. Both hands fly instinctively to his face, as blood leaks between his fingers from his newly broken nose.

But Tessa doesn't have time to thank the old woman. Ben is shouting, and Tessa turns back to Margot.

"I'll catch you," Ben is calling to her. "It's okay, Margot. Just let go. I swear to God, I. Will. Catch. You."

Her sister is still hanging from the eave of Fallbrook, but her hands are sliding closer to the edge.

Ben has rammed his SUV next to the house, pushing most of the debris out of the way, and driving over the rest. He's standing on the hood of the vehicle, with his hands outstretched. There's still empty air between Margot's feet and his hands, but he's there, reaching upward, waiting to catch her. Tessa knows, with every beat of her heart, Ben is not going to let her fall.

"You can divorce me if you want to, you can throw me out of our house, you can toss my golf clubs in the ocean. You can tell me you never want to see me again, but my God, Margot, you're going to have to tell me to my face. Let go now. I will catch you."

Tessa's muscles are tight, her breath raspy in her throat. She can't look away.

Margot lets go.

This time, when she falls, Ben is there to catch her.

Someone clears their throat, and Tessa turns to see the Donnelly sisters standing behind her, Deirdre leaning on her cane.

"The man with the gun, dear," Kitty says, gesturing toward the house.

Winters is gone.

"Jesus," Tessa cries, then runs toward the pile of debris that nearly blocks the front door.

"Top of the stairs," Deirdre calls. "There's access in the ceiling that opens into the attic, if the ladder is still usable. And be careful!"

Tessa squeezes past the mess cluttering the front of the house and falls through the nearly blocked front door Winters left open behind him.

Gunfire cuts through the air. It's coming from above her. But Oliver dropped his rifle when the balcony collapsed. Winters is shooting at an unarmed man.

He lied to her. He has no interest in bringing his daughter's body home to her mother. Or if he does, it's taken a back seat to his need for Oliver to pay for what he's done. Winters wants Oliver Barlow's blood.

Tessa takes the spiral stairs to the second floor, two at a time, refusing to think about the way they creak and groan beneath her. If they held Lloyd Winters, they'll hold her. She hopes.

At the top, a small set of stairs hangs down from a hatch in the ceiling. It leans alarmingly to one side, but Tessa doesn't stop.

She scrambles to the top as quickly as she can manage, ignoring the way the ladder swings beneath her. Pulling herself up, she looks around.

The roof slopes at the top of the house, what's left of it anyway. She can see the blue sky through the gaping holes where it's collapsed.

More shots ring out, louder now, and footsteps move across the roof, sending a shower of dust and dirt down from the rafters, giving her an idea of where Ollie and Winters are.

She moves closer to the lowest opening in the roof. She can crawl out behind them.

"And do what?" a small voice in her head cries. But she refuses to stop and listen.

The men are shouting at each other.

"You knew it wasn't me," she hears Oliver call. "You knew all along."

"So what?" Winters yells back. "So you served some time. I knew you had it in you, and I was right. You think I'm supposed to give a shit about your feelings?"

Tessa is on the roof now, watching as Winters stalks Oliver, who's taken cover behind a gabled section.

"Your daughter had a lot to say about you, Winters," Oliver calls, his words twisted with amusement. "She told me all about what a wonderful father you were. Before I killed her. How does that make you feel?"

"You bastard!" Winters rushes Barlow. His right foot collapses a section of roof beneath him, but he pulls it from the hole and charges forward, barely breaking stride. "You goddamn bastard!"

Winters levels his gun and fires, once, twice, *click, click.*

He tosses the gun aside. It spins across the roof and falls off the edge. Winters stands panting, his hands hanging loosely by his side like a raging bear.

He charges at Oliver again, but the other man is prepared to meet him. No guns, just two men trying to kill one another with their bare hands.

"Stop!" Tessa shouts. "Stop it!"

Neither of them listens. Shingles and boards give way beneath their feet, and the air is filled with the heavy thud of fists connecting with flesh.

Tessa moves closer, aware, as neither of the men seem to be, of the instability of the roof beneath them. She shouts again, but her words fall on deaf ears.

She casts around, searching for something hard and heavy. Anything she can use to break up the fight. There's nothing. Not unless she's willing to go back into the attic, and Tessa doesn't have that much time.

A choking, gasping sound pulls her gaze back to the struggle just yards away. Winters has his hands gripped around Oliver's throat. Ollie is taller, lean and sinewy from his years in prison, but Winters has him on brute strength and hatred.

His knuckles are white, and Oliver tries to pry them off, but Winters's grip doesn't ease.

"Stop it!" Tessa screams. "Winters, stop!"

Oliver's eyes are bulging, his face turning an alarming shade. Tessa rushes forward, determined to put herself between them, but Oliver changes tactic. All at once, he pushes forward with every bit of his weight.

Winters's grip doesn't loosen, but he stumbles backward, thrown by the other man's momentum. Oliver continues, barreling into Winters and keeping him off balance. Two pairs of feet shuffle across the roof, in a strange and awkward dance, but Oliver takes the lead. He pushes

Winters farther, shoving himself at the other man, even while his neck is closed in Winters's iron grip.

"No, no, no!" Tessa chants. With a sudden burst of clarity, Oliver's intention is clear. "No!" she shouts. She runs forward, but there's nothing she can do.

Winters, unaware and uncaring of what waits behind him, is focused only on choking the life out of the man who killed his daughter. Tessa reaches out. Her fingers touch nothing but air. With one final twist of his body, Oliver turns and takes the two of them crashing through the colored glass skylight that sits above Fallbrook's entryway.

Tessa's breath leaves her in a great and final whoosh at the sound of breaking glass and the impact of a body hitting the floor two stories below.

Hand still outstretched, Tessa is on her knees. She can't look. Yet she can't stop herself.

She opens her eyes, scoots forward.

Lloyd Winters's body is splayed across the entryway floor, one of his legs and his neck twisted at unnatural angles. Broken, rotting floorboards point upward at the sky where his weight cracked them in half.

But she doesn't have time to focus on the horror below. Another hand, belonging to another man, is gripping the frame of the skylight, broken glass cutting into his palm and fingers.

With a sharp intake of breath, Tessa reaches down and grasps Oliver, wrapping her hand around his arm the way he'd done for her sister.

"I've got you," she says, her heart beating in her throat.

He turns his face upward and meets her eyes. There's panic in his, a panic that Tessa has seen in the mirror.

"I've got you," she says, trying to keep him calm. "Reach up with your other hand."

But blood is sliding down his arm, working its way between their skin. Slick, slippery blood they have no way to stanch, and sweat runs down Tessa's face.

Oliver's arm slips a notch and she grips it tighter, willing her strength to hold.

This man, no matter what else he might have done, knelt in front of Margot when bullets were coming in their direction. She can't forget that. She won't.

His arm slips farther, and Oliver drops six inches more. She moves her other hand to help hold him, bracing herself as best she can.

"Please, Ollie, your other hand." Her voice is tight. She won't lose him.

But when he meets her eyes again, there's no more panic. A calm has settled on him, and he gives her a sad half smile.

"You were right, Tessa," he says in a preternaturally tranquil voice.

"Give me your hand," she pushes out through clenched teeth. "Do it, Ollie."

Images flash across her mind. She's sitting in Donna Barlow's living room, promising she'll try to help her son. She's hugging her as she cries. She's standing in the back row at the woman's funeral, quiet tears on her face.

She will not let him fall. She will not let another person fall.

Blood is pouring now, loosening her hold. It's sliding down her arm, pooling around her wrist, dripping from between her clenched fingers.

"It was a nice spot," Oliver says. Tessa can't process the words through her single-minded focus.

"Your other hand," she cries.

"A peaceful spot. Halcyon was the word you were searching for. I looked it up."

"Shut up, Oliver, and give me your hand."

He's slipping.

"Halcyon," he says again. Then he closes his eyes.

And releases his grip.

42

Tessa stumbles back down the stairs, lost and hurting. She can't stop the feel of Oliver's fingers sliding through her own, then grasping at air as gravity takes him.

The same as Margot.

No, not the same. It's not the same.

But she can't make herself believe it.

Bodies sprawl across the floor. Two lives gone. Wasted and gone.

She doesn't go to them. Doesn't look.

She could see from the roof that Oliver was dead, a jagged board protruding from one side of his neck. It's not something she can bear to face up close. Eyes averted, she stumbles to the front door, to the small opening that's not blocked, and squeezes her way through.

The sun is blinding.

Was it so bright before? Tessa's eyes search out her sister, who's clutched in her husband's embrace.

Safe. Margot's safe.

Tessa holds tightly to that.

When her sister spots her, Margot leaves Ben and rushes to her.

"What the hell were you thinking, running up there after them? You could have gotten yourself killed, you idiot."

Tessa doesn't have anything to say to that. She's cold, and she's beginning to shake. Margot grabs her by the arms, and Tessa studies her face.

They look so much alike, aside from those crazy curls. The world's not always fair.

"I've always been jealous of your hair," she says softly. She's so tired. She just needs to sit down.

Margot stares at her, confusion clouding her eyes.

"I think Ben might be tired too," Tessa says, looking over Margot's shoulder.

Her sister turns in time to see her husband collapse.

———

The Donnelly sisters stay with Tessa and Ben while Margot runs to the cottage to call an ambulance.

Tessa helps Kitty hold pressure on the gunshot wound in Ben's side.

When the ambulance arrives, Deirdre insists Tessa go too.

"There's no room," Tessa says, backing away.

"She's in shock," Deirdre explains to the paramedics, one of whom jumps out and herds her to the open doors where they've loaded Ben on a stretcher.

"I'm not," Tessa insists.

"Stop arguing and get in," Margot shouts.

Tessa does.

She can see Kitty and Deirdre standing, framed with Fallbrook at their backs, then Margot's car pulls in between the sisters and the ambulance, blocking her view. The ambulance takes them away.

"Ben, I really need you not to die right now," she says, leaning her head back and closing her eyes.

The emergency crew works between them, and Tessa puts her trust in their hands.

"If you're going to confess your undying love, Tessa, I won't stop you," he says weakly, ending on a hissing gasp as an EMT does something at his side. "But I need you to know. Margot wasn't a second choice. She was the right choice."

Tessa smiles but doesn't open her eyes. "I know that, but if it makes you feel better to think I've been pining for you for years, by all means, go ahead. I'd hate to disappoint a man on his deathbed."

"We never would have worked, Tessa. Your bedside manner is terrible."

"Thank you, Ben," she says. The tears are running freely now, and Tessa's eyes burn with them. "Thank you for always being in the right place at the right time."

"Yeah, well, next time it would help if I didn't have to track my wife through her phone because the pair of you keep hanging up on me."

"I'll keep that in mind."

"Mr. Russell, this might hurt," the EMT says.

When Ben finds his voice again, he has one more request.

"Tess, do me a favor? Could you steer clear of true stories for a while, at least if you're gonna get your sister involved? Try some fiction for once. Maybe a baseball movie. Everybody loves a good baseball movie."

Tessa smiles weakly. His voice almost takes away the slippery feel of blood dripping from Tessa's fingers as she grasps nothing but air. Almost drowns out the sound of Oliver's body crashing to the ground.

Ben is whisked away by emergency room attendants the moment they arrive at Westgate Memorial Hospital.

Tessa is taken to a different room where she's wrapped in a blanket, her feet elevated above her head.

"I'm fine," she insists, but the nurse continues to do what she does. Tessa gives up and waits.

The gash on her leg is treated and stitched. Her hands are inspected and cleaned, but Tessa's sure they're just wasting time now. No one will answer her questions.

Clad in a hospital gown after the staff insisted she remove her pants, Tessa waits some more, exhausted and impatient.

"You were right," Oliver whispers softly in her head. *"It was a nice spot. A peaceful spot.* Halcyon *was the word you were searching for."*

The curtain to her cubicle is pulled back with a clatter. Tessa sits up straighter.

"Ben's in surgery," Margot says. "They won't tell me anything else."

Tessa leans her head back against the crappy hospital pillow.

Margot looks around, spares a single glance for the uncomfortable-looking chair angled against the wall, then walks tiredly to the side of Tessa's bed.

"Scoot over," she says.

Tessa does and takes comfort in the warmth of her sister's body at her side.

They listen to the beeps of machinery and the rattle of hospital carts. The muffled voices in the hallway that proclaim the world hasn't changed at all.

"What do you think of when I say the word *halcyon*?" Tessa asks.

"Is this a quiz?" Margot asks, her eyelids still closed.

"No. No, it was just . . . something Oliver said. Before he . . ."

Margot opens her eyes. "I don't know. It's like . . . an ideal time from the past, isn't it? Halcyon days? I don't know, Tess. You're the one who went to college."

Tessa's brows knit together. "But what does it make you *think* of?"

Margot stares at the ceiling, blinking. "Before Dad died, I guess. When Granddad and Grandma Beth were both still alive. Sometime we were all together. All happy."

Tessa's heart beats at double time, and she sits up straight in the bed.

"Did you get the footage, Margot?"

"What?" Her sister shakes her head, confused by the sudden change in direction. "From your assistant? I don't know, I haven't checked my email. I was a little busy hanging from rooftops and trying to keep my husband from bleeding out."

"Where's your phone?" Tessa asks, ignoring the sarcasm. She jumps up from the bed and digs through her pile of dirty clothes. "Hurry."

"What's the matter with you?" her sister asks, leaning up on her elbows and glaring at her.

"Halcyon, Margot. A peaceful spot. Looking for some peace. *Halcyon*."

It's been right in front of her, this whole time.

43

KITTY

Something is there, right in front of her, but Kitty can't figure out what it is.

Red and blue lights flash through the trees from the police cars and ambulances that circle the big house.

Fallbrook is once again dealing with the dead.

Deirdre is still there giving her statement, but they've already questioned Kitty, not that she knows anything. One of the nice young men in uniform walked her home.

She sits on the porch, tired now, and watches for her sister to return. Aiden sits at her side.

The lights are bothering her, bringing back memories she wasn't looking for and doesn't want.

"Something's not right," she says in a quiet voice. The creak of her rocker is the only reply. Aiden is pretending not to hear.

"Aiden," she says, louder this time. "Something's not right."

He sighs. "Kitty cat, let it go."

She stares at him, surprised and hurt. "You sound like Dee. Don't treat me like a child."

"What do you want me to say, then?" he asks, but he's put out, irritated by her nagging.

"Something's not *right*."

Her rocker creaks faster, and she stares determinedly ahead. The lights keep flashing. Why do they keep flashing? Everyone is dead.

"Not everyone," a voice whispers in her ear. She turns her face away from Aiden and stares at the figure by her side.

"Who did she love, Kitty?" the figure asks. *"It wasn't Pynchon. That was just a little crush. Who did she really love?"*

"Mr. Pynchon," Kitty murmurs, but her voice is weak. Unsure. "She did."

"And?"

"Aiden, and me, and Mam."

The ghost at her side pulls a face.

"Ghosts shouldn't pout," Kitty says. She turns her face forward, her mouth set in stubborn lines.

"Let it go, Kitty," Aiden begs.

"Am I so forgettable?" the voice murmurs in her other ear. Kitty swats at it like a fly.

"Go away. You're dead," she says.

"Oh yes, I'm dead. But she still loved me best."

"Stop it!" Kitty shouts, but that hated laughter fills her ears. She holds up her hands, presses them to her head. "Stop it, I said."

"You know exactly what happened, Kitty. You don't have to ask. You know what happened. Because you saw."

The blood. Blood on someone's face and hands. Blood dripping down like tears, and a blank, hollow space behind her eyes.

Cora.

Standing in the entryway.

Cora.

Whom Deirdre loved the best.

Cora.

The hatchet falling from her hands.

It was Cora who swung the little ax. Cora who took their lives.

Tears cloud her vision, and colors swirl together. The green of the trees blends with the blood red in her memories, until a murky fog is all that remains.

Out of the fog comes a hand. A pale, shaky hand. The hand of a girl who grasps the handle of a fallen bloodied ax.

"No," Kitty cries. "No."

"Shh. Shh, now. What's all this?" Deirdre is here now. Deirdre. Her sister. Hers.

Kitty looks up at her with tears and fear pouring from her eyes.

"Cora killed them, Dee. Cora killed them all."

Her sister's outline wavers as more tears form, and Kitty's chest heaves in great, earth-shaking sobs. But Deirdre's arms come around her and hold her tight while she cries.

"I know," her sister whispers. "It's okay. I know."

"Then tell me the truth!" Kitty shouts, jumping from the chair and wrenching out of her sister's embrace. She stares at Deirdre's pale face, so old now. Old and incredibly sad.

"Tell me the truth," Kitty pants. "Deirdre, I need to know. Did I . . . did I reach down and pick it up? The hatchet was there, then someone picked it up! I saw it! Did I do it, Dee? Did I kill Cora? *Did I?*"

Deirdre's eyes close slowly, and her shoulders slump. She looks small suddenly. Small in a way she's never looked to Kitty before.

A woman with a lifetime of secrets carried on her back.

44

TESSA

"You can't go *now*," Margot insists. "We have two dead men lying in the middle of a house we own. The police are probably already on their way to question us."

They've watched the footage together. It took a while to find the right file, then there it was. Margot was right all along.

"Stall them," Tessa says. "Can I borrow your pants?"

"No!" Margot shouts.

"Margot! I can't walk out of here in these." She holds up her shredded, bloodstained trousers. "Please?"

Margot sighs and begins unbuttoning her jeans.

"Not a word about them being loose on you," she says. "I own a bakery, remember."

Tessa kisses her sister on the cheek and hands over her own pants to exchange.

"You look beautiful, have I told you that?"

"Don't suck up. It's gross."

Tessa bites her lip. "There's one more thing."

Margot glares at her.

"I need to borrow your car."

After a few choice words, Margot gives up her keys in return for the keys to Tessa's car, which is still parked at Bracknell Lodge.

"Thank you." Tessa pulls her sister into a quick hug.

"You need a shower," Margot says, but her arms are tight as she returns the embrace. "For the record," she continues, "this is a bad idea. Let the police handle it. Or at least wait until I can go with you. You don't know what you might find."

Tessa hesitates.

She knows what she thinks she'll find.

Valerie Winters's body.

"I have to be sure," Tessa says.

She's heading toward the emergency room exit when she spots two uniformed officers speaking with a man in scrubs seated behind the intake counter.

Quickly, Tessa ducks around the corner.

"You're not supposed to be here," a nurse says behind her.

"Hi!" Tessa replies brightly. Too brightly, by the suspicious way the nurse angles away from her. She dials it back. "Maybe you can help me. My brother-in-law was brought in earlier."

From the corner of her eye, Tessa sees the man in scrubs stand. He walks from behind the desk, then leads the two officers in the direction of Tessa's hallway.

She turns her body awkwardly so that her back is facing the police as they pass.

"Ma'am, you'll have to check with the medical receptionist at the main desk."

"Oh, is that not where I am?" Tessa asks as she tucks a strand of hair behind her ear, using her hand to shield her face from the people passing by.

"Uh, no," the nurse says slowly. She holds out an arm, ushers Tessa out of the hallway, and directs her to the information desk.

"Thank you so much," Tessa says, then turns and walks out of the double sliding exit doors that lead into the parking lot.

"Ma'am, that's not where you need—"

But Tessa doesn't look back.

———

In borrowed clothes and a borrowed car, Tessa speeds northeast.

She eases off the gas when she realizes she's twenty miles over the posted limit.

Lake Cormere is less than an hour away.

Oliver could have taken Valerie Winters anywhere in the northeast. Anywhere within a few days' drive. But he chose Lake Cormere.

She's sure of it.

Oliver was relaxed that day. It was a good day. He had bad ones, when the injustice of it all had rubbed him raw, and the magnitude of what he'd lost made his voice harsh and his eyes dark.

The bad days filled the editing room with hours of tough, emotional footage. The good days were easier. The days when his humor came through, and his heart.

"It's easy to see why you believed him," Margot murmured as they watched together. "Why the world believed him. Have you changed your mind?"

Tessa frowned. "I was convinced he was innocent of Gwen Morley's murder. The evidence just wasn't there. Winters even admitted there was another suspect. But Oliver confessed to killing Valerie." She shakes her head. "It puts everything in doubt."

"This wasn't in the series," Margot said, gesturing to the screen.

"You've seen it?" Tessa couldn't hide her surprise.

"Of course I've seen it. I've seen all your work. What kind of sister do you think I am?"

A short bark of laughter burst from Tessa's mouth, and Margot shrugged, a small smile on her face.

From the little screen on her phone, they watched as Tessa asked about prison life.

"How do you keep it from getting to you, Oliver?"

His mouth twisted a little and one shoulder came up. "Oh, you know. It does, sometimes. Lots of times, I guess. But when it gets too bad you just have to go somewhere else. You know what I mean?"

"Like meditation?" Tessa asked.

"No," he laughed. "Nothing fancy like that. No woo-woo in prison, Ms. Shepherd. That's a good way to get your ass kicked. Pardon my language."

"So what do you do?"

"You know," he said with another little shrug and a half smile. "You just lie on your bunk, like you're sleeping. You close your eyes and think about a time or a place when things were good. Or at least, not so bad. Someplace peaceful."

"Ollie, I hate to say it, but that sounds a lot like meditation to me." Her recorded voice was amused, and Tessa can remember how it felt to sit across from the man, fascinated by the humanity in his eyes that even a prison-issued uniform couldn't strip away.

"No," he said, laughing again. "It's just . . . thinking. Everybody does it sometimes. You don't have a place in your mind you go when things get hard?"

There was a pause. Tessa couldn't remember exactly what she was thinking at that moment on that day, but she had an idea what she was going to say next.

"Yeah, I guess I do, now that you mention it."

"You can picture it?" Oliver asked. He looked interested, like a friend would be. Like they weren't in a prison with concrete walls but seated across from each other at his mother's kitchen table.

"It's a lake," Tessa said. "My grandparents' cabin on Lake Cormere."

"What's it smell like?"

Tessa laughed, but Ollie nodded his head with a smile. "It sounds stupid, but if I think about a smell, it takes me back every time."

Tessa paused, thinking. "I don't know. It always smelled vaguely like bait. And campfire. Hot dogs. Bug spray. And that smell that fireworks leave behind."

Another beat of silence followed.

"There it is," Oliver said, nodding at Tessa, hidden somewhere behind the camera. "It worked. I can see it on your face."

"You're right. I haven't thought of that place in a long time."

"You looked peaceful." Oliver's expression was wistful, but proud almost, to have shared something good with her.

"That was a special place. One of those memories you wish you could bottle and take with you. There's a term for it . . ." Tessa paused. "It's on the tip of my tongue."

The rattle of keys came from somewhere behind them, and Oliver sat up straighter in his chair.

"Time's up, Barlow," a bored voice said.

The smile was gone, but Oliver spared Tessa another glance. "I'll look it up for you," he offered with a wink. "For next time."

"You don't have to do that, Ollie," she said.

He stood, and the camera caught the glint and rattle of handcuffs on his wrists before he moved out of the frame.

"No big deal, Ms. Shepherd. I've got nothing but time."

They never spoke of it again. Not that Tessa can recall. Not until that moment before his bloody hand let go of hers and he plunged to his death.

Halcyon.

It wouldn't have been hard for Oliver to find the address of the Ashwoods' cabin. A public records search would have pulled it up.

It was a nice spot. A peaceful spot.

When Tessa pulls up the long driveway that takes her to her grandparents' cabin, she's struck by the similarities to Fallbrook. Not the house. The cabin on the lake is simple and small, built of logs culled from the nearby forest. But the sense of isolation is the same.

Every memory associated with this place is good, and Tessa has a flash of anger that Oliver has tainted that.

She hopes she's wrong, but she's not.

Tessa parks the car and walks slowly toward the cabin. Lined by trees on both sides, Lake Cormere glistens behind it, water as smooth as glass, a shining reflection of the sky above.

She tries the door first, expecting to find it locked, and isn't disappointed. She rises on her tiptoes, feeling blindly for the key Granddad always kept on the ledge above the door.

Her fingers come away with nothing but dust and a few spiderwebs.

Tessa sighs and glances around.

Several hours away, there's a key hanging in her mother's cupboard, clearly labeled, Tessa is certain.

Still, she didn't come all this way to stop now. Tessa moves to the nearest window. She saw a jacket tossed in the back seat of Margot's car. She can wrap it around her elbow to break the glass if she needs to.

The jacket looked expensive. Margot will not be pleased.

Tessa tries to push the window frame up first, just so she can say she tried.

As she expected, it's locked.

She cups her hands on either side of her face and leans forward to peer through the glass.

Tessa screams and jumps back, her heartbeat thumping as blood pulses through her veins.

A face peers back at her from inside the cabin.

The face of Valerie Winters.

45

Valerie moves around the kitchen inside the cabin, quiet in socks and sweatpants, as she prepares two cups of tea.

The young woman's familiarity with the place is unnerving. Two tangential parts of Tessa's life she never expected to overlap.

The cups rattle against each other when Valerie takes them from the cupboard. Her hands are shaking, despite an outward mask of calm.

When she unlocked the dead bolt and held the front door open for Tessa, she asked only one question. "It's all over, then?"

She doesn't seem like a prisoner. And she's certainly not a murder victim.

"The world thinks you're dead," Tessa says in a hoarse whisper. "Your family thinks you're dead."

Valerie's hands grow still, the tea bag suspended midair, but she doesn't turn around.

She doesn't know about her father is the thought running through Tessa's mind. She's going to have to tell this woman her father's dead.

How do you find words to express something like that?

"I'm sorry, there's no milk," Valerie apologizes. She carries two cups in one hand and Grandma Beth's sugar bowl in the other. Her movements are as restrained as her words, and Tessa wonders if she's always this way or if it's a reaction to the circumstances.

"Does anyone know yet?" Valerie asks.

Tessa doesn't pick up her cup. She simply stares at the woman whose death was a weight she was prepared to carry for the rest of her life.

"I'm not going to try to hurt you if you say no," Valerie says with a small smile. "I'm just asking in case we're about to be overrun with police and reporters."

"No," Tessa whispers. "I mean, yes. My sister. She knows I'm here, but no one else."

Valerie's shoulders relax a little. "Then we have some time." She stirs a spoonful of sugar into her tea. "Does Oliver know you're here?" she asks.

Tessa hesitates. "Valerie . . . I'm not sure how to tell you . . . Oliver . . . Oliver's dead."

The woman closes her eyes, and her shoulders pull in as if to protect herself. She's shaking, but she holds herself so tightly, all her focus turned inward. From nowhere, Valerie's hand shoots out and slams onto the kitchen table, making the cups rattle. Tessa flinches, pulling back in her chair.

"I'm sorry," she says quietly. "I'm sorry." She wraps both her arms around herself, tucking her hands beneath her arms, and ducks her head, as if she's done something terribly bad.

She struggles to compose herself.

"I told him," she murmurs in a wavering voice, almost to herself. "I told him this was going to happen. I *warned* him to be careful."

Her words answer one question. Valerie Winters isn't here under duress.

"Was it my father?" Her head comes up and she spits the word *father* like it's something slimy and foul. "Did my father kill him?"

Tessa shakes her head. "No . . . not exactly. Valerie, I'm afraid . . . your father is dead too."

Valerie stares at Tessa. Other than a slight widening of her eyes, she has no reaction.

None at all.

"What happened?" she asks quietly.

It takes much less time than Tessa feels it should to share the events of the previous day with the woman the world presumes is dead.

By the time Tessa is finished, Valerie has gathered her emotions and safely hidden them away in whatever quiet place she keeps such things. Tessa may as well be speaking about the weather for all the reaction she can see on Valerie's face.

It's unsettling.

Valerie stands and walks to the kitchen counter without a word. She empties her untouched tea into the sink and carefully rinses the cup.

"I guess you're wondering what my part is in all of this."

Tessa doesn't bother to deny it. "Only if you want to tell me," she says.

Valerie turns and gives her a small smile. "Oliver said you were like that. Easy to talk to. Easy to like."

"He kidnapped my sister," Tessa reminds her. "He held her at gunpoint. I'm not sure that's how you treat someone you like."

Valerie leans her back against the counter and studies Tessa, her face settling into a sad sort of resignation.

"This is a beautiful place." She glances around, and her eyes pause on the view from the kitchen window. "Let's go outside," Valerie says suddenly, standing up straight. "I want to sit by the water one more time before it all ends."

So with the sun setting on the lake that gave Tessa the best and brightest pieces of her childhood, the two women sit side by side in the grass, and Valerie Winters tells her story.

"The first thing you need to know, Tessa, is that my father wasn't the man the world thought he was. I was seven years old before I truly understood that."

Valerie stares intensely at Tessa for a moment, as if she's weighing the impact of her words, then she turns forward to gaze at the water rippling over the surface of the lake.

"I don't know why he bought that stupid camper," Valerie says. "We weren't particularly outdoorsy and had certainly never gone on a family camping trip before, but there it was in the driveway one day after school."

A faint approximation of a smile flits across Valerie's features, there one moment, then gone the next.

"I was over-the-moon excited, as only a second grader can be. We took it out for the first time that weekend, to the Hazel Crest campgrounds. It was thirty minutes away from home, but it may as well have been another planet."

Valerie frowns. "For some reason, in my child's mind, I thought that the . . . the specialness of that day would keep everything else at bay. That it would protect my mother and me, like a magic bubble."

Valerie squints out over the horizon, and shrugs. "I was wrong, though. I dropped the last hot dog into the fire by accident. It's strange, the things that stick in your mind."

She shakes off whatever vision she's replaying and continues in her quiet, controlled voice. "My father lost his temper, and Mom stepped between us. She didn't always, but I remember that night she did, and my father turned on her. I suppose I should have been grateful to her, but I was so devastated. What had I expected? That a change of scenery and a little fresh air would turn my father into a different man?"

Tessa's heart breaks for the girl Valerie was. The little girl who deserved so much better.

"I ran," Valerie says. "I wasn't trying to escape. Not really. But sobs were building up inside, and I knew I couldn't let my father hear them. Tears only made things worse. So I ran into the woods, as far and fast as I could. Until I was lost. Or hoped I was. But then I burst upon another campsite."

The ghost of a smile is back. "The first time I met Oliver, he was kind to me. He and his brothers were camping at Hazel Crest too. The Barlow family had a bad reputation, and they'd had plenty of run-ins with my father and his men, but I didn't know that then. I just knew that there was a kind man who knelt in front of me and wiped away my tears."

Tessa can picture it, and that image helps her to bring back into focus the Ollie she thought she'd known.

"He held my hand, and he made me feel safe, and then he helped me find my way back to my parents. I didn't really want to go back, but I didn't want him to let go of my hand even more, so we went. And when we arrived, Ollie saw firsthand what kind of man Lloyd Winters really was."

Tessa sucks in a breath. "He never . . . he never told me this," she says, thinking of the hours of conversations she and Oliver had shared. He'd talked about the Bonham PD being out to get him, but Tessa always assumed that was because of his brothers' reputations. An assumption that Ollie never bothered to correct. "Why didn't he say something?"

A pained look crosses Valerie's face. "We were coming through the woods when we heard the sounds of my father hitting my mom. She was trying to stay quiet, but she couldn't hold back the cries of pain completely. I realized then what I'd done by bringing a stranger to witness this, and I stopped and pulled on his hand. *'You can't tell,'* I whispered to him, terrified. *'Please don't tell. If anyone finds out, he'll kill us.'*"

Valerie lets out a pent-up breath, but the tension still crackles in the air between the women.

"Oliver didn't want to go. He stood there, stock-still, staring at my father. Finally, finally, he promised. He promised me he wouldn't tell anyone. I ran back to the camper, but when I turned around, my father had stopped beating my mom. He was staring at the trees Ollie had disappeared into. I believe he saw Oliver that day. He saw him, and he knew his dirty little secret wasn't a secret anymore."

"Gwen Morley was murdered the summer after that," Valerie says quietly. "I didn't understand at the time. Not really. It wasn't until your documentary came out that I put it all together."

Valerie sits up and crosses her legs. She brushes off the palms of her hands and continues to stare out at the water.

"Growing up like that, I guess in some ways it made me strong. No matter how scary something was, it didn't compare to living in the middle of that. The careful way we were, with our actions and our words. Always so careful. *You don't want to upset your father, Valerie,*' was my mother's favorite phrase."

She sighs. "I confronted him. My father. Just once. It was the hardest thing I've ever done. He laughed at me, and I went away feeling as small and helpless as I had as a child. But I couldn't forget the things he said. Things he admitted, because he knew I'd never have the nerve to go public."

She pulls a blade of grass from the ground and runs it gently through her fingers.

"He told me about another suspect, a guy named Billy Tyson, who'd confessed to the crime. How he'd buried it. And he laughed. Laughed and admitted he was the one who planted that evidence in the first place, not the deputies. He was there for the search of Ollie's room. He saw his chance when they found the car, and he took it, then let his men take the blame. Neither one of them are in law enforcement anymore. Two more victims of his personal vendetta."

She turns and meets Tessa's eyes.

"Because it *was* personal. That's the one piece you didn't have. That no one had. People in Bonham believed my father acted in good faith. They knew what Oliver's brothers were like. They never saw Ollie as any different. They stood by their chief, one town against the world, because the world didn't *understand*, and they believed they did."

She turns away again, curling the piece of grass around her finger, then straightening it again.

"I should have spoken up. I should have told everyone the truth. Gone on the news and spilled my father's secrets but . . . he was right. I wasn't strong enough."

She flicks the blade of grass away, and it flutters through the air before it lands.

"It weighed on me, though. This sense that I was responsible for everything that happened."

"No," Tessa says. "Valerie, you were a child."

But Valerie continues as if she doesn't hear.

"It got easier when Oliver was released. A little. I wanted to believe everything was going to be all right then. He was free, and my father was under a cloud of suspicion. Things should have gotten better."

Tessa told herself the same thing.

"I became a little obsessed, to be honest. I followed him sometimes. Oliver. Parked on the road outside his house. I know how creepy that sounds, but I just wanted . . . I *needed* to see that he was okay. Happy. To know I hadn't completely ruined his life."

She shakes her head. "But there's no such thing as happily ever after. I knew about the lawsuit. It was in the papers. It sounded like a crazy amount of money. Thirty million?

"But I found out later his parents' house had been mortgaged three times, all to try and get him out of prison. The settlement the state offered wasn't going to save the house. Not after his dad lost his job. And Ollie's wife? They'd only been married a few months when he was arrested. She was pregnant. His twins were born while he was in jail. She'd had a boyfriend for years that no one told him about."

Some of this Tessa knows already, but she's ashamed of what she doesn't. She was supposed to be his friend, but she moved on and left Oliver alone to deal with the aftermath of the storm.

"Things were circling the drain, but winning that lawsuit could have helped. I was devastated when he lost. I know it doesn't make sense, but I felt like I'd personally let him down. Again. He found me across the street from his house, sobbing in my car like a baby. *'Hey, kid,'* he said, knocking on the window. *'Are you okay?'*"

Valerie runs her hands over her eyes, then pushes her hair back from her face.

"Everything came pouring out. Everything. He didn't remember me at first, and still, I was surprised by how kind he was. I guess I shouldn't have been. In the end, he didn't rage about the things I'd told him. All he cared about was making sure I didn't blame myself. He was a good person."

Her voice drops to nearly a whisper, and for the first time, Tessa can hear tears forming behind Valerie's words.

"I think Ollie could have weathered losing his wife, losing his kids, losing his mom the way he did. Losing fourteen years of his life only for people in Bonham to treat him like a pariah. Losing the lawsuit. His dad losing his job. The bank taking his parents' house. It was *so much*. So much loss for such a simple man. And I still think he'd have come through it in the end. But his father's suicide tipped him over the edge."

Valerie's face is calm again, her words stripped of the emotion she let slip out before.

"I gave him my number that day he found me in the car outside his house, but I never expected him to call. But he did, a few weeks later, and when I answered the phone, I knew something, I knew *everything* was wrong. Ollie found his father's body. And it broke him. He had nothing left to lose."

A shiver courses down Tessa's arms, and her heart hurts for the man she turned her back on.

"He called to say goodbye. He'd given up. But he . . ."

Valerie's voice breaks. She pulls in a shaky breath before she can go on. "He wanted to make sure I didn't blame myself for what he was going to do."

Valerie pauses to compose herself. Tessa wishes she could give some comfort to the self-contained young woman, but there are no words that will help, and she can sense that a physical touch, no matter how well-meaning, won't be welcome.

Instead, she sits with her, and she waits.

Eventually, Valerie continues.

"Everything that came after, all this—" She lifts her hands, then lets them fall. "This is all my fault. I kept him on the phone, and I jumped in my car. I sped toward his father's house. I wouldn't give him what he wanted. I told him over and over, *'Don't do this, Ollie. I can't live with the guilt. Don't do this to me.'*

"And he was so empty, so hollow and lost, that I was able to fill him up again. I filled him with my own anger. Years and years of anger at the man who stole my childhood as effortlessly and as thoughtlessly as he stole Oliver's life. I gave him a new purpose. A new reason to keep going.

"I infected him with my hate. I *used* him."

The air is thick with Valerie's remorse, and the tears finally come. She keeps going, fighting through them, and Tessa can feel her own begin to fall.

"I used Oliver for my own revenge. It was my idea. All my idea. Ollie told my father it was a cellmate who'd contacted him, but that was a cover story. It was all me. I wanted my father *destroyed.* I wanted the whole world watching while his sins were laid bare. To see him playact the grieving father before I brought it crashing down around him. I wanted justice for Ollie, but I wanted it for me more."

Valerie swipes her hand across her cheeks, pushing away the tears she's shed.

"I'm sorry about involving you. I didn't plan that. Everything just spiraled out of control. Ollie felt like you'd betrayed him. Said you'd be there to stand by him. Claimed you were his friend. He tried to call you first, that day, when he was planning to kill himself."

"And I didn't answer," Tessa finishes for her, regret in every syllable. "I hadn't taken his calls for months. When he needed me, I wasn't there for him."

"That's why he chose this place. Why he dropped your name into the videos. He knew you wouldn't have the answers the police were looking for. How could you? But he wanted you to know what it was like to be suspected by the whole world, to be vilified for something you had no control over. To have something you loved taken from you."

"Margot," Tessa whispers, taking the blow to her heart. "That's why he went after Margot."

"The last time Oliver and I spoke . . . he'd gone off the rails. My hatred ignited his, reminding him of everything he'd lost, and it . . . it burned away the man he used to be. *I* did that to him. And he took it out on you. I put you and your family at risk. I'm so, so sorry, Tessa. I never meant for that to happen."

But Tessa can still see him, shielding Margot from Winters's bullets. Grasping her by the arm to keep her from falling.

"He was still in there, Valerie," Tessa says. It's all she has to give. "He was still a good man. When it mattered most."

Valerie needs to believe that. And maybe Tessa does too.

Whether it's an effect of Tessa's words, or a coping mechanism of her own, Valerie summons the restrained calm that seems to define her.

"Well, it's done now. It's over." She stands and watches as the final rays of sun wink out over the horizon. "I sent the last video to the press an hour ago, right after you arrived."

Then Valerie turns and walks slowly back to the cabin, leaving Tessa alone in the grass.

46

CORA

A violin is crying somewhere above, and the baby wails her own discordant notes.

The kitchen is full of shouting, and the sounds are scratching inside Cora's mind. Her stepmother's voice, her little brother's cries. The baby upstairs, and always, above it all, the violin, rising to a crescendo that can't be stopped.

"You can't send them away," Peter cries again and again. "Please. Please!" Tears are coursing down his face, and he's too young. He doesn't know. No one cares if the world isn't fair.

"Let go of me," Helena says. "That's enough, Peter. It's done, and there's nothing you can do about it. Accept it."

But he doesn't know how.

Cora sits, still and silent, paralyzed by the scratching in her mind. The chaos swirls around her, flowing like ocean waves, beating them all against the rocks.

"But you can't! You can't! Cora, tell her. Tell her, Cora!"

Peter has cracked wide open, and all he's held inside pours out of him, only to float away on the wind. But Cora has broken inward, crushed without a sound.

She doesn't answer him. He shakes her by the shoulder, but she doesn't look at him, her sweet, too serious little brother. The baby they've raised who never knew his mother.

They were all his mother. All but Helena.

And the baby upstairs? Who will mother her?

She cries out, plaintive baby wails, but only the violin answers.

"Please don't send them away! Please, Mother, please!"

Cora swings her head, and her eyes find her brother now, clinging and begging at Helena's skirt. His words cut her, and steal her breath.

She rises to grab him to her. To shake him by the arms and shout, *"She's not your mother, you little fool. She never will be!"*

But her horror is dwarfed by the disgust on the second Mrs. Cooke's face.

"Never call me that!"

Her face is contorted, and the flush of victory has turned to something small and mean.

"Never!"

She pushes him.

Cora's hands reach to grasp him, to catch him before he falls and hug him tight.

"It's okay, Petey," she'll whisper, and carry him from the room, as he cries into her shoulder. "I won't leave you," she'll say. "I'll never leave you," until he cries himself to sleep and they wake together to face whatever pain the new day brings.

But there's nothing in her hands. Nothing but air. Cora can feel the loss of him, just out of reach, before she hears the sound of his skull connecting with the corner of the hearth.

The violin plays on.

They stand and they stare, Helena panting heavily as fear fills the room, taking the place of the shouts that were there just moments ago. But in Cora, there's nothing. What light she had dies with the spark in her brother's eyes.

Cora stands, hands against her ears, as the scratching fills her head.

Helena's mouth is moving. She's kneeling over his tiny, wasted body, nothing but muscles and bone now that will rot in a box in the ground. Useless to him, without his spark.

Cora can't hear Helena's words, can't care about the terror on her face when her stepmother shakes Peter. Slaps him and shouts at him, and the only response is blood pooling outward from the wound on his head.

And then the waves are pounding Cora against the rocks, pounding again and again, but it's her stepmother's fists. Cora's hands hang by her side. Hands that almost caught him but didn't.

"This is your fault!" Helena shouts, hitting at her, pounding, and her eyes are the eyes of a madwoman. "You did this! You!"

Cora's back comes up against the wall of the kitchen, next to the woodpile for the stove. The kitchen where her baby brother lies dead on the floor. The woman who took his life stands in front of her, spittle and hate flying from her lips.

Cora's hand reaches once again, but this time she grasps more than air.

Her fingers close tightly. Everything she has left inside, everything she could ever be, everything her brother will never be, rises up to fill her and give her strength.

Cora swings.

She swings and she connects and the terrible sound rends the air for the second time. The sound of a skull cracking while a baby cries and a violin plays.

Cora swings again. And again. She loses herself in the swings.

One. Two. Ten?

And then a gasp, and a clatter fills the air. Cora turns, her movements mechanical and stiff. Her face is a mask of blood that drips into her eyes. Her shirt, her hair, her hands.

Ruby comes into the room. Pretty Ruby. Cora stares at the red of her sister's lips, frozen in the circle of a silent scream, unable to escape.

Ruby turns to run, but Cora follows, running too. They haven't played this game in a long time, but Cora was always better at it.

Ruby looks back, her eyes wide with incomprehension at the monster that chases her. She stops. A mistake. And she opens her mouth to scream, but Cora swings again. And again. The scream dies in her sister's throat.

The baby cries. And the violin plays on.

She takes the steps slowly, dripping as she goes.

She opens the door to the schoolroom, where the tutor plays. Blood falls to the floor at her feet, but he doesn't turn around. His eyes are closed. Grace flows from the instrument to him and back again.

Cora tilts her head and watches. Listens. The baby cries again, but the sound is lost here, beneath the sound of the violin.

She can make the music stop. But there are terrible things waiting, and when the music stops, they'll come for her. The blood on her hands. The spark leaving her brother's eyes. They'll come, and without the music, there will be nothing to fill the air but her screams.

She turns and leaves him there, lost in his song, lost in a place better than this.

Cora goes down the stairs. She opens the library door. Her father's chair is turned away.

"Can't a man have some peace in his home, Helena. Is it too much to ask?"

On quiet feet, Cora walks to his chair. She's tired now. So tired. She's never been so tired. She'll rest soon. And then forever.

But when he turns, she swings again.

Cora's standing in the entryway when Deirdre comes, the violin washing over her. The baby is quiet now. Like she knows there's no one home.

No one but Deirdre. And poor, silly Kitty. Perhaps she should kill Kitty too.

But she's so tired.

She tries to raise her arm, but her strength is gone. The little ax drops from her hand and thumps on the floor.

She stares at it. Deirdre picks it up.

The baby cries again.

And the violin plays.

The darkness comes.

And Cora Cooke is no more.

47

TESSA

Tessa runs her hands through her hair and drops into one of the uncomfortable chairs in the hospital waiting room.

The police have come and gone, including Detective Morello. She was cool and professional, despite the circumstances.

Tessa might have spared her some pity. It was a hell of a story to sort through, but she's just so damn tired.

Margot walks into the room, which is deserted except for Tessa, and drops down beside her.

"They told you Ben's surgery went well?" she asks.

The sisters have barely had a chance to talk since Tessa arrived. The police were waiting, and the fallout from Valerie's final video has already begun. It spelled out, in no uncertain terms, the facts about Oliver Barlow and Chief Lloyd Winters. Despite any injunctions, the press ran with the story. It was too explosive to sit on.

Tessa has turned off her phone to stop it buzzing in her pocket.

"Yeah," Tessa says. "Full recovery, barring complications?"

Margot nods and leans her head back against the wall. "Yeah."

"You're not truly going to divorce him, are you?" Tessa asks quietly.

Margot sighs, but she doesn't open her eyes. "I should. I really should."

"You don't mean that."

"What if I do? Do you understand how big a betrayal it was for him to meet you in the city?" She picks up her head to meet Tessa's eyes.

"It was never romantic, Margot. That ended when I left home. You have to know that."

Margot's head falls back against the wall again. "I do know that. It was worse." She sighs, but when she speaks again, her words are quiet and heavy with everything they've left unsaid.

"When you called that one time, I held my phone in my hand and stared at your number. I couldn't believe it. Honestly. I couldn't believe it was real. It had been so long. I threw the phone down and marched out of the room. My hands were shaking. My whole body was shaking. I sat in the bathroom with the door locked and I cried."

Tessa stares.

"Ben knocked on the door, begged me to call you back but . . . I couldn't. I don't know why. I wasn't ready, I guess. You know what I said to him?"

Tessa shakes her head.

"I told him, if it was really important, *you'd call back*. I said it like it didn't matter to me any more than what color cart I got at the grocery store. He didn't say a word. He slammed out of the house instead. By the time he came back I'd pulled myself together as best I could. If he was going to be mad, then I could be mad too."

Margot studies the ceiling over their heads.

"It was our first real fight. When he packed a bag and said he was going to stay with a friend for a while, I didn't know if he'd come back."

Tessa knew how Ben spent the following days. He helped her through the admissions process at the best psychiatric hospital in the state.

"When he did come home, he acted like everything was fine. He let me believe everything was fine. Not once, in all the years since, did he think to mention that my sister, my twin sister, alone in New York, had suffered a breakdown, and when she did, it was me she reached out to. Not once."

Tessa lets out a breath she didn't know she was holding. She opens her mouth and struggles to find the right words to explain.

"I asked him not to," Tessa says. "I begged him."

"I know that now. It all came out after . . . after Mom died," Margot says. "But Tessa, no matter what you asked him, he's married to *me*. He should have told me."

She's right. And Tessa has no idea what to say.

"I'm sorry," she whispers, but the words are too small, nothing compared to the pain she caused.

Margot squeezes her eyes shut and shakes her head. "All this time, all these years. I was waiting, Tessa. I was waiting for you to need me. And when you didn't call a second time, I shoved away all the hope the sight of your call ignited. It was a fluke. A weak moment, nothing more. If you needed me, really needed me, you would have called again. You never did. And when I realized you didn't because you got what you needed from *Ben*, it was . . . difficult to swallow."

"Margie . . ." Tessa slips into the nickname she hasn't used since they were four. "That's not . . ."

"Fair?" Margot asks with a short laugh. "No, I guess it's not. But that's how I felt. How I still feel."

Tessa takes a deep, deep breath. Wonders how to explain eighteen years of anxiety and their cause.

"That's not what I was going to say." She braces herself and plunges forward. "Margot, I've needed you every day since I left. Every day. Without you, I don't function. It takes pills and therapists and mantras to get me through the day."

Tessa stares at the ceiling, counts the square tiles. "You . . . you're my compass. My true north. You always have been. Without you"—Tessa shrugs—"I'm perpetually lost."

She closes her eyes, lets the words float in the air between them.

"Then why, Tess?" Margot asks softly. "Why didn't you call again?"

"Because I was ashamed!" Tessa cries, turning to face her sister. "It was selfish, and needy, and pathetic. I wasn't the one who fought through physical therapy, day after day, just to walk again. I wasn't the one who had to lie in bed, in pain, after seven surgeries in two years. I wasn't the one who was supposed to *need* help, Margot. I had no right to ask you for anything. Not after what I did."

"What *you* did?" Margot sits up and stares at Tessa, and the anger she's become accustomed to is back in her sister's expression. "Tessa, what exactly do you think happened on that cliff?" she asks slowly.

Tessa tenses, fighting off the memories by instinct. But it never works. Even if she can keep them away during the day, they own her dreams. "I don't want to do this."

"I think we need to," Margot says. "I think we *have* to."

Tessa shakes her head, but she's been running for so long. She runs and she runs, but it's still there. It's always there.

"I talked you into coming," Tessa whispers. "You didn't want to. You never wanted to. You were terrified of heights."

She can't look at her sister. She closes her eyes instead and remembers the stars winking overhead and the splash of the water far below them. The sense of *possibility* that thrummed in her veins. Of the future opening in front of them, unfurling like the petals of a flower.

"But God, I loved that place. It made me feel . . . invincible. Like I could conquer the world."

Tessa goes back, willingly, for the first time in many years. For the first time maybe ever. And the night that changed all their lives washes over her again.

———

The three of them lounge on a blanket, far from the cliff's edge. Margot seems okay, as long as she stays clear of the drop-off. Tessa's skin is cool from the night wind, her bathing suit damp from her first dive into the lake.

She'd hurried to remove her shorts and T-shirt, then run for the cliff's edge as soon as they reached the top, just like when they were kids. Ben followed, his arms swirling in the air as he jumped. It was tradition, that first headlong kamikaze dive. Tessa first, with Ben by her side. They made the second trek up the trail where Margot waited, holding out towels with a bemused expression.

Their smiles are a little too wide, their laughter a little too loud.

Summer is ending.

She and Margot leave for NYU in a few weeks.

Tessa reaches over Ben, who's stretched out on the blanket next to her, and takes a bottle of water from the little cooler. It drips cold droplets on his stomach, but he doesn't open his eyes. Tessa offers the bottle to her sister.

Margot sits up and takes the drink, but there's a far-off look in her eyes. She leans forward, rests her chin on her knees, and stares into the moonlit night.

She hasn't said much since they got to the cliff, and Tessa wants her sister to smile. It's a celebration. An ending, yes, but a beginning too.

"New York's going to be great, Margot," Tessa whispers, but Margot doesn't smile.

Ben's staying in Pennsylvania. He registered for classes at community college but promised to transfer to NYU in a year or two.

Tessa doesn't mention that, though, because even when he said the words, she could hear the seed of doubt. His mom is alone now, and Tessa knows how hard it will be for him to leave her.

Margot opens her mouth to speak, but she closes it again. Then she takes a deep drink from the water bottle.

"What's your biggest fear, Tess?" Margot asks her.

Being alone.

"Snakes," she says. "You know that."

"Mine is heights."

"I'm sorry," Tessa says. "I shouldn't have made you come." She only wanted one night, one last night to celebrate the days and nights that have come before. But she should have chosen someplace else. She was being selfish.

"You didn't," Margot whispers.

Then she stands. Tessa raises her eyes, opens her mouth to tell Margot they can go. That she's sorry, it was a bad idea, but Margot's muscles are clenched, and Tessa realizes too late what she's going to do.

Margot's legs push forward from the ground, and she takes off at a run. Straight toward the edge of the cliff.

Without thought, without understanding the repercussions of what she's doing, without anything in her mind except to stop her sister, Tessa launches herself toward Margot, her hands flying in front of her, grasping, clutching.

For a moment, she has her, the skin and muscles and bone of Margot's ankle caught in Tessa's grip. But her momentum is too great, and Margot slips from Tessa's fingers toward the thing she fears the most.

Margot stumbles as she pulls away, unprepared for Tessa's grasping hands, and then she's gone. Over the side of the cliff. Falling. Falling to the hard plane of water that will break her.

———

Tears are leaking from the corner of Tessa's eyes, but she doesn't notice. She's lost beneath the heavy weight of guilt.

"It was my fault. If I hadn't grabbed you, you wouldn't have hit the water at the angle you did. I wanted to stop you, to keep you safe, and I almost killed you."

She risks a glance at her sister, seated beside her in the crappy chairs. But Margot's face isn't angry. There's no hatred or accusation. No blame.

One eyebrow is arched above the other, and her head is tilted slightly to one side. She's watching Tessa with an expression that can only be described as disgust.

"You're such an asshole."

Tessa's eyes widen. Margot's words are a lit match, burning away the atmosphere in the room, heavy with the fumes of Tessa's sorrow and regret. The only thing left behind is shock.

"Why is it always about you?" Margot demands. She stands up and stares at Tessa for a moment, then paces the small room. "*I* almost killed you, Margot. It's all *my* fault. *I* talked you into going up there, Margot."

She pauses, then turns back to Tessa, her eyes wide with mock suspense. "What if, for the sake of argument, we pretend for just a minute that you, Tessa Shepherd, are not the center of the whole goddamn universe? How does that sound?"

"I . . . uh . . ." But Tessa doesn't know what to say.

Margot's face softens, and her words are quieter when she speaks again. "Why don't we imagine for a moment, a girl. A girl who never had to make hard decisions because she let her sister make them for her. Imagine she liked it that way. It was easy."

"Did I do—"

"Shh," Margot interrupts. Tessa clamps her mouth closed. She watches. She listens.

"Now, imagine this girl is faced with the hardest decision she's ever had to make. But it's going to affect more than just her."

Tessa frowns, but she doesn't interrupt again.

Margot sighs. "Do you remember when I got the part-time job at the bakery?"

Tessa nods. That last summer was filled with pastries and cake samples Margot was always bringing home from work. They joked about putting on the freshman fifteen before classes even started.

"Now imagine my surprise when I realized, two months into the job, that I was *happy* there, Tess. Really happy. The same kind of happy that the thought of making movies made you."

Tessa's mouth drops open. "I didn't know that," she says on a surprised exhale of breath.

"You didn't know, because I didn't want you to know," Margot says. "We may be twins, but I can keep a secret when I want to. And I was keeping a big one. I didn't want to go to New York."

Tessa sits up straight. "But . . . but why didn't you—"

"Just say so? Because, Tess." Margot sits down next to her again. "I knew you didn't want to go alone. Never even considered it. We did everything together, and NYU had the film program you wanted. It didn't matter when we applied. I had no idea what I wanted. I thought I'd figure it out along the way, but the closer that day came, the clearer it was that I'd already figured it out. You belonged in New York, but I'd found my place already."

Margot watches as her words sink in. She studies Tessa's face while she absorbs the things she never knew.

"You didn't make me go to the cliff that night, Tess. *I* made me go."

"But . . . but *why*?"

"If I stayed in Linlea, that meant you were going to have to face your biggest fear, Tess. You were going to have to face the world on your own."

The bald truth of that stares Tessa down. When Margot asked, she said snakes. She always said snakes. But her sister knew her better than she knew herself.

"I couldn't ask you to do that without facing my own."

Margot shrugs. "So please, for the love of God, would you stop with the *all my fault* crap? It's tired and it's old. You didn't push me off that cliff, Tess. I made that decision on my own, and you grabbing at my foot isn't the reason I landed the way I did. I hesitated at the last minute. Fear got the best of me, but it was too late. That hesitation is why I hit the water the way I did. It wasn't you."

The idea is so foreign that Tessa can barely wrap her mind around it. A world in which she *hadn't* almost killed her sister? What would that even look like?

"And afterward . . . afterward was *my* fault, Tessa. Not yours."

A memory slams into Tessa of Margot's face, pale and strained, as the doctors tell her she might never walk again. They'll just have to wait and see.

"No," Tessa whispers.

But Margot shakes her head. "I can't describe the anger, Tess. Anger from nowhere. From everywhere. Anger like I'd never imagined. It hurts to think of it now."

Margot rubs both hands across her face, as if she can scrub the remnants of the emotion away.

"I was so *mad*. At Mom. At you. The doctors. At Dad for dying. At anyone and everyone, just so I didn't have to face the truth. I had made a terrible mistake, and I couldn't take it back. You and Mom. I'd ruined your lives. Mom was going to be stuck taking care of an invalid for the rest of her life, and you . . . you wouldn't even consider NYU. You took it completely off the table."

"I didn't want to leave you!"

"I know that, but I couldn't look at you, Tessa. I couldn't look at you every day, with your sympathy and your stupid, stupid guilt and know I'd taken the only thing you ever wanted."

"You never took anything from me," Tessa says.

"I did! I *did*, and you refused to even acknowledge it. *I* made a mistake, and *I* had to deal with the consequences. Me. Not you. And you wouldn't even give me that. It was always about how it was your fault, and if you'd only done this or done that differently. You, sacrificing your future to stay with your poor broken sister. But it was never about you, Tessa. It was about me. *Me*."

The heat in Margot's voice has risen, but she takes a deep breath and blows it out slowly through her nose. A trick Tessa learned in therapy.

"It was too much to process at once. It took a lot of time, a lot of self-reflection, and yes . . . a lot of therapy, to understand what I did to you. To us."

One side of Tessa's mouth twitches upward. "Anger management?" she asks.

"Oh yeah," Margot says without hesitation. "And then some."

Tessa looks down at her hands. Her nails are ragged and dirty, and she stinks. None of that matters right now.

"I pushed you out because I couldn't control the anger when I looked at you. Not with the shadow of NYU and a future you'd never have always at your back. I pushed you out and I channeled that anger into physical therapy. Into walking again. One foot in front of the other. On my own. Not because I blamed you, but because I blamed me. I said terrible things, truly awful things to you, and I've never said I'm sorry."

Margot reaches for her hand, interlaces her fingers though Tessa's. She clenches her hand as hard as she did after their mother's funeral. As hard as she ever has.

"When you didn't call, and the days stacked on top of one another and turned into years, I told myself I'd done the right thing. You didn't need me. You were better on your own. But inside . . . inside, I always secretly hoped that wasn't true, and a part of me, I'm ashamed to say, never stopped blaming you for listening. For leaving like you did. And I'm sorry for that too."

Tessa closes her eyes, dizzy at the sudden shift in the world.

It's tipped again.

This time, in the right direction.

48

Tessa parks near Fallbrook, which looks as if it's been through a war. In a way, it has. The debris of the fallen front porch and balcony has been pushed aside by emergency services, enough to give them access to the scene inside.

The bodies are gone now, of course, but yellow crime-scene tape still flutters in the wind.

It's all over, Tessa thinks. Or maybe it's just begun. Valerie's miraculous resurrection and final video have sent shock waves through the public and the legal system.

The footage begins with Oliver offering Lloyd Winters a chance to confess, publicly, to his crimes. The man doesn't know the exchange is being caught on tape. His response shows the world exactly what kind of person the upstanding Chief Winters truly was.

For the remainder of the video, Valerie and Oliver, together, lay it all out, everything Winters wasn't willing to say. The admission to his daughter that he planted the evidence himself. The burying of Billy Tyson's confession and DNA evidence. And the reason for his vendetta against Oliver Barlow in the first place.

Tessa can't watch it through to the end.

Seeing Oliver's face is too hard.

There have been some tough questions asked of the attorney general's office about the extent to which they were aware of Chief Winters's corruption, considering their months-long investigation into the matter, and whether they covered for him to save the state from paying out on a thirty-million-dollar lawsuit.

Tessa's voice mail is full of questions about her next project. It seems her professional reputation has recovered along with Valerie, both alive and well.

That's part of the reason she's here.

Deirdre Donnelly appears out of the woods, walking slowly along the trail from the cottage. Tessa waits, hands deep in her pockets, and studies the house where her mother spent the first year of her life.

Jane died, aware of the place, yet somehow willing to leave the house and its history in the past. Margot feels the same. But there's something in Tessa, something she doesn't understand, and certainly something her sister doesn't understand, that won't allow her to let it go so easily.

"You're back," Deirdre says. "I had a feeling you would be." She doesn't sound happy about that.

"I remembered the graves," Tessa says quietly. "We left them half finished. I thought I'd help you clear the rest."

Deirdre studies her, but the older woman finally nods.

"Come to the cottage with me and I'll get my things. You can choose roses from the garden to take."

They walk in companionable silence, and Tessa takes her time deciding which roses to clip while Deirdre collects her basket and gloves.

There's plenty that needs to be said, but they have time.

The forest is the same today, the same as it's been for hundreds of years. And will be for hundreds more, God willing. There's a serenity to be found in that, and Tessa lets the sounds of the birds and the brook soothe her jumbled thoughts.

When they arrive at their destination, Deirdre kneels at the graves. She's quiet, her hands resting in her lap, and Tessa wonders if she prays.

When she opens her eyes and reaches for her gloves, she doesn't look at Tessa when she speaks. "What is it you believe you know, Ms. Shepherd?"

She leans forward and clears away the grass and moss.

"Only what I've read," Tessa says. "There isn't as much as I'd expect. Not for a crime this big. It's like the world has forgotten them. But that's what you wanted, isn't it?"

Deirdre doesn't answer.

"I know enough to know I've been lied to," Tessa says, her brows knitting together. "Enough to know there's a story here. One you want to keep hidden. I have my own ideas about your reasons why."

Deirdre glances up with a look that says she doubts Tessa understands anything at all. "People lie for all kinds of reasons. And for no reason at all."

"You have a reason, though," Tessa insists.

Deirdre sighs. "I suppose I do. Are you going to make your movie, then? Is that what this is about?"

Tessa won't lie, not in this place. "I think they deserve their story to be told, don't you? To be forgotten this way . . . it's not right."

One corner of Deirdre's mouth moves upward slightly, but there's only sadness in her face. "Right and wrong. It's a nice idea, but a costly one."

Tessa stares at the woman and tries to tamp down her frustration. She's talking in riddles, as she has been from the beginning.

"Will you tell me the truth?" she asks softly. She can't ask more plainly than that.

Deirdre sits back on her heels and sighs. She reaches into the pocket of her sweater and removes an envelope, then runs her fingers across the front of it, slowly, carefully. Her gestures are telling. The writer was precious to her.

"This will explain better than I can," Deirdre says softly, then holds it up for Tessa to take from her hand.

The envelope is thick, yellowed and brittle from age. Deirdre must have collected it from the cottage while Tessa was clipping roses. She'd known Tessa would have questions.

Deirdre's name is scrawled across the front in ink that's faded from black to gray.

"A letter from Aiden," Deirdre says. "His last."

Tessa glances up at the elderly woman, who simply nods for Tessa to go ahead. She slips the folded letter from the envelope.

Her heart is fluttering in her chest, her fingers tingling with anticipation. What secrets are sealed in these pages, the words of a man so long dead?

Tessa begins to read.

> *To Dee, my sweet, sensible, unfailingly loyal sister. I beg your forgiveness, both for what I will do, and for what I've already done.*
>
> *I'm handing you the burden of my sins. I wish there was another way, but there are some truths you must know.*
>
> *This is my confession.*
>
> *For me, every story begins with Ruby. Always. My beginning and my end. My everything.*
>
> *I had no delusions she felt the same, but that didn't stop my wasted heart from wanting.*
>
> *Last year, after a night with my friends, I stumbled home, but my happy mood turned pitiful along the way. I would never have her. She couldn't love me, a poor Irish boy with nothing to my name.*

But drunkenness had loosened my tongue, and I called to Ruby's window from the ground, whispering loudly, tripping over my words. She didn't come, so I tossed up a pebble that bounced off the glass. The curtains moved. She was listening. I confessed my undying love in my clumsy, uncouth way. But the curtain didn't move again, and the window didn't open. I was no Romeo, and she had no interest in being my Juliet. Who was I kidding?

I staggered toward the barn, knowing I'd never hear the end of it if Mam saw me that way.

I curled up on the fresh hay, and I let the drink carry me to sleep. Even in my dreams, Ruby haunted me. Lovely, beautiful Ruby, who would never be mine.

And then she was there, slipping between my arms, her lips warm and sweet against mine. She did hear me, and she came to me, and my precious Ruby was mine.

I awoke the next day a changed man. I knew now she loved me back, and with all the swagger and confidence of a young man with a full heart, I searched for her until I found her, leaning against a tree by the pond with a book in her hand.

I crossed the distance between us and she stood to meet me. I didn't stop to think or second-guess, and that smile was still on her lips when I kissed her.

We told no one. It was our secret. We worried what her father would say, but we would have a future together, one way or another. Still, we hoped for the approval of our families, if they would give it.

The months that followed were full of so many things. Worry. Excitement. Wonder. New beginnings and fear of what those beginnings might bring to an end. Ruby and I were wrapped up completely in each other.

Mam looked at me knowingly a few times, like she suspected something was changing, but she accepted the excuses I gave.

And I wasn't the only one facing changes. Cora was sent off to boarding school. Ruby made an effort to please Helena, hoping perhaps she'd be on our side, when the time came.

But the months dragged past, and there never seemed to be a right time. Imogene was born, and Cora returned home sometime after. Then Lawrence Pynchon moved in. The world was moving on, and I was growing tired of secrets.

I can admit, my impatience grew seeing the way he looked at her. Pynchon.

She swore it was nothing. And I believed her. But I wasn't blind.

When Helena discovered us, it was a relief. No matter what happened then, the truth was out. No more hiding.

Mr. Cooke's acceptance was more than I ever hoped. He was a distant man, difficult to read, but seemed genuinely pleased for the two of us. And my world was right.

For a little while, my whole world was right.

If only I could have made things right for Cora.

To say I didn't know of Cora's feelings would be a lie. I knew. Ruby and I both did. We spoke of it once, of Cora's jealousy of her sister. I'm ashamed now of the way I laughed it off. A silly schoolgirl crush. I was flattered, when I bothered to think about it. Which wasn't often.

When Cora came to me after Ruby and I became officially engaged, I was barely listening. And once I realized what she was saying, I could hardly comprehend.

It wasn't Ruby in the barn that night, Dee. Ruby never came to me, never let me hold her in my arms. It was Cora, who only wanted me to notice her. Cora.

In my drunkenness, I took her, and she let me.

I can barely write these words, Deirdre. Just the thought of it makes me sick. I'm a monster. I committed a terrible, terrible deed. Upon a child who trusted me. Someone I loved, though not in the way she thought she wanted. But I did love her, Deirdre. I still do, as a brother to another little sister, and never anything more. Please, even if you can't find it in your heart to forgive me for what I did to your friend, please know that's true.

I never wanted to hurt her. But I did hurt her. And then, in my shock and my stupidity, I hurt her more.

She'd brought the candlesticks, Dee. They were her mother's, she said. It wasn't stealing. We could sell them, and run away together.

Just the two of us.

And the baby.

The baby? Deirdre, I stared at her like she'd gone mad. For one shining moment, I hoped she had. That something had gotten into her blood, poisoned her, and all her wild talk was nothing but the fantasy of a deranged mind.

I shouted. I took her by the arms, trying to shake the madness out of her. I told her we weren't running away together and we weren't kidnapping her baby sister.

And then she smiled, Deirdre. She smiled and, in that moment, I understood. My life was over.

She smiled sweetly, and she put her hand on my cheek, and my blood went cold.

Not my sister, Denny, she said. Our daughter. Our little girl.

Deirdre, they knew. Cora's parents knew. There was no boarding school. Helena faked a pregnancy, knowing a baby would have to be explained somehow. Cora claimed Everett forced Helena to do it, but that she didn't want to be a mother. She'd never love Imogene like we could.

I had used her, Deirdre, then her parents had hidden her away like something to be ashamed of. She wouldn't tell them who the father was. To protect me, she said. Because they wouldn't understand. So she was sent away.

In a home for unwed mothers, Cora gave birth to a baby girl who was taken from her arms and given to the woman she hated most in the world, to be raised under her nose as her sister. And the person she believed she loved, the father of her child, was going to marry her other sister.

And at that moment, when it mattered most, I failed her further still.

My only thought was for Ruby.

I told her to go home, and my voice was harsh and cold when I crushed her hopes.

I took the candlesticks from her, and I sent her away with nothing but loss in her eyes.

I went straight to Ruby and confessed my sins. I had no choice. I was on my knees, Dee, begging her forgiveness the way I should have begged for Cora's. At that moment, Cora was far from my mind.

Ruby was quiet and still. Her face was so pale and her limbs didn't move. She swayed in her seat, and I was afraid she might faint. She couldn't look at me. She sent me away, just as I had Cora.

I was devastated. Destroyed.

I took the candlesticks back to the dining room, to return them where they belonged, the only thing left that I could put right. But Helena caught me along the way.

Deirdre, I didn't even care.

Things couldn't get worse. And then they did.

Ruby burst into the room and accused me in front of her father. The hatred, the pure contempt in her eyes, it ground what was left of my heart beneath her heel.

And I deserved it all.

Everything that happened after, every step along the way, was a chain of events I set in motion with my callous, thoughtless actions.

Cora was not to blame for what she did. I treated her with careless indifference, believing somehow that her feelings didn't count, didn't run as deep. Just childish things, things she'd grow out of soon enough.

And now lives are stacked like cordwood at my feet. My sweet Ruby. Her family. Even Lawrence Pynchon. News of his death has reached me just this hour. And I find it's one too many. The death of a man guilty of nothing but being in the wrong place at the wrong time.

The price for my carelessness is too high. I cannot face it, day in and day out. Tell Mam I'm sorry. So sorry. The rest, I leave with you, Deirdre. You always were the strong one.

Forgive me,
Aiden

Tessa wipes at her cheeks, taken low by Aiden's words. The paper and ink have blended together in places, stained by tears. How many were Aiden's and how many Deirdre's, it was impossible to say.

She folds the letter carefully back along the crease.

"Aiden hanged himself after he wrote that," Deirdre says quietly. "So much death. It leaves a scar on the earth. There was another, you know. One with no grave at all."

Deirdre looks up at Tessa with a frown. "I always leave an extra rose for that forgotten life. Helena was pregnant herself, at one time. She came to Mam, hoping she would help her, but when Mam refused, Mam believed she found what she needed somewhere else."

Tessa stares. "And Cora?" she asks.

They were all forgotten, by everyone but the woman kneeling in front of her. Cora, perhaps, most of all.

"There's a great deal I still don't know and never will. I've wondered how Mam could have been fooled by Helena's fake pregnancy, considering how much she knew about midwifery. Or if she was never fooled at all but held her tongue for Cora's sake. Would she have recognized the signs of pregnancy in Cora before she was sent away? How and why she kept her secrets from me of all people, I . . ." Deirdre shakes her head. "But it makes no difference now."

"Cora killed them."

Deirdre nods.

"She was just a girl."

"Fifteen, the same as me. Tessa, a girl's mind can break as easily as anyone's," Deirdre says. "She suffered so much, alone and in silence. I don't believe she killed Peter, though." Deirdre's voice is adamant, daring Tessa to argue. "I refuse to believe that. They said he died from a fall, and I think . . . I think his death pushed her over the edge."

She's clearing the last grave in the row. Gently she lays the roses Tessa has chosen and slowly stands, brushing off her hands.

Tessa walks to her side, reads the names and the dates carved there. "What happened to her, Deirdre?" she asks quietly.

"You know the answer to that already, don't you?"

Tessa studies the woman by her side, the softness in her expression as she stares down at the graves. A softness that Tessa's rarely seen in her before.

A single, silent tear slides down the old woman's cheek.

49

DEIRDRE

Dee flings the little ax as far as she can, but it's broken now, and the iron blade falls at her feet, while the handle clatters across the air through the entryway, toward the stairs. Her hands are shaking. Kitty is shaking.

Fallbrook is shaking, coming down around their ears one piece at a time, and that horrible violin is playing its death knell.

"Stand right here," she says to Kitty, who looks at her with huge, empty eyes. There's blood splattered across her face.

"Don't leave me," Kitty says.

"Don't move!" Deirdre grinds out in a harsh voice. "I have to get the baby!"

She runs. She won't look at the bodies on the floor. She won't look again through the library door or into the kitchen. They're not people anymore, just obstacles in her way. Eyes forward. Eyes forward.

She must get the baby.

Imogene is whimpering in her crib, forgotten and ignored for far too long.

"Shh," Deirdre whispers, bundling her up. "Shh, now."

The little thing curls against Dee's neck, hot from her tears, and desperate for someone, anyone, to hold her and make it right.

"We have to go now, little one," she whispers, holding the tiny life tightly in her arms.

She rushes back down the stairs, around the things lying in her path. Around them, out of the belly of this dying beast. Away from that hated, haunting violin.

"Move, Kitty!" Deirdre hisses, and Kitty follows, thank heavens. Deirdre doesn't have the strength to carry them both.

They hurry through the woods, down the trail to the cottage. They burst in on Mam, who's packing a bag and wiping away her tears. There's no time for that now.

There's no time.

Aiden has gone into town to try and find a ride for them all to the nearest bus station after being thrown out of their home. The baby has fallen asleep against Deirdre's shoulder, listening to the crazy beat of her heart.

"Please," Deirdre says, begging her mother to fix it. To somehow, some way, make it all better. "They're dead, Mam. They're all dead."

The confusion in Mam's face gives way to shock, but only for a moment. She takes in the sight of them, this trio of girls who need her now more than they've ever needed anyone, and a calm comes over her. Her shoulders straighten and she moves quickly, in a flurry of practical hands.

"Outside," she says as she gently takes the baby from Deirdre's arms. "We have to get you cleaned up."

The seconds are melting off the clock, and every one of them feels like a knife to Deirdre's chest. This can't work, she thinks, but she blindly trusts in her mam.

Their mother asks only a few questions, which Dee answers as truthfully as she can. There's no time for lies.

When the police are called, Deirdre glances at the clock. So little time has passed, yet nothing will ever be the same.

She's not present at Fallbrook when the police arrive. She's standing over a baby girl, watching her sleep, trying desperately to keep her story straight. She and Kitty had taken the baby for a walk, which they often did. Nothing out of the ordinary. And when they arrived back at Fallbrook, everyone was dead.

Everyone was dead.

———

Tessa listens quietly as they walk slowly back to the cottage, and Deirdre can feel each day that's passed since that one, deep in her bones. The younger woman doesn't interrupt with more questions, not yet, but Deirdre knows they're coming.

"Some say Lawrence Pynchon was still playing his violin when men with guns burst into the room, but I doubt that's true. The other tale is far more likely. That they found him, clutching Ruby's body to his, wailing and spouting incoherent words that made no sense. About Tchaikovsky, and death, and how he found them that way. They were all just . . . just dead."

No one intended for him to take the blame for the murders, not at first. Not even Mam. At least that's what Deirdre chooses to believe. They simply didn't spare him a thought.

When it became clear that the police felt they had their killer, the Donnellys had a choice to make.

An echo of Mam's words come back to haunt her, as they have so often. *"My hope for you, child, is that you're never forced to put those fine principles to the test."*

Deirdre's youthful arrogance, when right and wrong were simple, feels like a dream she once had.

"No one believed him," she says. "The handle of the ax was by his side. He must have picked it up, then dropped it again. And he was covered in Ruby's blood." She sighs. "If there'd been a trial, he may have been able to convince a jury of his innocence. The evidence didn't add up. But he never got the chance."

Deirdre has spent a great deal of her life avoiding thoughts of Lawrence Pynchon, the innocent man who died a violent death in jail. Not because she was in love with him. Her feelings for Pynchon had been nothing more than a girlhood crush, in truth.

He liked women. Enjoyed their attention and their appreciation. That much was clear, in hindsight, at least. He'd flirted with Deirdre just as he'd flirted with Helena Cooke. And Ruby. She suspects his feelings for Ruby, while unrequited, might have been a bit deeper, but how much deeper she couldn't know.

All she knows for sure is that she's spent a lifetime with the weight of his death upon her heart. That he paid such a price for their lies was the most shameful stain upon Deirdre's soul.

They've come to the end of the trail. Deirdre spots the cottage up ahead and Kitty, seated in her rocking chair. She stops and turns to the young woman by her side.

"Have you made things right with your sister?" she asks. It's not her business, but still, she'd like to know.

Tessa frowns, her gaze trained on Kitty as well.

"I have," she says without turning her head. "As much as I can, after so many years of hurt."

Deirdre smiles a little. "I'm glad."

But Tessa is still watching Kitty, her mind on the story she's been told. On everything she's learned and all she hasn't.

The time has come, as Deirdre knew it would from the moment she found out who Tessa was.

Imogene's daughter. *Imagine that.*

"Are you sure you want to know the rest?" Deirdre feels a flutter inside. Nerves, after all this time. She's kept these secrets for so long. Because they aren't her own to give away.

But Kitty's mind is betraying her. Dementia has stirred up the truth and mixed it with lies, and her sister can no longer tell the difference. If she ever could.

"Every story has an end," Tessa says. "And Cora's didn't end in a grave in the woods."

"No," Deirdre says.

There was only so long the pretense could continue, as Deirdre had understood from the beginning. She'd read the truth in Tessa's eyes when she arrived. The younger woman had known what they'd find when they finished clearing the graves. And she'd known what they wouldn't find.

Six graves.

Aiden. Ruby. Peter. Helena and Everett Cooke.

And Saoirse Donnelly.

"What happened to her, Deirdre? What happened to Cora Cooke?" Tessa asks.

Deirdre meets her eyes. There's a resemblance there. Nothing specific, but it's present, all the same. A tilt of the head. A light in her eyes. A hint of Cora. Tessa's grandmother.

"She was sent away," Deirdre says. "Adopted, along with her baby sister. No one knew they were mother and child. Not then. Only that they were orphaned and needed a home."

Tessa doesn't speak, and Deirdre continues, filling the silence with the last of the elusive truth.

"The Ashwoods were good people. They tried. But Cora was too much. A young girl plagued with night terrors and a broken soul. She didn't make it easy for them. The baby adjusted, as babies do, but Cora . . . she only wanted one thing. Cora wanted to go home."

"Home to Fallbrook," Tessa whispers.

"Yes. To Fallbrook, and to the family who'd always treated her as their own."

Kitty rocks slowly in her chair and, even from a distance, they see her smile. Her lips move, speaking as if someone is standing by her side.

"I know it's difficult to understand, Tessa. It's true that she was Cora Cooke in another life . . . but Kitty, the girl who ran wild through the woods, raised by Mam in all but name, the girl who preferred the pet name Mam gave her even before her own mother died . . . that girl was more real than Cora Cooke ever was.

"So while Imogene became Jane, Kitty simply became the girl who, in her heart, she'd always been."

"People must have known that Kitty and Cora were one and the same," Tessa says, and Deirdre can see she's struggling.

She nods. "The townspeople knew. But Snowden has always been a small place, especially back then, and Mam was well liked. Something like this, it rocks a community, and there was a sense of closing ranks. Protecting Cora was something tangible they could do, when very little else could be done. Years passed, and eventually what was once an open secret simply became the truth."

Deirdre pulls the edges of her sweater tighter around her middle.

"My grandparents knew," Tessa points out.

Deirdre nods. "Mr. Ashwood was unsure about the future of Fallbrook for some time. He could have sold it, but with the house's bloody history, people were hardly lining up to buy it and certainly not for the price it was worth. Instead, he kept us on as caretakers, Mam and Aiden and me. A few months after the murders, when Cora insisted on coming back, he set up the estate trust to ensure that she would be provided a permanent home, with people who loved her as family. And baby Imogene—Jane—was raised without the specter of the past hanging over her head. It seemed the best solution for everyone."

"My mother didn't know who Kitty was?"

"No," Deirdre says, shaking her head. "Mam and Mr. Ashwood decided it was better that way. Kitty was having a difficult time. Aiden was . . . *gone* by the time Kitty returned. And she wasn't the same girl she'd been. She never spoke about that day, or the months leading up to it. In fact, she barely spoke at all, not for a long time. We didn't press her. Only Mam's imaginary stories of Aiden seemed to bring her alive. We didn't want to upset Kitty, and as for Jane . . . the Ashwoods decided they'd tell Jane about her true family history, and about Cora, when they felt the time was right."

"That time never came," Tessa says. "She knew nothing about Fallbrook until after my grandparents died. And even then, his letter never mentioned Cora."

"I never saw Imogene again after she was taken in by the Ashwoods. But she wrote to me once," Deirdre says. "Not through a lawyer that time, but directly to me. It was many months after her father died. I suppose she'd read about the murders in an old newspaper somewhere. She asked if I knew what had happened to Cora Cooke."

"What did you tell her?"

Deirdre takes a deep breath and straightens her back. "I told her that Cora had moved away and I never heard from her again. To my great relief, she never dug any deeper. Not that I'm aware of, at least."

Tessa studies the old woman, the wrinkles in her papery skin and the frown lines that life had carved into the space between her eyes. "Why did you lie?" she asks quietly.

Deirdre sighs, and Mam's voice drifts through her memories. *"A lie told out of kindness is less of a sin than the cruelty of a harsh truth."*

She's not sure how she feels about that, even now. But the time for regrets has long since passed.

"For the same reason I've always lied, Tessa. To protect my sister."

"It couldn't have been easy." Tessa frowns. "For any of you."

Deirdre shrugs. "Nothing ever is, Tessa. But for over seventy years, it's somehow worked. Kitty has lived the most normal life we could give her. After a while, even Mam seemed to forget that Kitty wasn't her daughter from birth. And they had their stories. Stories about Aiden." She shrugs again. "She was happy. They both were." Deirdre sighs. "Then Mam died, and it's been just me and Kitty and our secrets ever since."

50

TESSA

Tessa's head is spinning.

Some of what Deirdre has shared Tessa already suspected. News reports of the day listed the victims of the Fallbrook Family Slayings, as they were termed, along with the names of the survivors. Two sisters, Cora and Imogene Cooke.

The search for Cora is what brought her back here. But the weight of the truth, once given, is shockingly difficult to bear.

Deirdre studies her. "What happens now is in your hands, though. Have you come to a decision?"

Tessa doesn't meet her eyes. "This is what I do," she says slowly, frowning at the aftertaste of bitterness the words leave in her mouth. "I tell stories on film." There is uncertainty in her voice, and Tessa stares into the distance. She reaches for a note of confidence, and almost manages to convince herself it's real. "This story . . . Deirdre, this story is too big to walk away from."

So why does the idea of telling it make her feel like a ghoul?

The elderly woman by her side nods slowly, unsurprised by Tessa's answer. "All right, then."

Deirdre says nothing more. She doesn't attempt to persuade Tessa that she's making a mistake. There are no pleas to leave them be, to let them live out the years they have left in peace. Her sad acceptance wraps itself around Tessa's heart like an anchor.

She opens her mouth to speak, but Kitty has spotted them from the little covered porch.

"Tessa," she calls, and stands to wave. Tessa gives a wan smile and a wave in return as she swallows the rest of the unformed words on her tongue. Deirdre begins to walk toward Kitty, and Tessa follows.

"It's so good to see you," Kitty says when the pair reaches her. She rises to pull Tessa into a hug. The scent of citrus shampoo surrounds her, and Tessa embraces her tightly in return.

"Come sit with me," Kitty says, smiling in pleasure. "Deirdre will make us some tea."

Tessa meets the older woman's eyes only briefly, and a moment of sadness passes between them. An acknowledgment of words left unspoken, perhaps. At least for now.

Deirdre nods, then walks inside and leaves the two of them alone.

"I have something I want to show you," Kitty says, her face alight.

With the weight of both the future and the past tugging at her conscience, Tessa nods and pulls a chair close to Kitty.

The grandmother she never knew she was missing.

"Kitty, can I ask you a question?" Tessa says gently. "Someone locked a door inside Fallbrook while I was there." She's careful with her words, careful not to sound accusatory.

Kitty looks sheepish. "I'm sorry. I hope you're not mad. I just . . . I was afraid you would leave." She gives Tessa a blinding smile. "But you've come back."

Kitty leans over and picks up a little wooden chest from the small table between them. It has tarnished brass fittings and a small rectangular hole for a key.

It's heavier than Tessa expects for its size. She holds it in her hands, studying it, while Kitty fishes in her pocket for the key.

"I haven't looked in here for a long time," she says. "Not since Aiden came home. But I hoped you'd be back, so I retrieved it from my hiding place."

Tessa can't look away from the box in her hands. A long-held memory, private and precious, blooms in her mind.

"I've never known what it unlocks, but I suppose the mystery is part of the appeal."

Kitty holds out her hand, palm up, to offer Tessa a small, old-fashioned brass key.

Tessa takes it and stares. Then she slips a chain from around her neck and lays the pair of keys side by side. An exact matched set.

"Well, my goodness," Kitty exclaims. "Imagine that."

But Tessa doesn't look up. Her eyes are fixed on her mother's key and on the box in her lap.

With trembling fingers, and her breath trapped in her chest, Tessa slips the little key her mother gave her into the lock mechanism.

Slowly, she turns.

"Take it with you, Tessa. Let it remind you that you always have a home to come to, no matter how far life takes you."

The latch clicks and the lid springs open, just the barest inch.

Tessa lifts the lid the rest of the way. Her vision is cloudy behind a watery pool of tears, but she squeezes her eyes closed and lets them fall down her cheeks.

She doesn't wipe them away.

The box is filled with faded postcards. Postcards that Kitty has saved, written out of love by the woman who was her mother in all ways that mattered. She must have left the other key with the baby girl she couldn't keep, a moment lost somewhere in Kitty's faulty memory.

"They come from all over," Kitty says, pleased to share her treasures. "Italy and Spain. Ireland. Morocco. What a life Aiden's lived. Can you imagine? I think it would be a wonderful addition to your movie."

Tessa doesn't trust herself to speak.

Footsteps come from inside the cottage and across the porch as Deirdre joins them. Tessa wipes her eyes and takes the offered cup of tea. She sets it on the small table between her and Kitty, grateful for the chance to pull herself together.

"These are incredible, Kitty," she says, clearing her throat and striving for a normal tone.

Tessa lifts the postcards from the box. There are so many. More cards from more places than a single man could visit in three lifetimes. She fans them out. None have postmarks.

"Do you think they'll be useful?" Kitty asks. Her eyes are bright with barely contained excitement.

But Tessa doesn't answer. She's transfixed by what she sees at the bottom of the little box.

It's a piece of metal, rectangular in shape, and the reason the small chest is so heavy. One end is thicker than the other, and the thinner edge is curved.

A small piece of broken wood protrudes from a circle on the bottom.

The entire thing is discolored by a dark substance. So dark it's nearly black.

Tessa slams the box closed, so hard it falls from her lap. The blade of the hatchet rattles inside, and for one terrible minute, Tessa wonders if it's trying to escape.

The postcards have fallen as well and scattered across the porch.

"Oh," Kitty cries. She lowers herself on elderly knees and reaches to collect them before the wind takes them away.

Tessa is panting, her eyes wide, her breath coming in short, hot bursts, but the sight of the old woman's dismay as she gathers her treasures brings a new reality crashing around her.

"Kitty, I'm so sorry," she says as she hurriedly drops to the porch and helps her collect her postcards, her voice and her hands shaking uncontrollably.

"That's all right, dear," Kitty says. "I can be clumsy myself. Just ask Dee." She smiles briefly up at Deirdre, who is watching the pair of them with shock on her face.

"No, Kitty," Tessa says. She pulls in a deep breath. "It's not . . ." Tessa reaches out and places a hand on Kitty's arm. "I need to tell you. I . . . I'm so sorry to disappoint you, but . . . I'm not going to be making that movie after all."

Kitty stops and stares at Tessa. Some of the light dims in her face.

"Oh. But Aiden . . ." She casts her eyes around, at the postcards strewn about.

"Kitty." Tessa scoots forward and takes the old woman's hands in her own until she meets her eyes. "Kitty, in your heart, you know he isn't a murderer. Whatever sins he might have committed, he's paid for them. Let that be enough, Kitty." She searches Kitty's face. Understanding would be too much to hope for, but Tessa will settle for acceptance. "Let it be enough."

Kitty meets her eyes. Finally, she smiles sadly and nods. "All right, then. If you think that's best."

Tessa helps her rise to her feet, then collects the last of the postcards and stacks them on the table. She can't bring herself to touch the little box again.

"Goodbye, Kitty," Tessa says.

She walks quickly down the steps, away from the fairy-tale cottage. It takes everything she has not to run. She wonders if she'll ever return.

One day, perhaps. When there's no one else left to tend the graves.

There will be no documentary, of that she's finally sure. Maybe she'll take Ben's advice. Tessa can see the appeal of fiction, with a clear-cut version of good guys and bad. A story where you know who to root for, and you're never wrong.

And long-lost grandmothers don't keep a bloody hatchet in a box.

Tessa bites back a hysterical laugh. If she lets it out, the screams will follow, and she might never stop.

"Wait," Deirdre calls. Tessa forces herself to slow.

She breathes deeply. Once, twice. Three times.

I am afraid. But I am not in danger.

When the older woman draws even with Tessa, she hugs her. Tessa can feel the bones just beneath her skin. The embrace is brief. Deirdre runs her palms down Tessa's arms as she pulls away, until she reaches her hands. She squeezes them in her own.

"Thank you," she whispers. There are tears in her eyes. "You made the right decision."

Tessa glances over her shoulder, to where Kitty is rocking in her chair again. She's subdued now, not shining as brightly as she did before.

"Do you think she knows?" Tessa asks quietly.

Deirdre shakes her head. "The truth is in there. Somewhere deep, deep inside." She sighs. "But some things are best left buried, don't you think?"

There was a time Tessa would have disagreed.

But that time has passed.

The key her mother gave her is still gripped in her hand. Tessa opens her fingers and lets it fall. She doesn't need a talisman anymore.

She starts her car and points it away from Fallbrook.

Tessa knows her way home.

51

DEIRDRE

Deirdre joins her sister as Tessa walks out of their lives. Kitty picks up the cup that was left on the table, and Deirdre hurries to take it from her hand.

She pours the tea onto the ground by the edge of the porch.

Kitty protests.

"I'll make you another," Deirdre assures her. "That one was cold."

"I like it cold," Kitty says, but she's already distracted, thumbing through the postcards she brought out from wherever they've been hidden.

"Then you can let it get cold again," Deirdre says, though Kitty's no longer listening.

In the kitchen, Deirdre rinses the cup carefully, then pours the pot of tea she made earlier down the sink. Enough for all of them. Tessa, Kitty, and herself. She replaces a small tin box on the upper shelf of the pantry that Kitty can't reach. The tremor in Deirdre's hands begins to subside once it's out of sight.

As the fresh tea brews, Deirdre glances out the kitchen window to her mother's garden. Her gaze falls on the foxglove that grows there. A beautiful flower, with bold purple petals in the shape of a bell. Lovely. Delicate.

And deadly.

One day, perhaps, if she must. If Kitty's in danger of being left behind with no one to care for her, or if the past again creeps close enough to devour them whole, Deirdre will be forced to make a cup of tea for them both, using the dried leaves and petals she keeps in that tin box.

Kitty will never understand the lengths Deirdre is willing to go to keep her safe, or why, but that's okay. It's for the best, really. As for herself, Deirdre accepted her role long ago.

A single tear makes a path down her lined, paper-skinned cheek. Deirdre takes a deep, cleansing breath and wipes it away.

She is her sister's keeper.

52

KITTY

In the early afternoon light, Kitty sits next to her sister on their front porch.

They don't speak, but Kitty's not bothered.

She doesn't mention it to Deirdre, because her sister worries too much, but Kitty's rarely alone.

"Keep my secrets," a voice whispers in her ear. "For my secrets are yours."

A ghost of a memory, back to greet her as an old friend might.

Kitty frowns. "Do you remember the gravedigger's bell, Dee?" she asks.

A small dark seed of worry burrows down deep, settling in.

Something is rising.

If only she could remember what it is.

ACKNOWLEDGMENTS

Writing a book is a lot like making soup. There are some standard things you need. A pot. A spoon, a base, and some seasoning. After that, the sky is the limit. But the best part about soup is sharing it. Some will like it. Some won't. (And that's okay.) There's a sense of satisfaction in the creation and, if you're very lucky, a few who will finish the bowl and ask for seconds. There is immense joy in that.

If you've made it this far, thank you, from the bottom of my heart.

I owe a debt of gratitude to a great many people for their guidance, generosity, and support along the way. Katie. Chris. Gabe. Faith. Miriam. You don't need me to tell you how amazing you are, but I'm going to say it anyway.

Jason, Isabel, and Max . . . *I love you* doesn't seem like enough letters, but I suppose it will have to do until they create a few more.

ABOUT THE AUTHOR

Eliza Maxwell is the author of *The Shadow Writer*, *The Widow's Watcher*, *The Unremembered Girl*, *The Grave Tender*, and *The Kinfolk*. She writes fiction from her home in Texas, which she shares with her ever-patient husband, two impatient kids, a ridiculous English setter, and a bird named Sarah. An artist and writer, a dedicated introvert, and a British-cop-drama addict, she enjoys nothing more than sitting on the front porch with a good cup of coffee. For more information, visit www.elizamaxwell.net.